What the Neighbors Saw

What the Neighbors Saw

A NOVEL

Melissa Adelman

MINOTAUR BOOKS
NEW YORK

First published in the United States by Minotaur Books, an imprint of St. Martin's Publishing Group

WHAT THE NEIGHBORS SAW. Copyright © 2023 by Melissa Adelman. All rights reserved. Printed in the United States of America. For information, address St. Martin's Publishing Group, 120 Broadway, New York, NY 10271.

www.minotaurbooks.com

Design by Meryl Sussman Levavi

The Library of Congress Cataloging-in-Publication Data is available upon request.

ISBN 978-1-250-87656-0 (hardcover)
ISBN 978-1-250-87657-7 (ebook)

Our books may be purchased in bulk for promotional, educational, or business use. Please contact your local bookseller or the Macmillan Corporate and Premium Sales Department at 1-800-221-7945, extension 5442, or by email at MacmillanSpecialMarkets@macmillan.com.

First Edition: 2023

1   3   5   7   9   10   8   6   4   2

You're gone, gone, gone away
I watched you disappear.

—"Little Talks," Of Monsters and Men

What the
Neighbors Saw

$1,699,000
5 Beds 4.5 Baths 5,100 Sq. Ft.
51 Shadow Road

Exceptionally located on a dead-end street of $3M+ properties in highly coveted River Forest, this expansive 1927 house is waiting to be restored or rebuilt as your dream home! Original hardwoods, extensive millwork, and two wood-burning fireplaces (may need repairs) are just some of the many charms of this historic home, which has been lovingly cared for by the same owners for 35 years. The home boasts an excellent floorplan for both gracious entertaining and comfortable family living, with an embassy-sized dining room, multiple living spaces including an airy sunroom and a cozy den, as well as a powder room—all on the main floor! Four bedrooms and three baths up, and a lower-level au pair/in-law suite complete this perfectly laid out home. Mature landscaping graces all parts of the 0.75-acre property, and there is plenty of room for a pool! River Forest is a wooded oasis just a few minutes' drive from downtown D.C. as well as Northern Virginia's finest shopping and dining destinations. Homes in this exclusive neighborhood rarely go on the market and never at this price point. It's a once-in-a-lifetime opportunity, and it won't last! Please note, property offered AS IS.

2013

Alexis

The listing popped up on my phone last night. I scrolled through the pictures at least a dozen times, then tried to conjure the house's full layout in my mind's eye as I fell asleep. Now, over breakfast, I am looking at the pictures again and trying to make my only-one-a-day-during-pregnancy espresso last, while Sam struggles to convince Caleb to eat the Cheerios on his highchair tray. Last night it had seemed like a good idea to schedule a 9:00 a.m. showing, but now we are running late and I have to text our realtor.

"Dammit, Alexis, can you help me out here?" Sam snaps after Caleb sweeps a chubby hand across his tray, knocking most of the cereal onto the kitchen floor. I jump to attention and quickly clear the small island, dumping our coffee mugs in the sink for later. "Don't curse, he's old enough to repeat you now. Just give him a yogurt pouch and I'll get the rain jackets."

Our weekends often devolve into a chaotic and unproductive exercise in domesticity, especially compared to the order and calm of our weekdays. Monday to Friday, we hand Caleb off to his nanny at 7:00 and take turns coming home early enough to give him dinner and put him to bed. I love the nights when it's my turn. I'll let him babble and splash in the bath until the water gets cold, while I sit on the floor next to the tub just grinning at him. Then, against all principles of our overdue sleep training, I hold him in my arms long after he's fallen asleep, inhaling the clean smell of his curly auburn hair and running my fingers along the chubby curves of his delicate, new-fawn skin. Somehow, on the weekends, both of us fumbling to parent together is harder. It makes me worry how much worse things will get when the new baby comes.

As we cross the bridge over the Potomac into Northern Virginia, the mottled brown and green wall of trees clinging to the river's steep western bank rises up in front of us through the mist. "I'm really excited about this house, Sam."

"I'm sure you are. It's too expensive and too old." He smiles out at the squeaky windshield wipers and takes one big hand off the steering wheel to reach over the gearshift and squeeze my knee.

"But it's supposed to be one of the nicest neighborhoods inside the Beltway, and old houses have a lot of character." For the next ten minutes, I rattle off the house's features, having memorized the listing description, while Caleb dozes off in his car seat. Sam alternates between quiet chuckles and long sighs, letting me know he's skeptical, but doesn't interrupt me.

When the GPS instructs us to turn into the neighborhood, I stop mid-sentence and actually say "Wow." We've abruptly left behind the featureless principal roads and strip malls of D.C.'s close-in suburbs and turned onto a narrow, curving street. Thick woods on both sides open up every few hundred feet to postcard-perfect scenes of residential affluence. Manicured lawns, large houses set back from the road in a variety of tasteful architectural styles, and high-end cars casually parked in driveways combine to make me suddenly and painfully aware of the old Honda hatchback we are driving. We inherited it from Sam's parents years ago—a perfectly fine car for people who live in the city and park anonymously on the street. Not a car for this neighborhood.

"Wow," I say again. "I can't believe we've never been back here before. We'd have to really step it up to fit in." I'm almost whispering now, as if someone might hear us.

"We could just throw a new car into the mortgage while we're at it," Sam mutters, slowing down to look around himself. I can tell he is impressed.

Two more turns and we find ourselves on Shadow Road, pulling up to a large, pale blue house partially hidden behind a trio of tall evergreens. As Sam tentatively pulls into the house's semicircular driveway, our realtor steps out of the bloodred front door waving with nearly frantic excitement.

"Good morning, Crawfords! I've got to say, I did *not* think you could get into this neighborhood!" she practically yells to us from the portico as I help Sam strap Caleb into the baby carrier on his back. Now that I am pregnant he's grudgingly accepted this load, but he's so tall that I have to get on the tips of my toes to do it, clutching a jumble of carrier straps pulled as long as they'll go. I resist the urge to tell our realtor to shut up, and quickly finish all the clips so I can cut off her broadcast of our inadequate finances.

Even in the gloom, the house is beautiful. It is a Cape Cod Revival, sprawling but symmetric, with a steeply pitched roof and dormered windows sheltered by a frame of additional fully grown trees on both edges of its wide lot. As I climb up the brick steps, I notice the large house numbers spelled out in serif script above the front door and smile at the indulgence. A house worthy of writing out its numbers.

"Let me tell you this even before we go in, the house needs *a lot* of work, but this street is fabulous. Seriously, if I were you, I would make an offer on it *today*," she continues emphatically as we step through the front door.

We worked with the same realtor when we bought our row-house, and I had called her a few weeks ago, the day after my positive pregnancy test. She knows how focused I am on finding an as-close-to-perfect-as-possible house before the baby comes, and we don't waste time anymore on pleasantries.

The front door opens onto a large foyer with an elaborately detailed triple archway to the living and dining rooms, and what looks like a sunroom beyond. "Gracious entry to formal entertaining spaces," narrates our realtor as we walk in.

"It smells musty," Sam says, doubtful.

"Well, this house was built in the 1920s, and it's only had two owners, can you believe it? Some of it must be additions, but it all flows together seamlessly." She gestures to the left, past the intricately carved staircase, "There's a den and powder room over there," then pivots to the right. We follow her through a narrow doorway and enter an indeterminate but long-past era of poor taste—muddy-colored linoleum floors, tiny, veneered cabinets clinging to oversized soffits, and a fruit-themed backsplash.

"The kitchen is at the *front* of the house, which is unusual, and *clearly* this one has seen better days," she continues. But beyond the main kitchen is a breakfast room, enclosed on three sides by divided-light, floor-to-ceiling windows, and another living space with a gray-veined marble fireplace surround and hearth. "Wood-burning, may not be functional," she goes on. "This room would be an *excellent* playroom. You'll be needing one of those."

The basement is damp, Sam hits his head on the ceiling going up the stairs to the second floor, and all the bathrooms desperately need updating. But neither of us has ever lived in anything nearly as gracious, or as big. Our narrow rowhouse downtown is a new construction box, full of light and not much else. Sam's parents' house is perfectly fine, but its aluminum siding and identical neighbors hold little charm. My mother and I always lived in apartments—run-down rentals I'd just as soon forget. In fact, I can only think of two houses that gave me the same feeling I have right now: the Federal-style mansion of my former boss, a lifelong strategy consultant who worked in a dozen countries before buying a half block of Georgetown for one person, and back in college, the expansive Connecticut estate of my freshman-year roommate who'd taken pity and brought me home with her for a long weekend.

In this house, it feels like the same good taste and sense of wealth could be mine. Dentil and egg-and-dart moldings crown several rooms, the subtle irregularities of the thick plaster walls feel special, and the narrow-plank white-oak floors are original— according to our realtor—and quite lovely, if profusely creaky. I am enamored.

"Maybe we can get more for our rowhouse than we've been thinking," I whisper up to Sam as I tickle Caleb under his soft chin. Our realtor leads us through the living room to a set of French doors opening to the backyard, her heels clicking. She must be in her late sixties, at least, and dresses up for showings on the weekend. We pad along quietly behind her in sneakers.

"Alexis, come on, this is too expensive, and I know you.

You're going to want to change everything in here." But before I can respond, Sam turns his attention to the yard.

We are standing on a crumbling brick patio, overlooking a wide, gently sloping expanse of green that ends at a towering line of deciduous trees. Through the patchy branches, I make out what looks like an even larger backyard, a pool covered over for the season, and the stacked glass and concrete boxes of a modern mansion beyond.

"Those trees must be a hundred feet tall," Sam says, surprised. "Definitely room back here for a pool . . . we could have some really good parties."

Sam likes to pretend that he is a middle-class kind of guy, a Midwesterner with sensible, modest tastes, like his parents. But the truth is that he is as dazzled by nice things as I am. The first year he worked at his law firm, when we were trying to save up for a down payment, he spent half of his bonus on a watch. I didn't try to stop him. Now I feel his mind working, imagining the people he could impress with this house, and I know that this is my opportunity.

"Can we go for a walk around the neighborhood, see how it looks, and then give you a call?" I ask our realtor.

"Of course. Down the road," she points a red manicured nail toward the right, "you'll hit a cul-de-sac almost immediately, and between two of the properties there's trail access down to the Potomac River. Going back the way you came will take you to many other beautiful streets."

She steps toward us and leans in as if she has a secret to tell. Her face is close enough for me to see the foundation settled into the crow's feet around her eyes. It reminds me that I forgot to put anything on my face after showering this morning. She must think we are a mess.

"And I'll tell you, the listing agent just texted me, there are three other showings this afternoon, and he's expecting a *big* crowd at the open house tomorrow." She looks knowingly from me to Sam, and back to me.

My fingertips are beginning to tingle. I know we have a lead, but the race is on. "You'll hear from us soon, one way or the other," I say over my shoulder, as I follow Sam around the side of the house. It is already 10:00, and we don't have much time.

After grabbing hats from the car, we turn toward the cul-de-sac, walking quickly as Caleb starts to babble on Sam's back. "Trail directly to the river, now that's something," Sam says, absentmindedly rubbing at the ginger stubble on his cheeks. We both run and have spent enough crowded mornings in Rock Creek Park to know how valuable this is. 52 Shadow Road is across the street, a large yellow farmhouse with a front porch running the span of the façade, centered on what must be a double lot. A white-haired man is sitting on the porch with a blanket on his lap and appears to be engrossed in a magazine.

"This neighborhood is so much nicer than any of the others we've seen," I say to Sam, as the man lowers the magazine to his blanket and raises a hand to wave. "Doesn't it feel so exclusive? There probably aren't too many young children, but still, these people must all be really successful, don't you think?"

"Ya that's pretty obvious," Sam laughs. "I think one of my senior partners lives somewhere around here. This street is amazing, it's exactly the kind of place I thought we'd live eventually. But that house is in rough shape."

"Exactly, how else could we afford to live here?" I continue without waiting for him to answer. "Look at the size of these lots, and the trees, and we'd never have to move again, this is the top school pyramid in the area. We could renovate slowly.

The kitchen is the only thing that would really need to be done right away. I mean, we can't live with a kitchen like that."

I'm not sure whether my monologue is swaying Sam, but I can tell the walk is. 53 Shadow Road is next, separated from what I hope will be our house by a narrow but dense grove of trees. It is an oversized new construction built in a modern Tudor style, with an austere white stucco façade broken up by the dramatic peaks and swoops of a black roof. Only one mature tree remains in the front yard, and it looks like most of the first-floor lights are on against the morning gloom. I imagine a happy family inside, enjoying the type of cozy and relaxed Saturday morning I hope we will eventually have. The wide cul-de-sac is now straight ahead, carved into three equally grand properties.

"God, all these houses are huge. They're practically estates," Sam says appreciatively. "I'd better make partner next year, we'll need the money."

We notice the house on our left first, 54 Shadow Road. It is a massive, white Federal-style mansion with black shutters, thick columns, and an elegant row of dormered third-story windows. This is the house of my dreams, anyone's dreams really. I say "Wow" for the third time this morning.

Sam goes on, "You should reconsider going back to your old firm too. Country club memberships don't run cheap."

"Come on, Sam, why are you bringing that up? You know we can afford the house. That's the only thing we're talking about buying—" I stop myself when we see them, coming around one side of their house in a loose huddle, relaxed and laughing.

First, the husband—a square-jawed, dark blond man with a rake in his hand—followed by three teenagers, each a different shade of blond. The tallest of the three, a boy, is cradling a large bag of soil, while the other two hold shovels, rakes, and gloves.

The wife brings up the rear empty-handed, a slim woman whose sandy blond hair is pulled into a low ponytail. Even from fifty feet away, I can see that she is quite good-looking. The five of them are dressed in subtly coordinating quilted pullovers and rubber boots, comfortable in their affluence—exactly the type of people I had expected to live on a street like this. Sam makes a joke about vanity gardening, since everyone in this neighborhood must hire a landscaper. I am still smiling at this when the wife sees us.

We have been staring at their house, and I suppose that is why she starts walking toward us, leaving the husband and children to begin their work near the garage. "Hi there," she calls out in a bright, expectant voice, almost as if asking a question. I clear my throat reflexively, my mind scrambling to compose a satisfying explanation for our presence.

"Good morning!" Sam answers before I can.

"Hi!" I add quickly. "We were just touring the house that's for sale and wanted to get a better feel for the neighborhood. We're thinking about making an offer."

"That's great!" the woman replies, taking in the picture of our family as we had just done with hers. "I hope you like what you see. Your little one is adorable!" She dismisses us with a big smile, turning back toward her house before either of us can answer.

We immediately start walking again, quicker than before, propelled by the eyes of this catalogue family on our backs and the wet chill of the day creeping between our toes. We must look like shoddy prospective neighbors, with Sam's tall frame all a crumple of rain jacket and baby carrier straps. Without needing to look in a mirror, I know I'm even worse—in a faded old windbreaker that barely zips over my already showing belly, and frizz poking out from my old knit cap and sticking to my face in the dampness. But here we are. There is no time to go home and pull ourselves together for a better first impression.

55 Shadow Road is a hulking orange-brick Colonial facing 54, likely a product of the 1990s—perfectly fine and exceedingly large, but nothing compared to its neighbors. 56, sitting at the apex of the cul-de-sac, is an imposing stone house with at least four chimneys. Next to its mailbox stands a plinth of matching stone, with a little silver plaque mounted on it. The plaque is engraved with a paragraph explaining that the house was the Colonial-era manor of the area and that the original owners' descendants—lucky them—had slowly sold off all the surrounding parcels over the last two centuries.

We do not stop long to look at either house, having spotted the green county sign denoting the trailhead with pictograms of a pedestrian, a cyclist, and a small wave with an "x" through it. The sign stands neatly on what looks to be a no-man's-land between the side yard fences demarcating the property lines of 55 and 56, a gravel trail about six feet wide leading straight into dense woods. A "no parking" placard immediately below the green county sign signals exclusivity, and Sam is thrilled.

As we turn to walk back toward the house, he says, "You'll be shocked to hear this, but I think you're right. We should make an offer. This neighborhood is unbelievable."

"Really?" I counter.

"Yes, really. What? Now you don't want it anymore?"

"No, of course I want it. Worst house, best block, it will be a great investment. Let's do it," I reply, grabbing his big hand and smiling to show him that we are on the same side about this. There is no need for an argument.

We keep holding hands and marveling to each other about

the passing landscape. We make a brisk loop past 51, to the end of the block where Shadow Road intersects with Sunrise Lane, and back. Sam wonders aloud if the houses on Sunrise command a premium for being on a more hopeful-sounding street, and we both laugh.

It is past 10:30 when we return to the driveway of 51 and Caleb is getting fussy, but before unlocking the car doors, I glance down the street to see if the family in the white Federal is still in their front yard. I'm mortified by the possibility of them seeing us get in the Honda. Happily, they are nowhere in sight.

I call our realtor while Sam drives us home, and the deal is done by the time I start the dishwasher after dinner—a full-price offer with no contingencies, and the quickest closing our lender will commit to. Every other house we've seen has been so obviously problematic—new construction awkwardly towering over modest ranches, a coffee shop around the corner but a convenience store sign glaring in the backyard—I was starting to think we'd be stuck in our skinny rowhouse, forever climbing stairs and tripping over toys. This house—our new house—will have problems to be sure. I've read that old houses always do. But the bones, the lot, and the location are just so good. It feels like we've purchased it by an incredible stroke of luck, so quickly and easily do our lives shift course for Shadow Road.

Blair

Teddy's tired voice calls to me from the mudroom, "Hey babe, we're back." I don't answer, and instead just let myself enjoy each familiar sound: sports equipment clattering to the tile, kids dropping onto benches to peel off smelly socks then grudgingly tucking all their stuff out of sight, into the custom built-ins I designed for this purpose. Since we told my mother not to stay, and Whit failed his driver's test yet again, Teddy was on game duty today. He had to get all three kids out the door practically at the crack of dawn to make it to Whit's cross-country meet, then run to catch the second half of Jamie's soccer tournament. Poor Rob just got dropped off and had no one to cheer him on at badminton. But it's his own fault for having picked a back-yard pastime as his fall sport.

It's a good sign. Usually, when Teddy's angry he'll only call me by my first name in this fake, cold tone that I just can't stand. So childish. Last night we went out for a gorgeous dinner at Dolce del Mar on the Georgetown waterfront, to compensate for the trip we should have been on and talk things through. But we just ended up arguing for hours. This morning I told him I had a migraine and stayed in bed with the drapes drawn until they all left the house.

Now I'm sitting at the island, waiting for him. "Hi Mom," each kid calls over their shoulder as they head straight upstairs for showers. They know I'm not interested in sweaty hugs.

"Hi honey," I finally answer, as he comes into the kitchen and reflexively leans down to kiss me on the lips. I keep my eyes open, and notice that the three horizontal lines on his handsome forehead look a little deeper today.

"You feeling better?" he asks, straightening back up.

"Much. How about you?" I keep my eyes on his face, wanting to know if he's realized I'm right, as always.

Teddy gives me one of his charming sideways smiles and nods slightly.

"I'm glad." I follow as he heads toward the fridge and wrap my arms around his broad torso from behind. "Oh, and listen to this, the open house at Dr. Robinson's didn't happen today. The realtor didn't even show up."

"Huh, maybe somebody swooped in and bought it already," he answers, his head deep in a shelf.

"That place? It's falling apart. Who would want that?" I say into the warmth of his back.

"I have no idea, but Jim would know," he answers as he pulls himself out of the fridge with a gleaming red apple in hand. Jim is one of Teddy's golfing buddies and runs the agency selling the place. I let go and turn to grab my cell phone off the counter. I have his number and dial him on speaker.

"Jimmy, it's Blair Bard, how are you?" I say into the phone and wink at Teddy, who's sat down across the island.

"Blair, to what do I owe the pleasure my dear? Don't tell me that you and Teddy are thinking of selling that gorgeous house of yours?" Jim's affable voice fills the kitchen.

"You wish," I laugh. "I'm just calling as a nosy neighbor. You know the old Cape your agency is selling on our street? There was supposed to be an open house today, but nobody showed up, not even the realtor."

"Ah, well, it hasn't closed yet of course, but a couple saw it yesterday morning and just fell in love. They made a strong offer and the Robinsons decided to accept. You'll have new neighbors very soon."

I get off the phone with Jim and raise my eyebrows at Teddy, "Do you think it was that couple with the baby that walked by?"

"Maybe, why not?" he shrugs, then finishes off his apple in three bites.

"They didn't look like they could afford it, with all the work it needs," I continue.

"How do you know? I hope you're not saying that because the wife was a minority." Even with a mouth full of apple flesh, the self-righteousness in his voice is hard to miss. Teddy prides himself on the right thing—thinking it, saying it, doing it—even if it might mean hurting me. I can't stand this about him, but I don't want another fight, so I let it go.

"Oh come on, I don't even know what the wife was. I'm saying that because of their awful clothes and crappy car. Anyway, the Robinsons should really just have sold it to a developer, to do a gut reno. It's too charming to tear down, but only just barely."

Now I'm talking to myself. Teddy's thrown out the core, pulled out his own phone, and is engrossed in typing out messages with his thumbs. He's already decided, and it doesn't matter what I say. I open my mouth to complain but hold myself back again. It's been too long of a weekend already.

2014

Alexis

We move on a miserably typical mid-Atlantic winter day of incessant, cold rain. Caleb, his nanny, Elena, and I pack into the Honda and follow behind the moving van to Shadow Road, while Sam stays back at the rowhouse to supervise the cleaning crew. I am five months pregnant, and full of nervous energy watching the movers methodically unload the disassembled furniture and neat stacks of boxes we paid extra for them to pack up yesterday.

The three months since our offer was accepted have been a blur of business trips, doctor's appointments, and holidays, overlaid with a steady stream of expensively bad news about the house. I'd refused to discuss the possibility of placing our dishware in a kitchen caked with the muck and dust of strangers, and convinced Sam to pay extra for a rush order on new cabinets. We also paid our general contractor extra to work through the holidays, only to get a call the day after Thanksgiving that the main heating system, an ancient furnace powering the original network of radiators, had given out and his crew had gone home due to the intolerable working conditions.

Early December brought tidings of mold in the basement and a rodent infestation in the attic that had destroyed whatever insulation once existed. Sam and I agreed not to buy each other any presents for Christmas as a cost-saving measure. In a small show of affection, I bought him a deep green cashmere sweater along with a framed photo of Caleb for his office. He, on the other hand, stuck to our agreement and did not get me anything. But to his credit, Sam did save me most of the headaches of dealing with the contractor, visiting the house nearly every day to check on progress. That was gift enough, and now, at least the kitchen is almost complete.

As I try in broken Spanish to explain to one of the moving crew that the bed frames have been placed in the wrong bedrooms, the rusty chimes of the doorbell cut in and drown me out. Elena reaches the door as I come down the stairs, and I signal to her that she can open it. She is also part of the move. We've convinced her to live in the basement rather than endure an even longer daily commute, at a fraction of the rent she's been paying for a run-down studio apartment in an outer suburb. She is a diminutive and quiet woman, nearing sixty, and on her third decade of shouldering multiple relatives' expenses back home. I wonder sometimes if they have any idea what it's like, living in a foreign country, barely speaking the language, and draining her bank account every two weeks for the school fees and prescription medicines of people she barely knows anymore. She hadn't actually needed much convincing about the basement and seems relieved at the prospect of saving some money.

"Hi!" I hear the bright voice and immediately know who it

is—the woman with the Federal mansion and gorgeous family. I come up behind Elena, who quietly fades back into the house.

"Oh hi! I'm Blair, from the white house just across the street," she says, gesturing with her blond ponytail behind and to her left. She's in a red rain jacket that looks like it was tailored just for her, and tall black galoshes. "Welcome to the neighborhood!" she grins and holds out a basket of artisanal baked goods, wrapped with a large, sage-colored bow.

"Wow, thank you so much," I fumble to receive the basket while trying not to look mortified. The house is, obviously, a mess of boxes, dismembered furniture, and construction dust from the kitchen. I am also a mess, wearing the only clothes I'd found that fit after having packed up nearly everything—a pair of pajama pants and my sleeping-bag-size Yale sweatshirt. My hair is sticking out in all directions thanks to the rain, and I can feel every pore on my face fighting for attention.

"I'm Alexis," I manage to smile back. "Sorry for the mess, we're just starting to move in, and I don't know where I put most of my clothes," I add, vaguely gesturing to myself.

"Oh don't apologize, moving is such a headache, that's why I wanted to drop this off today. Everyone could use a few carbs on a day like this," she laughs, and I do too. "I remember you from a few months ago. Was that your . . . mother? Here helping you?"

"No, it's our nanny. She'll be living in the basement. I need all the help I can get, we have another one on the way," I explain, patting my belly through the folds of my sweatshirt.

"Oh that's wonderful, a live-in is so much more convenient. Our kids are too old for it now, but I never did manage to convince Teddy to have someone else in the house." Blair is not the first person to have mistaken our nanny for my mother—we both have brown skin and dark hair, after all. But she brought me this beautiful basket, out in the rain and with a big smile on her face.

"God, where are my manners, please, would you like to come in?" I ask.

"No, no thanks, the last thing I want to do is get in your way, we'll have plenty of time to get to know each other." With that, she waves a slim, manicured hand, pulls up the hood of her jacket, and is off. I watch her cross the street diagonally, aiming confidently for her garage without looking back. I bring the basket into our dusty kitchen, and fish out a card from between the folds of the damp ribbon. It's a single piece of heavy, cream-colored cardstock embossed with the thick, navy blue initials "BB" at the top. A short message is handwritten in spare, flowing script: "Welcome to the neighborhood! Blair and Teddy Bard, 54 Shadow Road."

I have crossed paths with many women like Blair. They exude the confidence and comfort that must come from never having been deprived of anything, or ashamed of anything. It starts when they are children, really. At the elite, all-girls high school I went to, "scholarship student" might as well have been tattooed on my forehead, it was so obvious that I—and a few other lucky ones—had to work to be there. Anxious and sweaty from the long walk from the bus stop, I'd hurry past all the full-freight girls, my single uniform skirt scratching at my shins, while they strolled in bored and oblivious, their one-of-a-closetful-of-skirts tailored to barely cover their behinds. And in some ways, it got worse after school. At my first strategy consulting job out of college, they were the ones in confidence-inspiring designer clothes and centrally located condos that their parents bought them, while I looked like an intern in polyester from the sale rack, still running in from public transportation. Those women used to make the envy rise in my throat like vomit. But I've gotten used to them. More than that, Blair is my neighbor, and she'd been so warm, it's hard for me not to like her.

Saturday / March 15 / 11:15 PM

After an hour in bed losing a wrestling match with my body pillow, I get up to unpack the last box from our move. Even though I'm exhausted, it's been getting harder to sleep as my belly gets bigger and lights up the pains that had gone dormant after having Caleb. "Old lady pains," Sam calls them, which makes me cringe. Sam is not home tonight—more depositions in New York, and this time he's decided to stay the weekend and visit some old college friends who still live in the city. "Go ahead," I'd told him when he proposed it. "It will be much harder to do things like that once we have two."

But the truth is things already feel hard. Stupidly, I'd hoped another baby would bring us closer. He couldn't keep his hands to himself when I was pregnant with Caleb, but we've barely touched each other in months. Work is to blame, at least partly. One of us has had a business trip nearly every week, and the constant grind of being on the move has pulled us each into a separate orbit. A whirlwind of solitary, pseudo-glamour— business class and concierge floor, high-stakes meetings and upscale dinners—suddenly spirals back to suburban life, with laundry that needs doing and toddler handprints on freshly painted walls. It's like a slap in the face, walking in the door. At least, that's how I feel, and judging by the look on Sam's face sometimes, the same thought has crossed his mind.

Sam is working even harder than I am, trying to drive home the case for promotion at his law firm, and maybe deserves more empathy. But it's sloppy thinking for him to assume that he can slack off at home just because he is putting in the time at work. When he's too tired to play with Caleb, or can't be bothered to take out the trash, I usually let him know how awful he's being. This only makes things worse, of course. He just mocks my admonishments as unreasonable whining, instead of trying harder. We've had the same argument dozens of times, and it's just become more bitter for all its mundaneness.

Even more stupidly, I also thought that the new house would make us happier. Sam would have more impressive entertaining space, the children and nanny would have grass and fresh air, and I would finally feel like we'd made it. For the past few months though, the house has done nothing but add to our arguments—how to handle unexpected repairs, which renovations to prioritize, and how to pay for it all. Whenever I complain that he works too much, he snaps back at me, "Remember that huge mortgage you wanted to take on? For this dump? You need at least one partner's income to keep you afloat, old lady."

For reasons I cannot understand, Sam thinks it's funny to reference our age difference, as if it matters. I am nine months older but was a year behind him in college, because my mother didn't enroll me in kindergarten the year I was supposed to go. When I eventually figured out that I was always turning a year older than my classmates and asked her why, she'd told me that it was for my own good. The old woman who ran the basement day care where I'd been going refused to come pick me up at the bus stop—she said she was too arthritic to corral the little group of kids for a four-block walk—and my mother figured a six-year-old had a better chance of navigating the walk alone than a five-year-old. So she kept me at the day care for an extra year. After that, I trudged to that basement every day after school until I was eight, when the day care woman decided I was too old to keep coming.

Sam also likes to point out that he makes more money than me, even though that's only been true since I downgraded to a smaller, more modest consulting firm. He'd argued from every angle to try and convince me not to, but I'd gone ahead anyway. It's been more than a year, but he won't let it go, bringing it up almost every time we talk about money, as if I could just unmake my decision and go back to my old job. I don't want to anyway, our schedules would be ten times worse if I did, but sometimes it feels like he doesn't care at all about what I'm saying.

Nights like tonight, when my body pains flare up and our latest fights won't stop replaying in my mind, sleep seems impossible. So I finish with the box—dusty DVDs and books we haven't read in decades—and decide to take it out to the recycling bin and go for a walk. Two days ago, the high temperature didn't break freezing, but tonight the air feels nearly warm, and I throw on a light jacket that is too small to zip up over my belly. At least at this hour I don't have to worry about being seen.

It's nearing midnight, but the sky is clear and the moon is almost full, so I can walk along the street without using the flashlight on my cell phone. The streetlights are few and far between, presumably because the homeowners took issue with light pollution rather than any neglect on the county's part. But even in the dark, I feel self-conscious—a pregnant Black woman strolling alone along this kind of street—and think again about getting a dog to give me a legitimate excuse to wander.

It's not that the neighbors are unfriendly. Blair was the first, but in the week after we moved in nearly a dozen stopped by with expensive plants, baked goods, and scented candles. Every house in the cul-de-sac, except for the empty stone manor, plus a handful of people from further up the road who'd known our house's old owners, had come. I'd taken the week off, so was usually the one who answered the door when the bell rang. Twice, the unwitting welcome wagon smiled warmly at me, gift in arms, and asked to speak to the owner of the house. I couldn't just shut the door, so I smiled back and explained, committing their faces to memory so I can ignore them in the future if the opportunity ever presents itself.

A third time, after Elena reached the front door first and called out to me, I found an elderly couple holding up a lush fern between them. *"Oh good morning, we just wanted to welcome you all to the neighborhood,"* the wife started off enthusiastically. *"You . . . are you . . . is this your house?"* she tripped herself up trying to be polite, while craning her neck to see past me into the foyer, in search of a more plausible-looking neighbor. Caleb was wrapped around one of my legs with only a diaper on, and I hadn't yet showered, but still. *"Yes, my husband and I moved in last week, and this is my son,"* I'd laughed, patting Caleb's head. *"That's great!"* the husband had said, a little too loudly. *"Where are you from?"* he went on as they both leaned in to deposit the fern at my feet. Caleb grabbed at a frond with a chubby hand, and I called for Elena half in Spanish, to come scoop him up before giving them an answer, *"Well, we're just moving from the city, and I grew up not too far away actually, around Baltimore."* Relieved of their generous burden, they looked eager to have a conversation. *"Oh is that where you're originally from?"* the wife asked.

Usually, I answer the question that they can't quite politely formulate—*why do you look like you do*—before it devolves into an awkward guessing game, but that morning I had just wanted to take a shower and get on with my day. So I'd grinned as wide as I could manage as I answered, *"Born and raised! I really apologize, but I've got to get back to my son now. Thank you for the gift!"* and shut the door.

I walk toward the intersection with Sunrise and consider continuing past it, but even with a spotless local crime map, the late night murmurs of the trees prickle at the back of my neck. I decide to turn back. I pass our house and continue toward the cul-de-sac. All the houses are dark, except for a faint light coming through one of the first-floor windows at Blair and Teddy's. I haven't spoken to Blair since the day we moved in, but we have waved at each other multiple times. All the neighbors wave here, not like on our old street where resentment seemed to be the predominant feeling between the young-ish professionals betting their financial futures on appreciation, like we had, and the longtime residents watching their property taxes rise. Here, everyone's property taxes must be astronomical, but they can afford it.

Sam and I have talked about having a small housewarming party, to reciprocate the graciousness of all the gifts. No one had even stopped by to introduce themselves when we moved into our rowhouse. A party would also help clear up any remaining doubts that I am, in fact, a co-owner of the house. I haven't told Sam about any of the misunderstandings. Not because he wouldn't be sympathetic—he would be. He'd call them idiots and laugh at them and tell me not to worry about it.

But he'd also find a way to ask if I might have done something without meaning to—just a little something—to have made them ask. Like a few years ago, when I'd called him on

the verge of tears after four days with a client who kept thinking that my Sam-like analyst was the newly minted team leader,
instead of me. Sam had listened and made fun of the client,
joking that I must have traveled back in time instead of to an
office park in Dallas. But he'd also asked if I was being assertive
enough, if I could try a little more to act like I was in charge. My
first weekend home from that trip, he'd cheerily suggested we
go to the mall so I could get more "team leader appropriate"
clothes. I'd said no, just don't worry about it, and he'd gotten
annoyed, like he usually does.

I am standing directly in front of Blair's house now, wondering what she is doing up at this hour. Maybe she's laughing over
a drink with an old friend in what must be her gorgeous kitchen.
A housewarming party would also be a good way to start making friends with some of the younger neighbors—the woman
next door in the Tudor, Jennifer, looks like she's in her thirties,
at most, and some couples, like Teddy and Blair, are probably
in their forties. But the weeks have slipped through my fingers
and the opportunity has gone stale. I wouldn't know how to do
it even if I had the time. Making, much less keeping, friends
has never been my strong suit. When Sam and I got together, it
was easy to start forgetting this weakness, because his friends
became mine too, by default. Dorm room parties, summer road
trips, post-work happy hours—I've always had a secure role to
play as Sam's girlfriend, then wife. But now that the children
have started coming and the migration to the suburbs is on, it
feels like couples are closing ranks. Husbands prioritize their
favorite buddies for those rare rounds of golf they are allowed
to play, and wives select the friends they actually like for their
book clubs. It turns out that Sam usually makes the cut while I
do not.

He's told me, more than once, that I should try harder—call up old roommates, be more enthusiastic about those colleagues that he has over—but he doesn't appreciate that I have tried, and failed. I even joined a new-mothers group after Caleb was born, but the glassy-eyed discussion rarely deviated from diaper contents and mastitis. I was simultaneously bored and humiliated in every meeting, afraid I'd never care about anything else again yet worried I actually didn't care enough.

I look around the cul-de-sac. No one is out. I hesitate for a second, then start moving slowly to the left, toward the side of Blair's house, keeping close to the tall hedge that separates it from 52. I'm not sure if I am doing this out of nosiness or restlessness, but something attracts me to that faint light. Halfway toward the house, I realize that I know nothing about the property—they may have a dog, or motion-sensing lights—and stop still. Nothing happens, and after a few seconds, I move closer.

Four floor-to-ceiling windows are set on this side of the house, toward the back. The shades are open, and a soft light illuminates what looks like an elegant great room, decorated in a muted palette of creams and whites. Blair is propped up on a deep, clean-lined sofa in the middle of the room. She is naked, her head thrown back and her hands clasped around Teddy's head in between her legs. There is no reason for them to close their shades I suppose. The hedge against which I am lurking is probably twenty feet tall and shields their house on this side. They likely never considered the possibility that a neighbor would wander back here in the middle of the night. I should not be here, but I am frozen to the spot, ashamed and, absurdly, jealous.

Blair

God it feels good to be fucked by Teddy. I've been in love with him since the day we met. It's so cheesy to say, but we were meant to be together. Even after all these years, and three kids, we still have times like last night where we practically rip each other's clothes off, the urgency is too much.

I'm staring up at the ceiling of our bedroom, thinking about last night and about our first time, back in . . . I can't even remember the year, Jesus. Middle age makes me feel ancient sometimes. But I was living in a ratty studio apartment in the West Village, and we were making so much noise on my squeaky full-size that the downstairs neighbor started pounding on the ceiling.

I'll have to wake him up soon. We've got Sunday brunch at the club in two hours, and I promised Jennifer that I'd stop by this morning to look at her new dining room rug. I already know that I'll be lying through my teeth. That woman has awful taste and, tragically, an unlimited decorating budget thanks to her husband, Jeff. I should have found her someone else when she first asked me. There's a designer out there for every persuasion. But I liked her. Even worse, after we'd talked for a while, I felt sorry for her.

She's been through things. She was still in high school when she had her son, and has worked some truly awful-sounding, menial jobs. Yet she's managed to keep both her sense of humor and her good looks intact. Even now, lonely and floundering in the house of her dreams and more money than she ever thought she'd have, she's still sweet and funny. It's mostly her own fault, I know, but Jeff deserves some thanks for her misery too. I do my best to avoid him at parties. He's a humorless and unpleasant guy whose only shows of emotion, I'm told, are flashes of anger. Every morning must be awful for her, waking up and remembering who she's married to. So when she asked for my help I couldn't say no, and now I'm stuck just trying to steer her away from the worst of her design impulses.

I should be hunting for my own new rug, for this room, and maybe new light fixtures. Sitting up on my elbows and looking around, I realize the whole master needs an update. It's been at least three years since I went gray, splashing it all over every surface in here, and I'm ready to move on. One room won't be enough though. I need a more substantial project. I thought I had one, but now I'm not so sure.

Last year, before things got so complicated, we talked about getting a place in the mountains, to lure our kids back to us. Soon they'll be in college, and we'll need to use everything we can to keep ourselves attractive. Skiing, hot tubs, a lax alcohol policy, whatever it takes. We'd booked a flight to Colorado for the long weekend in October to house-hunt, and I'd even started pulling together boards for the design: leather and linen, unpolished brass and dark wood, big windows and a massive fireplace. I could see it all coming together.

Then, the night before our flight, my mother arrived. We'd asked her to come down from Philadelphia and stay with the kids, but she'd shown up with some seriously unpleasant baggage. Her voice was even, nonchalant almost, as she spoke her ugly words, but I knew she was drunk. Besides the faint stench of vodka, she'd mismatched her two pairs of caramel-colored Tod's driving loafers, with suede on one foot and leather on the other. But the liquor wasn't enough to make her sorry, either for telling us something so awful or for not having told us sooner.

We'd canceled the house-hunting trip, of course, and sent her home the next morning. But instead of ignoring my mother's drunken visit until it fades into never-happened (which is the only reasonable thing to do) Teddy can't seem to focus on anything else. Sometimes I think he's actually lost his mind, what he says is so unbelievable. We're just stuck on the same nonsense, and every day it grows, that nasty feeling in the pit of my stomach that this won't end well. We haven't talked about the mountain house in months. But last night gave me a flicker of hope. Maybe we should get a little place in Manhattan, just for ourselves. Maybe, eventually, we'll do both.

Teddy rolls onto his back and opens his cobalt eyes just as I'm getting out of bed. "Blair, last night was . . ." he starts in his husky, just-waking-up voice. He's staring at the ceiling and stretching his arms past the pillows to the headboard, his features already distorted by what I'm afraid is regret.

I lay back down and pull his unhappy face into my breasts to stop him from talking. He doesn't pull away. I kiss his warm forehead and grip the back of his still thick hair, just like I did last night.

Alexis

It rained all morning, but around noon the clouds dispersed as if scared off by the sun, and a gorgeous, clear-blue afternoon emerged. Sam, the children, and I are sitting out on our crumbling brick patio, enjoying the briefly perfect weather before summer's humidity pushes us back inside.

I gave birth to a baby girl, Carter, in the middle of May, and the past two weeks have been a blur of diapers, feedings, and bleeding. Every inch of my body aches, and I don't think I've uttered a fully coherent sentence in days. It is Saturday, and I have a glass of wine in my hand for the first time this year.

Sam's parents flew in the day we came home from the hospital. I appreciate their help, but I can only be around them for a week before suffocation creeps in—maybe less. The constant effort to listen with interest to his father's stale stash of stories about Sam growing up, to feign appreciation for his mother's unsolicited advice, and to pretend I don't notice the pity in the way they look at me, their poor daughter-in-law, orphaned and adrift in the world . . . It's tiring.

Sam had insisted on giving them the "grand tour" as soon as they'd walked in, house-proud in a way I'd never heard him before. From the sprawling main floor—*"We've got a playroom, a living room, a den, and a sunroom. The four of us could be here and not see each other all day!"*—to the somehow-still-slightly-damp-smelling basement—*"We waterproofed this whole damn thing. Elena doesn't mind though, it's basically a one-bedroom apartment that she's got down here."*—to the narrow halls of our second floor—*"It's a little tight up here, but the layout's great. Did you see how the stair rails are carved?"*

I'd followed along behind, cradling Carter and qualifying everything he said. *The half-empty rooms will get filled, just as soon as our savings recover from all those repairs. Don't mind the yellow acrylic shower liner in the guest bath, all the bathrooms need to be redone. The utility bills might kill us this summer, what with five thousand drafty square feet to cool. What were we thinking.*

Sam's parents had nodded along supportively to our opposing commentary, genuinely impressed but also worried that we might not land the leap from a brand-new, hermetically sealed 1,500-square-foot rowhouse to our aging estate, as Sam called it. They'd almost choked on their pizza slices when we told them we'd paid over a million and a half dollars for a fixer-upper and seized on the idea that we should move closer to them. We could get a much newer tract house, half the size for a quarter of the cost. Sam's mother even remembered that a neighbor down the street from them is considering selling, in case we might be interested. It was all more than a convalescent should have to endure.

I'd gently declined their offer to stay a second week, and Sam had not put up a fight. But as we pulled away from the departures curb at Reagan, he'd casually asked, *"So since when did you turn on the house?"*

I'd told him I didn't know what he was talking about, honestly, and he'd laughed, *"I should have recorded it and made you listen to yourself. You spent the whole week trashing the house to my parents, as if it were a dump somebody forced you to buy."*

"No, I didn't. I love our house. I'm the one who dragged you there, remember? But it's such a mess, more than we thought it would be."

"Love? Come on, if you loved it, you wouldn't be so obsessed with talking about its little flaws all the time. Like did you have to tell my parents that the bathroom they were using is the ugliest one you've ever seen?"

"I don't think I was revealing any secrets, they have eyes don't they?"

"You can complain as much as you want but we're not redoing the bathrooms now. You're so negative all the time, you know that?"

We'd gone on like that for the rest of the drive home, with Sam insisting that my increasingly long list of mundane renovations—windows, floors, tiles—is nitpicking and unnecessary, and that we should be focused on the things that would make the house more fun, like a pool. I'd ended the argument there, with my uterus cramping, before he started getting mean.

He's reserving his paternity leave for after promotion decisions, and I'm glad for it—if he were in the house all day, we'd be having these fights constantly. Besides, Elena and I are managing between the two of us. In addition to taking care of Caleb and Carter nine hours a day, she helps keep the house presentable in between the cleaning ladies' biweekly visits, makes Caleb's breakfasts and lunches, and lends an extra pair of more versatile hands than Sam's for all the drudgery required to keep things running—dishes, laundry, and all the rest. She's also been helping me with the baby nearly every night, so we gave her this entire weekend off.

Yesterday after dinner, a cousin came to pick her up so she could spend two days with extended family near Richmond. I've never met any of them, but I know much more about Elena's family than I do my own. They all came from Honduras at some point in the last thirty years, following a long and winding migration chain through unexpected places. Maybe that's why I'd insisted we hire her, back when Caleb was a newborn and I anxiously counted the days until I could get back to work. Down in Richmond, I like to imagine Elena relaxing in a lawn chair, surrounded by cousins and laughing about old times in rapid, aspirated Spanish. Getting a break from us, and—to be honest—us getting a break from her.

Sitting out here now with just our little family—Caleb quietly playing with his blocks, Carter fast asleep on her newborn lounger, and Sam scrolling through news articles on his phone—I feel like I can breathe. A breeze is making the trees sway slightly, their full coats of green shimmering in the afternoon sun. The grackles are taking turns pecking at the lawn for their dinner, and their intermittent calls mixed with the rustling of young leaves lulls me into closing my eyes. I could fall asleep like this, balancing the nearly empty wineglass on my deflated belly. Then I hear it.

It starts out faint, barely distinguishable from the leaves. But it quickly gets louder and closer, until it fills the air around us—the high-pitched whine of an ambulance siren that now sounds like it's stalled outside our front door. This is the first time we've heard sirens here, and for a moment in my drowsiness I think we are back in our rowhouse downtown. Miraculously, the baby doesn't stir, but Caleb is startled and begins to bawl. I put down my wineglass and jump up to console him. Sam and I look at each other.

"You think Mack across the street croaked?" he jokes, but I can see a shadow of concern behind his grin. Mack is our neighbor in the yellow farmhouse, a widower who refuses to move closer to his grown children out west. He is only in his late sixties I'd guess, but perched every weekend morning on his front porch with his balding head sticking out above the day's reading material, he seems old and frail.

"Well there's only one way to find out. Why don't you go see what's happening?" I suggest. "I'll stay here with them."

Sam slowly gets up and goes around the side of the house farther from the cul-de-sac, where we have an undeveloped, heavily wooded lot for a neighbor. A few minutes pass in silence. Caleb has calmed down, and Carter is still sleeping. My curiosity is growing, so I carry Caleb inside, to the kitchen, leaving the French doors open in case the baby wakes up. We didn't have the budget to move the kitchen to a more dignified position in the back of the house, but we did enlarge the window over the sink "to bring in more light and expand the view" as I'd read on a design blog. Through the new window, I can see Mack's house straight ahead, obscured somewhat by the hemlocks in our front yard, and to the right I have an angled but clear view of Blair's house and beyond.

The ambulance is not at Mack's, but at the end of the cul-de-sac, parked in reverse with its back doors splayed open as if swallowing the trailhead. The lights are still revolving, silently now, and a small group of neighbors is gathering at a respectful distance. I see Sam chatting with Mack and with Jeff, who lives next door to us in the modern Tudor. He is in the midst of an unhealthy middle age, judging by the paunch pulling at his polo shirts, but his wife, Jennifer, is no older than me—mid-thirties—and looks like a vintage pinup girl, with thick waves of black hair and generous curves in just the right places. Despite the beautiful wife and no children, Jeff's face looks dragged down by exhaustion and creased by anger, with dark bags under his small eyes and jowls flapping at the sides of a permanent frown.

The couple in the hulking brick house, Laura and Shawn, walk down their driveway and join the group. Their two pre-teens are nowhere in sight, but Shawn is wearing a black-and-white youth soccer referee shirt, the polyester shiny-tight across his thick chest and straining around his biceps. His blond head, buzzed down nearly to baldness, is bent down toward his wife, who stands barely taller than his elbows. Even from this distance, they're a strange-looking pair, with Laura—nearly as wide as she is tall—a dark, soft blot next to her pale, muscular husband.

I see all of their heads bob up at the same moment that I hear it—the whirring of helicopter blades. "Someone must have fallen into the river," I say to myself, bouncing Caleb on my hip to keep him calm. The whirring sound falls away then rises again, as the helicopter circles back over our neighborhood and out to the river. On its third pass, as the sound briefly fades, I hear the baby's small cry out on the patio. "Shit," I say out loud. I'd forgotten about the baby. "I'm sorry Caleb, that's not a good word to say, let's go get your sister."

We settle back down on the patio, Carter hungrily sucking at a bottle while Caleb goes back to his blocks. The helicopter keeps circling, and a few minutes later we hear the whine of police cars arriving on the cul-de-sac. I use my free hand to check local chat boards and news sites on my phone, in case any-one has already posted about what is going on. But I won't drag two tiny children out onto the street just to see for myself. What would the neighbors think? At least twenty minutes pass. I can't find anything online. Just as I start formulating a respectable excuse for going out there after all—I need Sam to watch the children so I can get dinner ready—one patio door swings open, and Sam comes out with a protein shake in hand.

"What is it?" I ask as he closes the door behind him.

He looks at Caleb, who is engrossed in trying to balance a modest block tower on the low wall that edges the patio, and shrugs. "Apparently a fisherman spotted a body on the rocks below the trail. He was on a boat but managed to call 911. The ambulance guys couldn't get to the body, so they had to send in the water rescue team or whatever they're called, with the helicopter."

He stops and takes a gulp of his protein shake. Since we had Caleb, he's become obsessive about his own fitness, but I can't believe he took the time to make a shake before coming out to talk to me. There's no point in mentioning it now though. I want to hear more.

"Oh my God, that's horrific," I answer as Carter finishes the last dredges of her bottle. "Did any of the neighbors out there with you have any idea what happened?"

Sam shrugs again. "Who knows? You know that trail has some pretty dicey stretches, so maybe the person was going too fast and lost their footing. In that case, their family should sue. The trail really needs to be better maintained by the county. We were just discussing it. Apparently there've been petitions to the council, but they've been ignored because it's such a low-traffic trail."

"You always think someone should sue," I can't help but laugh.

"Most of the time, I'm right." He gives me a small smile before taking another swig of his shake.

Later, after the children are in bed, we manage to watch about half of a movie on the couch before I fall asleep. Carter's crying wakes me up around 11:00, and she and I spend a long night rocking together in her nursery.

Blair

After dawn, I blacked out for a couple of hours, but gasp back into consciousness now, thinking I hear Teddy's voice. The weight of what's happened this weekend immediately crushes me, and I remember that I am all alone in my house. I couldn't have heard anything.

On Friday night the kids and I drove up to my mother's, the big house on the Philadelphia Main Line where I grew up. Teddy hadn't wanted to come, using a complicated deal at work as an excuse, but I hadn't actually invited him in the first place. The call came twenty-four hours after we arrived, on Saturday just as we were finishing Thai takeout in my mother's dining room. I didn't recognize the number but stood up from the table anyway, letting my chair tumble back onto the thick Persian rug with a muffled thud.

Am I speaking to Blair Bard? A deep voice on the other end of the line asked as I walked through the butler's pantry into the kitchen. *Mrs. Bard, this is Detective Thomas Kim. Can you confirm your address and your husband's name for me?* I grabbed at the refrigerator door handle with my free hand and braced myself as I answered. The detective sounded genuine when he finally revealed the gutting punch line—*I'm very sorry to tell you that your husband's body was found today.* . . .

When I walked back into the dining room, my three kids and my mother all looked up, confused. I'd mumbled something about an emergency and needing to go right away. I'd added, unconvincingly, that they shouldn't worry. It had taken me more than three hours in highway traffic to get back to Virginia, to the morgue where Teddy's body was waiting. This was just a few hours ago, but I can't remember exactly what happened when I got there. Maybe it's because I've barely slept since. I couldn't, not after having to call my kids and tell them he was dead. There was silence, and then their quiet sobbing. I couldn't get the sound out of my mind all night. It felt like they were crying right next to me as I looked at old photo albums through the dark, empty hours between midnight and morning.

My whole body aches now from the two hours of sleep on the family room floor, and it takes me many minutes to make it to the kitchen. I am staring into an empty coffee mug when the doorbell rings. It feels like the front door is a mile away. By the time I pull it open, the two men on my front steps are looking around, probably wondering if anyone is home.

"Mrs. Bard?" the older one of the two asks as they both hold up badges for me to see. They could be props from the toy store for all I know, but it doesn't matter. I don't look at them. I just say yes and invite them in.

"I'm Detective Thomas Kim, we spoke on the phone last night, and this is my partner, Detective Rich Bryan. We're very sorry for your loss."

Detective Kim is taller than his partner, with thick black hair and salt-and-pepper stubble sprinkled across his square jaw. An attractive Grim Reaper. His partner looks like a choirboy, small and pale, and wearing a tie for the occasion.

"I appreciate that. Come in, please." I lead them back into the kitchen and gesture toward our long breakfast table. "Would you like some coffee?"

"No, thank you ma'am," the choirboy speaks up as the three of us pull out chairs and sit, the two of them across from me.

"Mrs. Bard, we're still waiting on the medical examiner's official determination, but your husband's death does not appear to have been accidental," Detective Kim breaks the news with his hands clasped on the table and his eyes focused on me.

"What do you mean? He jumped?" My tongue feels heavy in my mouth, and I wish they'd accepted my offer of coffee.

"It doesn't appear to have been suicide," Detective Kim answers flatly.

"What does it appear to be then?"

The choirboy jumps in, "Homicide, ma'am. Your husband suffered from injuries that he didn't receive from falling into the river."

I blink at each of them in turn, but neither continues. They are waiting for me. "Teddy was murdered? That's insane. There's no one who would want to murder Teddy. He was the best . . ." My voice catches and breaks in my throat, and I don't go on. I'm not interested in crying in front of these men.

"We understand this comes as a shock to you, Mrs. Bard. But it's very important for us to gather as much information as we can, as quickly as we can. Right now, our colleagues are out on the trail above where Mr. Bard was found, and anything you can tell us could be helpful."

The choirboy and I are both nodding along as Detective Kim

speaks. "So Mrs. Bard, did you notice your husband's absence yesterday?"

"No, my kids and I were in Philadelphia. Well, just outside the city, at my mother's, for the weekend. Teddy and I spoke on Friday night, and, I don't know, Saturday just got away from me. When I called and he didn't answer, I just figured he was busy and would call eventually. He always did."

Detective Kim still has his eyes on me, but the choirboy has pulled out a little notebook and is scribbling while I talk. He stops his pen and looks up to ask, "Did anyone else see you in Philadelphia, besides your mother and kids?"

I have to think for a long moment before answering. "Yes. On Friday I had a drink with an old high school friend. Saturday morning, I dropped into the florist, and around lunchtime that day a charity service picked up some of my mother's old furniture. Would you mind if I make some coffee? I didn't sleep."

The two men glance at each other before Detective Kim says sure.

"Don't worry, I'll make enough for three," I manage to say before dragging myself up from the table. "And please, we can keep going. I'm listening."

"Did your husband often use that trail, Mrs. Bard?" The choirboy sounds soft and slightly nervous compared to his partner.

"Every Saturday morning at dawn. It's his long and slow run. Eight miles total, out and back. On Wednesdays he runs through the neighborhoods, fast and short. Well, fast for him. The runs are really important to him. We have a home gym, in the basement, but he doesn't use it much anymore. Didn't, I mean."

I say all this while popping capsules in and out of our

espresso machine. I can't think straight enough to measure out ground coffee.

"And do you ever run, Mrs. Bard? Maybe with your husband?" Detective Kim asks from the table.

"Me? Oh no way. I've had three kids. It's too high impact. And I get bored. I haven't run in decades."

We go on like this for more than an hour. The detectives are an endless fount of questions, about how Teddy spent his time, who he was and wasn't close with, whether he had any problems. I do my best to answer them all. When the choirboy finally closes his little notebook and Detective Kim thanks me for my time, I almost don't want them to leave. The house will be empty until tonight when my mother gets here with the kids. But I can't bear to call anyone I know.

Once the front door clicks closed behind the detectives, the sobs start coming. I climb the stairs to the second floor on all fours, crawl into our bedroom, and lock the door behind me.

Alexis

I wake with a start. Elena is batting aggressively at the wall in the hallway with one of Carter's burp towels. Through the doorway, I can see the muscles in her thin brown neck tensing every time she pulls the towel back to strike again. "Miss Alexis, there are flies again!" She turns toward me with a concerned look on her face.

I try to remember where I am. Carter is fast asleep on my chest, and I'm slouched low on the rocker in her nursery. I rummage for my phone to check the time and find it stuck to the bottom of my left thigh. It's already past 9:00. I think it's Monday. Caleb has music class.

"Elena you should be getting ready to leave, it's almost time for Caleb's class," I whisper angrily. Even after two years, she still has a hard time remembering the schedule.

"But Miss Alexis, flies in the house are a bad sign. They mean poverty is coming, that's what my father always said to us," she says to me from the doorway, the burp towel hanging limply in her hand now. How can she repeat such stupid, awful things? I want to tell her that I'm not interested in her Central American superstitions, but instead I just hiss, "Please, go now, you're going to be late. These classes are expensive, I don't want him to miss any of it."

After carefully placing Carter in her crib, I pick my phone back up to check the news. Saturday is still fresh in my mind, but I haven't yet been able to find an update online. Now, finally, the banner story on a local news site starts with a stock aerial shot of the river and reads:

UPDATE (7:45 a.m.): *Police identify man found deceased on banks of the Potomac.* Police have identified the man whose body was found on a rocky outcrop along the western bank of the Potomac River in Virginia as 49-year-old Theodore Bard. Bard, a prominent local businessman and representative to the state legislature, had not been reported missing. County Police say the body was spotted by two local fishermen in a small speedboat just after 5:00 p.m. on Saturday, May 31. The location of the body could not be accessed by emergency responders on land, but a joint air-water rescue team was ultimately able to recover the body. The cause of death has not yet been confirmed.

Theodore Bard . . . Teddy Bard. Blair's husband. Teddy is the dead man? I blink a few times, and reread the paragraph, wondering if sleep deprivation is playing tricks on me. The story doesn't change. Teddy is the dead man splayed out on the rocks.

In my limited experience, death likes to surprise. A coworker died last year of some vicious form of cancer that took him from running half marathons to hospice in months. A couple of students in college committed suicide. I hadn't known them, but everyone who had seemed shocked. My mother spent her short adult life in numb disbelief after a particularly excessive surprise. When she herself died, at the end of my junior year of college, I'd been telling people I was an orphan for three years. But it still caught me totally off guard.

Teddy's handsome, smiling face comes back to me now — playing basketball with his children in the driveway, jogging slowly past our house, waving to us as he emptied his mailbox. At a distance, he looked much younger than he was, with his thick, dark blond hair gleaming. He was a little shorter and a little stockier than Sam, which to me looked like a man who knew how to keep his vanity in check. It always made me smile to see him. He was middle-aged Ken, married to Barbie, complete with the dream house. I wonder what went wrong.

I try calling Sam but he doesn't pick up, so I text him the news article with a line of exclamation points, then take a quick, scalding shower to wake myself up. As I get dressed, gingerly putting on maternity clothes that I'm ashamed to still be in, Sam texts back. "That's insane. Blair is definitely going to sue." Carter starts to scream from her crib, and I hurry to finish. In her room, I pick her up and we go through our usual ritual. I change her diaper, give her a bottle, and rock her gently, humming into the wisps of hair on her head. It is jet-black, much darker than her brother's, and her skin has yet to mellow from its fragile newborn flush and reveal its full color.

She is a sweet baby, and I silently congratulate myself for taking the full six months of paid maternity leave my new job offered as she falls back asleep on my chest. With Caleb, I had been so eager to stay on top that nearly every day of leave filled me with anxiety about what I was missing at work. We'd hired Elena and I'd started back full-time two months after he was born, only to find that what had made me so successful before—singular focus, perfectionism, an inability to not constantly check my email—was nearly gone, replaced by resentment. I did my best to ignore it, but when my assistant caught me throwing up in the ladies' room, I knew something had to change.

The small firm I'm at now was a good choice—slightly less travel and far more modest ambitions. There are no more illusions about how successful I'll be, and since I've already decided to fall off the fast track, the anxiety of being home only occasionally surges. Mostly I think about the house instead of work. I fall asleep with Carter still on my chest, wondering if our roof might be in worse shape than the inspector suggested, and wake up to the sounds of Caleb and Elena giggling together as they come in from his class.

/ 9:15 PM

I am emptying the dishwasher when Sam gets home from work. He looks exhausted. "Hi Alexis," he calls as he drops his briefcase by the front door. We only have a one-car garage, so narrow that the hatchback's doors hit the walls. After almost impaling myself on a sideview mirror, I grudgingly gave up on pulling it in. Sam also parks his new BMW in the driveway. Despite all his grumblings about money when we bought the house, he'd insisted on a second car as soon as we moved, since we are far from public transit and both of us work downtown. We'd agreed that he would park it close to the street, to distract from the Honda.

He comes into the kitchen and pokes at the pot sitting lidded on the stove. "What's for dinner?"

"It's just chicken and rice. I left some in there for you." In truth, the only person who'd eaten any was Elena. I think she felt obliged, after hovering in the kitchen giving me unsolicited recipe tips and teaching me ingredient names in Spanish. Caleb had just pushed rice around on his tray until I gave up and let him have two puree pouches for dinner. I am aiming for only one meal a day for myself—lunch—so didn't have any either.

The shadow of Teddy's death has hovered around me all day, and I approach to give Sam a hug. He smiles and pulls me in toward him, leaning down to kiss me on the forehead. I don't remember the last time he's done this, and even though I'm swollen and raw, the affection feels good. "I can't believe that was Teddy," I say with my head against his chest, his steady heartbeat in my ear.

He sighs, deeply. "Ya, and did you read the latest? The police are saying it was a murder."

My reaction is shameful. I pull my head back and look up at him. "Seriously? Oh my God, that's terrible for our property value. A murder victim across the street? Did they say if it happened in his house, or out on the trail? It might be better if it happened out there."

Sam considers my face for a second, and sighs again. "That's a good point, I guess. What I read online was pretty short on details. The article just said that it was definitely a homicide. They didn't say exactly what killed him, but apparently it wasn't falling from the trail."

I start making him a plate as he pours two glasses of cold red wine, left over from the weekend. "Well, there've been three police cruisers parked in the cul-de-sac since this morning. Also, there were at least five cars parked at Blair and Teddy's house. I guess she's getting lots of support."

"Thank you, neighborhood watch. So glad we sprung for the extra-large window. You really are an old lady." He smiles at me as I hand him his plate. I am about to protest when I hear a hard knock at the door. We look at each other, concerned. It's past 9:00 and dark out. I walk toward the door, with Sam close behind me.

Through the peephole, I see a clean-cut young man standing under the bright lantern light of our portico. He can't be much over thirty, wearing a brown windbreaker over a buttoned-up white shirt with a dark blue tie. I think he might be a Mormon missionary, sweating in his dress-up clothes, and turn back toward Sam, silently shaking my head no. A second knock, and this time the young man announces, in a surprisingly authoritative voice, "This is the police. I'm here to speak with you about an investigation."

I open the door, and the man flashes his badge at us without a smile. "Good evening folks, I'm Detective Rich Bryan. Sorry for coming by so late, but my colleagues and I are trying to talk to everyone in the area about the death of Theodore Bard. I'm not sure if you're aware . . ."

"Yes we are!" I answer, too loudly.

"In that case, could I ask for a little bit of your time? We are speaking with all the homeowners in the neighborhood." He's holding my gaze, and I feel uncomfortable without knowing why.

"Of course," I step aside so he can come in. Sam asks, inappropriately I think, "Would you like a drink?"

Detective Bryan shakes his head. "No, but thanks for the offer. Where is a good place to talk?"

I lead the detective and Sam, who's grabbed our wineglasses, through the arched doorways to our formal living room, the only part of the house I've fully furnished and actively keep tidy precisely for times like this—unexpected visitors. Sam and I sit next to each other on the couch, me nervously perched at the edge and him sitting back with his long legs farther apart than I think is polite. The detective, who's barely taller than me, settles comfortably into one of the two barrel-backed armchairs across from us. I make a mental note to thank Sam later—he's the one who pushed me to buy the floor models last month because they were 20 percent off. I was angry with him, and convinced they were flawed, but if he hadn't been so insistent, the three of us would now be awkwardly crowded onto our couch, still waiting for chairs to be made and delivered. Detective Bryan pulls a small notebook and pen from his windbreaker and asks us a series of simple questions. Our names and occupations, a full roster of household members, how long we've lived here, and so on.

He asks if he can also speak to our nanny. "Sure," I answer, "but her English is not perfect, and she was in Richmond from Friday night until last night visiting family."

"That's not a problem, I'll come back another time with an interpreter," he says, his eyes down as he scribbles notes. "Now, can you folks tell me, how well do you know the Bards?" He looks up now, back and forth between us, waiting for reactions.

I've only spoken to a police officer twice in my life. Once, for a speeding ticket in Nebraska, because Sam and I moved from New Haven to San Francisco and decided to drive. When the officer pulled me over, I'd apologized so profusely that he'd yelled at me to please stop and just focus on being more careful so that I wouldn't have to be so sorry. Sam made it worse by laughing about it until the Wyoming border. I'd just kept my eyes on the speedometer, too annoyed to tell him that being close to an officer had sent me back, to the first time.

During middle school, they found a little girl's body in one of our apartment dumpsters and police had canvassed the whole complex, knocking hard at the door like Officer Bryan just did tonight. The somber officer had towered over us in his uniform, at least in my memory, and pressed my mother and me for any information, anything that we'd seen. But we couldn't help. My mother was gone fourteen hours a day, working, and I always followed her instructions—walk quickly from the school bus straight to our apartment, don't talk to anyone, and lock the door behind me. The wallet photo of the girl that the officer showed us looked a bit like me, and familiar, but I couldn't remember anything at all about her. It made me feel so awful, and petrified.

Now, my heart is racing even though I know logically there is nothing to panic about.

"I guess I can start?" I ask, looking from him to Sam and back. They both nod slightly. "Well, we've only lived here since January, like I said before, so the truth is we barely know them. But they seem, seemed, like a really wonderful couple, and family. Blair Bard was the first person we met in the neighborhood—the first time we saw the house last October—and then the day we moved in, she brought us a really lovely gift basket."

"Did you ever interact with Mr. Bard?" Detective Bryan asks.

Just like with the little girl's case, I feel awful that I can't help, but it's not my fault. If anything, I'm angry that this is happening. We didn't move here for this. Detective Bryan himself doesn't inspire much confidence either, despite the self-assurance in his voice. He can't have a lot of experience, given how few murders are committed around here and how young he looks. I wonder if this is all an act, pretending to know what he's doing.

"Teddy? No, I mean, we always waved when we saw each other outside. He seemed very cordial. We've been meaning to invite them over, invite the whole block for a little housewarming party maybe, but since we just had a baby, we haven't had time." I realize this is beside the point. "Anyway, no, I never spoke to Teddy directly."

"And what about their kids?" he asks, his eyes narrowing.

"Their children? They have three, we've seen them. But again, I've never spoken to them. They look like good kids, polite. They always wave at neighbors."

"And you, Mister . . ." He pauses to check his notes. "Crawford. Mr. Crawford, have you had any other interactions with the Bards?"

"No. Like Alexis said, we met Blair late last year. I wasn't here when she came by the day of our move. And I've only seen Teddy from a distance," Sam answers.

"All right," the detective continues. "Now, can you each tell me about where you went and what you did this past Saturday?"

This time, Sam starts. "Okay sure. I woke up around 6:30 and went for a run. Since it was looking like rain, I decided to run through the neighborhood instead of the woods. I did a five-mile loop and was home before the rain actually started, must have been right before 7:30. I had my phone with me in case you want to check my route? Alexis was asleep when I left, but when I got back she was up feeding our newborn." He pauses to take a long drink of his wine. Officer Bryan is taking notes and doesn't look up, so Sam continues.

"We basically spent the day taking care of the kids. I made pancakes for breakfast, helped out with the laundry. Around noon, Alexis made our son lunch, then I put him down for a nap. While he was napping, I worked on my laptop. He woke up around 4:30 I think, and the four of us went out to sit on the back patio for a while. That's where we heard the sirens. I suppose that's as far as you need me to go?"

"That's fine, thank you Mr. Crawford," Detective Bryan nods. "And you?" he turns toward me.

I give a similar account of my Saturday, minus the exercise and the work, plus more child care. It's true that Sam had pitched in and done some loads of laundry, for once. A few additional questions—if we noticed anything out of the ordinary leading up to Saturday, what we've heard from the neighbors— and Officer Bryan seems satisfied. Our wineglasses are empty now, it's nearing 11:00 p.m., and Carter will be up soon. I also need to use the bathroom and start shifting uncomfortably on the couch.

"Just one last question. Do you folks happen to have any security cameras on your property, like a doorbell camera or anything like that?"

Sam and I both shake our heads no. We hadn't thought we'd need anything like that here.

"Well that's fine. The houses all around here are set pretty far back from the road, probably wouldn't catch much," the detective says as he slowly closes his notebook and tucks it back into his windbreaker pocket.

From the other pocket, he pulls out a business card. "I think

I've got what I need for tonight. Call me if you think of anything else, or if you notice anything at all. Don't hesitate to call."

We walk him to the door, and my curiosity wins out over decorum. "Detective Bryan, was he definitely murdered? Do you have any leads?"

"Yes, the medical examiner ruled Mr. Bard's death a homicide this morning. We're working on a number of leads, and like I said, if you notice something—anything—let me know." He opens the front door himself.

"Okay, thanks so much," I say, stupidly, and wave at his back as he walks out to the street. Even if it was an act, it was a pretty good one, and I am hoping, for Detective Bryan's sake and ours, that one of those leads he mentioned gets him to an answer. When that little girl was found, the flurry of police activity died down in days, and then it was as if nothing had happened. They never caught whoever killed her—I look it up every few years to check. But this, I reason with myself, is a different world—a richer, whiter, and safer one. The murderer won't be allowed to go unpunished. The neighbors would never stand for it.

Blair

Even after a week of lying alone in this bed, tonight feels like a new torture. I piled pillows into the void on Teddy's side to give myself the feeling of someone next to me. But now I can't keep my eyes closed for fear that it's all going to come crashing down and smother me while I sleep.

The whole day, really, has been awful. It would have been our eighteenth wedding anniversary, but instead I had to bury Teddy's broken body in the nearest respectable cemetery I could find. We hadn't quite gotten this far in our life planning, picking plots and whatnot, and it all felt so rushed and arbitrary. His brothers and sisters wanted to take him up to Ithaca and bury him next to his parents. I told them to fuck off, in so many words. We'll be resting eternally together, and there's no way I'm going up there.

All I remember from the funeral service is a graphic sea of white and black. White flowers, mostly roses, ringing a massive sea of black-clad mourners. There were so many that some had to stand in the back behind the last pew. I wasn't surprised, everyone's always loved Teddy. He was the kind of man whose easy self-confidence bolstered the people around him and made them feel like all was right with the world. That's part of what made me love him too, for so many years. I remember one of our early dates, weeks before that first sweaty night in my apartment, sitting at a little sidewalk restaurant with big bowls of pasta and laughing over ridiculous family stories. I realized that night I'd found a better, kinder version of myself and just kept hoping to God that the sex would be good.

The CEO of his company, his oldest brother, and the president of the club all gave eulogies, but I haven't got a clue what any of them said. All I could hear was the kids sniffling in their brand-new funeral clothes on either side of me, and my own voice in my head urging me to run up to Teddy's coffin, throw open the lid, and climb in.

The worst part wasn't watching him go into the ground at the cemetery, but afterward at our house. My mother directed the whole show, insisting that I remain on a specific armchair in the living room, and I did as I was told. It was infuriating, having to sit there quietly as a current of condolences threatened to pull me under. If these people had any idea who we really were, they'd be whispering behind our backs instead of grabbing at my hands and offering help I don't need. The kids were given permission to hide in their bedrooms. When the rush of guests slowed to a trickle, she ordered a server to leave plates of catered funeral food outside each of their doors. She knew better than to offer me any.

Five years ago when Dad died, I remember being so impressed with how gracefully she wept at his graveside and how solemnly solicitous she'd been with all the guests afterward. To the point where I could tell that more than one person had to stop themselves from commenting on the way out about how great of a time they'd had. That's Beryl for you, always setting an example that can't be followed. She's taking the kids with her to Philadelphia on Monday. They don't have camp for another few weeks, and she doesn't think it's good for them to have to see the police buzzing like flies around their father's body (Beryl's words). She's right, they've been through enough already, but I dread being alone in this house again. I can't even manage to sleep alone in this bed. But what I need isn't of much concern to my mother. No, Beryl's main concern has always been about keeping up appearances. Doing what looks good and making sure everyone walks away with the right impression. I guess I learned from the best.

Alexis

It's Sunday again. The weeks are passing through me like a fog, condensing one into another. Nothing much distinguishes day from night, Monday from Thursday. I remember this feeling from my first maternity leave, of being disconnected from all the rhythms of the week. No more rushing out to make a meeting or a flight, or checking restaurant reviews while riding the metro ahead of the weekend. That first time, I had anticipated liberation — long walks pushing the stroller, reading novels while the baby napped — but instead found myself, day after day, staring at reality shows on television, barely comprehending the hackneyed premises.

If no one is expecting you somewhere, if no one notices that you didn't take a shower, what's the point? I had tried to articulate this feeling of disorientation in my new mothers group and had been met with furrowed brows and a printed list of postpartum depression resources. I feel the same way this time, but not as badly. Elena is here, and her presence is enough to shame me off the couch and into the shower more or less regularly.

I am also worried about Teddy's murder. For his family, of course, but if I'm being honest with myself, mostly for mine. Those first few days after they found his body, I made a point of claiming the kitchen sink, and its window to the street, as my territory, letting Elena know that I prefer to wash Carter's bottles myself. She didn't put up a fight but moped around the house as if offended. Usually I would apologize and relent, but I need to be able to watch what is going on behind a respectable excuse, so she will just have to get over it this time.

Teddy's obituary is prominently featured in today's paper—a glowing description of a golden life. He had been the youngest of five, raised in elite Northeast circles. His father, James, was a respected chemistry professor at Cornell, and several patents early in his career made him and his wife, Susan, rich. All the siblings held Ivy League degrees and impressive job titles. He had come to D.C. to work on Capitol Hill after college and, through what his obituary described as his "sharp intelligence, innate leadership capabilities, and deep knowledge of our country's military priorities," had shot through the ranks to become a senior executive at a large aerospace and defense company. "These same talents" combined with a "commitment to service" led him to run for state office in 2005, and win reelection ever since. I couldn't help but raise an eyebrow—maybe his prep school connections and a wife toiling away at home had also helped—but felt guilty begrudging a dead man his success. The obituary mentioned that he and Blair were married for eighteen years, and that he is survived by three equally golden children, ages thirteen, fifteen, and seventeen.

I had read the obituary on my phone around 4:00 a.m. while feeding Carter in her nursery, and now, as I'm helping Caleb

get scrambled eggs from his plate to his mouth, a fresh article
pops up on our local news site:

> UPDATE (7:30 a.m.): *Investigation continues into local*
> *leader's murder on the river.* The investigation into the
> shocking murder of Theodore Bard, area business leader
> and long-time member of the Virginia House of Dele-
> gates, continues. Bard, whose body was found on May
> 31, was laid to rest yesterday at St. Paul's Cemetery fol-
> lowing a funeral service attended by over 200 mourn-
> ers. Police have released limited information regarding
> Bard's death, citing the ongoing investigation. However,
> confidential sources independently confirm that Bard
> sustained the injuries that caused his death prior to enter-
> ing the river. Sources also confirm that Bard was dressed
> in workout clothes, and that he fell or was pushed from
> a point along the Skyview Trail. The 12-mile-long public
> trail runs along the steep western bank of the Potomac and
> is popular with hikers and trail runners. Bard's body was
> spotted on the riverbank below the trail approximately
> two miles from its only access point, within the upscale
> River Forest neighborhood where Bard lived with his fam-
> ily. Anyone with possible information about this case is
> asked to call the TIPS Hotline. $200,000 will be rewarded
> for information that leads to the apprehension of the
> perpetrator.

I already knew his funeral was yesterday because the whole
street had been filled with luxury cars all afternoon. I had
wanted to walk by with Carter in her stroller but thought it

would look too obvious and nosy. From the kitchen window, all I could see was a large white wreath hung on Blair and Teddy's black front door. The stream of visitors had continued for hours, only tapering off after sunset. "Lucky guy to have so many friends," I thought to myself, guiltily, after every Mercedes cruised past.

This new article makes me think about the trail. I've only been on it once since we moved in. Our first weekend in the house, Sam and I got up early to check it out while Elena prepared breakfast for Caleb. We were bundled up against the January wind and the trail started off gently enough, the flat gravel path leading from the cul-de-sac, between the two houses, and into thick woods. After just a few minutes, the roar of the river filled our ears and the trees began to thin, giving way to massive clumps of bedrock. This is where the path turns to dirt and starts to narrow and wind, quickly climbing then falling abruptly, as it traces its way along the cliffs.

That day in January, I'd been hesitant to go on, but Sam had insisted, and we continued walking slowly for another forty minutes or so. Around that point, all the vegetation buffering the trail from the river falls away. We found ourselves on a narrow ledge looking down at a hundred-foot drop to large boulders half submerged in the icy gray water. My hands were clammy and trembling, and I had insisted on turning back, much to Sam's disappointment.

I have no way of knowing, but for some reason I am sure that this is where Teddy died. Where everything falls away and it feels like there is nowhere to go but over the edge. I try to imagine the scene. Maybe he'd run into a psychotic hiker, tried to defend himself, and ended up falling. Maybe he'd stumbled into something sensitive at work, a matter of national security, and been followed. Or maybe one of our neighbors was the killer—a psychopath settling a seemingly insignificant grudge, a serial killer type who hadn't meant for Teddy to be discovered so soon. I hadn't looked for long, but my impression had been that anyone who went over would most likely end up wedged between boulders, out of sight, or swept into the river and eventually out into the Chesapeake Bay. It was Teddy's good luck to have landed on top of a rock.

Of all the mildly outlandish hypotheses running through my mind, the bloodthirsty wanderer and the insane neighbor are the two that concern me most, because they mean that someone else could be next, that we are not safe, and that I made a mistake bringing my family here. When they didn't find that little girl's killer, my mother picked up even more hours at work and six months later we moved to what she hoped was a slightly less dangerous complex. The idea that we are now in a similar position is both absurd and overwhelming. After all the effort Sam and I put into finding, paying for, and patching up this old house in this expensive neighborhood, here we are—double-checking all the locks and researching alarm systems.

I am thinking about the trail, and about how we ended up here, when Sam comes in from a run, sweaty and still breathing heavily. "Jesus, it's hot out there already," he pants. "It's also hot in here."

I look up at the wall clock—a modest, pointless housewarming present from my in-laws—it's only 7:45 a.m. I'm still sitting at the breakfast table, but I've released Caleb to the playroom on the condition that he leaves Carter, peacefully sleeping on her lounger, alone. I love this about our house—I can see them from where I sit, the morning sunlight filtering in all around us. It's beautiful, even if the air conditioner's having a hard time keeping up with this early heat wave.

"Sam, how many people are usually out on the trail?"

"Usually? Beats me. I've only been out there a few times. But I've probably run into four, maybe five, people on my entire run each time. Why? You feel like taking a hike today?"

I ignore his joke. "Doesn't it seem weird to you that no one saw anything? I mean, it's a public trail, and there's only one way in and out."

"Ah, your favorite subject. I doubt anyone else is standing at their kitchen window as much as you, so it seems pretty easy to go by without being seen." He mixes up a protein shake on the counter, obliviously spattering tiny flecks of chocolate-flavored powder that he won't wipe up all over the gray-veined marble I'd picked to coordinate with the playroom fireplace. I glare at his sweat-stained back.

"And a good rock climber could probably get off the trail and back to civilization without coming through here," he adds.

"It's been two weeks and no arrests or anything—that can't be a good sign. They must not have much."

"Plus, we don't have any idea of when it actually happened," he keeps going, ignoring me. "Maybe the poor guy got dragged out there in the middle of the night."

"Shhh," I interrupt him, nodding my head toward Caleb. Sam shrugs and grabs a banana from the fruit basket to add to his shake. "You're the one who brought it up."

"It's just so shocking. I feel really bad for Blair, what a terrible hand to be dealt. Left with three children, and I don't know if she works. I mean, they look rich, but still, for their sakes, I hope he had a lot of life insurance."

"So sentimental. Have you talked to her since?"

"Me? I barely know her. I don't want to be the nosy neighbor who gets off on other people's tragedies."

Sam just smirks at me over the rim of his big plastic cup, so I continue. "I just don't want to intrude. It's not like she's alone—you know how many cars have been through here."

Sam is still smirking, but he doesn't say anything, and we turn our attention to Caleb.

Blair

The detectives are back. They called five minutes ago and invited themselves over. I don't mind, since I don't have much else going on, just the numbing repetition of accepting food we won't eat, turning down ridiculous invitations to "not be alone," and deflecting intrusive questions. I thought I was done on Saturday after the funeral, but it seems like a significant share of the metro area's population knows one of the five of us. Yesterday, the headmistress at Jamie's school kept me on the phone for nearly half an hour and Rob's badminton coach brought over a dozen croissants (of all things) with tears in his eyes. An old design client I hadn't seen in years showed up with a casserole at 8:00 p.m., apologizing that she'd made it as fast as she could after seeing Teddy's obituary in the paper.

The kids are upstairs packing, and my mother went out to breakfast with a friend. She's not one to let her son-in-law's death interrupt her social schedule. At least while the detectives are here, I'm momentarily shielded from everyone else's pity.

I silence my phone and make the coffee without asking first, and this time they sit at the kitchen island.

Detective Kim doesn't make small talk. I don't think he's even ever offered me a sympathetic smile. "I don't have good news for you. We received the final results of the analysis on Mr. Bard's body, and unfortunately there was no genetic evidence."

They'd been hoping for a scrap of someone else's skin under one of Teddy's fingernails, or a drop of someone else's blood on his clothes. But there was nothing.

"Also, as you know, Mrs. Bard, we believe that a rock was used to murder your husband. Our teams have searched the woods around the trail as well as the riverbank itself, but we have yet to find it," he goes on with his disappointments.

"What about the tip line? Have you gotten any good leads?" I ask hopefully.

"We're working several. We'll see if they turn out to be any good," Detective Kim answers.

Choirboy Bryan adds, "But the line is still getting a pretty high volume of calls. The reward amount is probably driving some of that."

The county had offered a $100,000 reward, in light of the disturbing nature of Teddy's murder and his prominence in the community. I'd doubled it.

"Is there anything else I can do?" I don't know what else to ask.

"For now, no. But please don't hesitate to call if you remember anything that might be relevant, for example if anyone at the funeral jogged your—" Detective Kim stops mid-sentence and looks over my shoulder.

I turn to see Jamie's white-blond ponytail disappear up the back staircase.

"I'm sorry gentlemen, I guess we had an eavesdropper."

"That's fine. We'll let you go deal with that," Detective Bryan offers, and they both push themselves up from the island bar-stools. I quickly see them out and run upstairs to knock on Jamie's bedroom door. I should have been more careful. I'd for-gotten that her room is right above the kitchen.

"Jamie, honey, I'm coming in now."

She's lying facedown on her bed and doesn't move as I step in and close the door behind me. Her room is all lilac and wood tones. We redid it last summer, before she started high school. I'd taken her to the stores with me, helped her think about shades and patterns and scale. It was the closest I'd felt to her in a long time. Sometime during middle school, she started being so hard on herself, and on the rest of us. It's like what other people think of her suddenly became an incredibly important thing. Maybe the most important. I know where she got it from, but still, it had caught me off guard.

I realize I haven't been inside her bedroom in a few weeks. An overlay of teenage clutter obscures all of our good design work. Schoolbooks and loose papers cover her white-oak desk. Sports medals and ribbons are tacked all over the abstract flower wallpaper. Clothes are thrown over both her desk chair and armchair, and stuffed animals from the fair at the beach are lined up in the window seat. I'll have to ask the cleaning ladies to do a better job, and also consider building her another closet.

"Jamie? Sit up honey, we need to talk for a minute." I sit on the edge of her bed and gently rub her back. After a few seconds, she lets out a long grunt and pushes herself up to sit next to me. I try to grab her hands, but she pulls them away and wraps her arms around her body.

"Mom, why haven't they caught the person yet?"

"Because solving murders is hard," I sigh. "Especially when

it happens out of nowhere and no one is there to see it. But they will, don't worry."

"My friends said that most people are murdered by someone they know," Jamie says and leans forward to put her forehead on my shoulder.

"Which friends told you that honey? Your friends on the police force? The ones who work at the courthouse?"

"Mom." She's annoyed. "Don't be stupid."

We both let out a little laugh, and then Jamie starts crying. I pull her closer and wrap my arms around her. She lets me.

"It's just so awful. I miss Dad so much. Why did this have to happen to us?" she asks as fat tears roll down her flushed cheeks. It's so hard not to wipe them away for her, but I know she wouldn't like that.

I want to tell her that she's right, Teddy didn't deserve this. None of us did. But there are worse things than losing your dad at fifteen, even if she can't imagine them right now. I want to tell her, but I never can. Instead, I just keep holding her for as long as she'll allow it, rocking us slowly as she sobs.

Alexis

Sam shut himself up in the office again, right after he got Caleb to sleep, without even telling me what he's working on. As soon as Carter went down, I walked to the office door, but hesitated before knocking. After his parents left, the murder happened, and now partner promotions are in just a few weeks. It's a lot to deal with—on top of a newborn and a toddler and a postpartum wife—so I decided to leave him be and came downstairs intending to pick up a book.

Instead, I find myself sitting at the breakfast table with my phone, scrolling through a seemingly inexhaustible stream of home interiors better than my own. It should be inspirational, but it's just depressing, and after nearly two hours I get up to make my way to bed. I keep looking at my phone while clicking off the lights and almost miss it, except for the next picture that comes up. A room so similar to the one I've been sitting in— but professionally decorated—that I glance over my shoulder to see if my divided-light windows have suddenly been graced by floor-length curtains. They are bare of course, but in looking back I catch a pinpoint of yellow light outside, in the blackness of the undeveloped lot beyond our narrow side yard.

While sitting in my bright, quiet kitchen, doors locked and newly installed alarm activated, I'd been oblivious to the world outside the panes of glass, already accustomed to the inky stillness that envelops us every night. But now, standing in the darkness, I can see that there is clearly a light, wobbling in those dense woods. No one should be out there—our realtor assured us that whoever owns the land has no intention of developing it, and besides, it's nearly 11:00 on a Friday night. The options start running through my mind—an odd neighbor walking their dog through the woods, some teenagers looking for a thrill, who else? I should let Sam know about this, and start typing a text message, but when I look up again the pinpoint is brighter and I can see a faint streak of yellow as whoever is holding the light sweeps its beam across the ground. My fingers are shaking but manage to find Sam's number. He answers just before it goes to voicemail.

"Sam, come to the kitchen right now," I whisper before he can say anything.

"Why?" He sounds annoyed.

"Someone's outside, in the lot next door. They've got a flashlight or something, in the middle of the woods, and they're walking toward our house."

He doesn't answer, but in seconds I hear his heavy steps on the stairs.

"Where?" he asks coming into the breakfast room, but then curses before I can respond. "Who the fuck is that?"

"I think we should call the police," I say as I duck behind him, grateful for his size and, for once, his fitness obsession.

"No. They won't get here in time. I'm going out there." He's already walking toward the foyer to grab his shoes, not waiting for my response.

I call after him, but he's disengaging the alarm and putting on his sneakers. "This can't be a good idea. What the hell are you going to do?" I'm trying to dissuade him even as I frantically search the shoe rack for a pair of sandals to follow in.

We are out the door and headed around the side of our house toward the empty lot, Sam striding fearlessly and me fumbling to keep up behind. I'm still clutching my phone and turn its flashlight on. "Turn it off!" Sam hisses at me over his shoulder.

There is no fence separating our property from the woods, and in minutes the trees have closed in around us. The dark doesn't slow Sam down, but my flip-flops are sinking into the layers of leaves and muck underfoot, and the sour smell of decomposition on the thick air makes it hard to breathe. I can feel that he is getting farther ahead of me, and I want to ask him to wait but can't make the words come.

Now his movement has faded into the trees, and I realize I'm not sure which way he's gone. I stop still, trying to breathe slowly and hold off panic, but the scent of decay fills my nostrils. Slowly reaching my arms out in front of me, all I touch are branches and leaves. The blackness is disorienting, and I'm scared.

"Sam?" I whisper as quietly as I can, straining to see in front of me. But instead, the noise comes from behind, and suddenly the faint flashlight pool of yellow is trained on my back.

"Who are you?" a man's voice asks, firm and unnervingly close behind me.

I hold myself as still as possible, even as mud starts to ooze onto my bare feet and an insect's furry wing brushes against my cheek.

"I'm Alexis Crawford, my house is just right behind us." The tremor in my voice is obvious, but I've managed to speak loudly. I hope it was enough for Sam to hear me.

"Alexis, okay, didn't mean to scare you—" the man starts to answer when Sam comes crashing back toward us.

"Who the hell are you?" he yells, running past me, but stops short to shield his eyes when the man trains the flashlight on his face.

"Calm down buddy, it's me, Shawn, your neighbor," he laughs, strangely relaxed, and points the flashlight up at his own face to prove it, then clicks it off.

"Jesus! What the fuck are you doing out here?" My eyes are still readjusting to the dark, but I can hear in his voice how angry Sam is.

"Whoa, you've got to cool it," Shawn barks back, the dark mass of his muscular body stepping forward, challenging Sam. I reach out and manage to grab the edge of Sam's T-shirt, tugging him backward toward me and away from a fight that I don't think he'd win.

"We almost called the police, you really scared us!" I say meekly, trying to cut the tension.

Shawn lets a few seconds pass before reverting to his friendly voice. "I really didn't mean to scare you folks. I'm just looking for something I lost, that's all."

"Couldn't you wait till morning?" Sam's regained his composure but doesn't bother to hide the suspicion in his voice.

Shawn doesn't answer the question. "Don't you notice that stench? I just about fell over the antlers of a huge buck over there, dead in the middle of these woods."

"What exactly did you lose?" Sam asks.

Shawn hesitates before answering. "One of my best drones.

It crashed somewhere around here, and I need to find it tonight. There's rain in the forecast."

"A drone?" Sam and I both say simultaneously, incredulous. Sam keeps pressing, "What the hell are you doing flying a drone around at night? Does it have a camera? You know that's illegal right?"

"Hey, a murder was committed, almost on our street. Isn't that why you're out here frantic?" Shawn asks without pausing for us to answer. "I'm doing what the police won't and keeping an eye on things. You're not going to turn me in for that." This last part clearly sounds like a threat.

"Can we please move this conversation to our driveway?" I ask as the leaves at my feet suddenly rustle with the movement of some small animal.

"You folks should head inside. I really need to find this thing now."

"No, I'll help you," Sam says, stupidly unintimidated. "Alexis, I need your light. Be careful walking back to the house." He grabs the phone from my hand and turns to follow Shawn before I can argue, leaving me to make my way alone through the humid darkness.

By the time the clouds finally burst, I've checked on the children, taken a shower, and researched trespassing laws on my laptop. Sam comes through the front door soaked as I'm rearranging the shoe rack, with scratches on his arms and the faint stench of animal death still clinging to him. "Did you guys find the drone?"

"No, he led me around and around the woods, talking about his fucking flock of drones and what each one can do, night vision and high-resolution video, like that's something to be proud of," Sam says as he peels off his muddy sneakers and socks. "Then it started pouring, and he just laughed, said the rain won. The whole thing was fucking suspicious."

"Do you think he's lying?" I ask from the kitchen, where I've run to grab a plastic grocery bag to limit the mess. "Is he dangerous?"

"He very well could be. I don't trust him." Sam hands me my phone, battery drained and damp from his shorts pocket, then pulls his wet shirt over his head and drops it into the bag I'm holding open for him.

"Hopefully he's just some kind of paranoid soccer dad, creepy but harmless." I try to laugh but instead find myself blinking back the sting of tears. From exhaustion I guess, and relief that nothing worse happened tonight.

Alexis

I've been thinking about Blair. What kind of a person am I, hiding inside worrying about my property value, when my neighbor's been widowed? It hadn't even occurred to me to reach out to her before Sam mentioned it. At night, after all her visitors have left, she must be miserable and maybe even scared, with the trail that swallowed Teddy just outside her windows. Thinking of Blair like this makes Shawn's creeping around in the dark for his drone seem even more perverted. Instead of playing police, he should be concerned about her and her family. We all should.

I know how awful it is, being alone and afraid. One of my early memories is of being alone in an unnervingly quiet apartment, eating dry cereal off of a paper plate. I was terrified that if I made too much noise chewing, someone would hear me and something bad would happen. It must have been before my mother found the basement day care. She wasn't home most of the time, but even when she was, her mind usually seemed to be somewhere else. Now, I'm certain my mother was thinking of Honduras, where she was from. But as a child, really up until recently, I thought she didn't want to be where she was—with me—and that I was alone in the world. There was no one else. We had no family. No one to visit for holidays, no one to talk to or talk about.

Only the barest facts behind this were known to me—she'd come to the States by herself after a hurricane, and a few years later, she'd had me. Through it all, she worked long days and studied nights, slowly working her way up from menial labor to low-level administrative jobs. My mother wasn't one for telling stories, so if it weren't for school projects and a few rare bouts of courage, I probably never would have known more. My questions and her terse answers come to mind at the strangest times now.

When thunder splits the air during a summer storm,

"Which hurricane was it?"

"Fifi. A silly name for an evil storm."

When I'm struggling to get a cute picture of Caleb and Carter together,

"Who did you live with when you were little?"

"My parents, of course. And six brothers and sisters. I was the youngest."

"Why don't you talk to them anymore?"

"They're all gone. They died in the hurricane."

Sitting in the title agent's office, signing dozens of sheets of paper to close, both times,

"Where did you grow up?"

"In a village by the sea. Stop asking all these questions, it's giving me a headache."

I pieced it together eventually, with the help of the internet. In 1974 Hurricane Fifi triggered massive flooding that killed thousands of people along the Caribbean coast. Her town was one of many that disappeared overnight. My mother, in her early twenties and studying at the national university in Teguci-galpa, was the only survivor in her family. All six of her siblings had been pitching in to pay her tuition and, just like that, they were all dead. Her parents and nieces and nephews and cousins and neighbors and friends too. After Fifi, she decided to leave. There was nothing left for her, and besides, she'd told me once or twice, being Black there was nearly as hard as it is here.

It's not much, but I've always held tight to these details. It's all I have. For the other half of the story, she wouldn't give me anything. Whenever I asked about my father, her answer was always the same. *"We are not talking about this."* If my cour-age were really up and I insisted, she would grab me by the arm and push me into my room to be grounded for stubbornness. On rare occasions, when my timing was really unfortunate, I'd ask or say something that would ignite her always smoldering anger. Once she knocked a tooth out of my mouth for some snide comment I'd made about always having to wear second-hand clothes. To be fair, the tooth had been loose already. But af-ter the flash of fierceness faded, she would come into my room, to hug me tightly and kiss the exposed scalp of my middle part, a brief swell of affection that momentarily sucked me under. I hated that feeling, and would squeeze my eyes shut and dig my elbows into my ribs until she let me go.

The morning is almost over, but I'm still in my pajamas. Elena took Caleb to a playgroup, and Carter is asleep in her crib. I am on the floor of her nursery, stretched out on the pale pink polka-dotted rug with a price tag that had made Sam roll his eyes, slowly moving my arms and legs through the poses of the Vitruvian Man. The pains are flaring up again as my bones and muscles, relieved of their burden, shift back into place. Splaying myself out like this helps. It also makes me wonder what position Teddy's body was in when the fishermen spotted it. I turn my head slowly to the left, and my eyes settle on the void between the radiator and the wood floor. A layer of white specks covers the oak under the radiator's painted metal fins.

How could I have missed this? We were so worried about the sale going through, and not losing out to someone else, we just believed what we were told. Our agent said not to worry so much about lead paint, as long as it's intact and undisturbed, it's not dangerous. She'd even cracked a joke about telling our children not to lick the walls. But now, here I am—looking at paint chips on the ground, probably getting paint chips in my hair, and poisoning my baby. I hold my breath and curse myself silently. I curse Sam too, as I grab my phone off my belly and search for lead abatement services. We'll need to talk about how this happened, how we let ourselves be so negligent.

After finding three options, I leave Carter's room as quietly as I can, and call to schedule home visits. A scalding hot shower is the only thing I can think of to do next. As I scrub a second round of shampoo out of my hair, the fight I'll have with Sam plays out in my mind. He'll be defensive, like he always is, and say that it's not his fault, that I'm the one who went crazy for this house. I know we are both responsible—the prospect of living in a neighborhood like this seems to have blinded us to all our house's problems. But really, Sam could have known better. He has parents. He has friends. People who could have warned him, if he'd bothered to ask. Who could have warned me?

It's exhausting—painstakingly building up my life, brick by brick, only to have it crumble right in front of me, then struggling to patch it all up on my own. I wonder if Blair is feeling something like this now. She has people, of course. Plenty of them. But her steady stream of visitors seems to finally be drying up, and this morning I haven't seen a single car parked in their driveway.

Maybe on this point, Sam is right—the neighborly thing to do is reach out to Blair. Maybe she'd like to know at least that we are here for her. Whatever that means. I quickly get dressed and look up "kind gestures after a death" on my phone. It seems that the appropriate thing to do is bring over some food, but my cooking skills are severely limited. I only ever learned a couple of dishes from my mother, by watching quietly from the far end of whatever tiny kitchen we had, but instinctively I know that kind of food wouldn't be familiar to Blair. It took me long enough to get Sam used to it. Purchased food will have to do.

I drive to the grocery store at midday and wander the aisles. It's Monday, so my only fellow shoppers are slow-moving elderly people and harried-looking stay-at-home moms. We've been getting our groceries delivered, and the aggressive air-conditioning and long, overstuffed aisles of this in-person experience are overwhelming. As I slowly navigate past the produce stands, I remember the beautiful basket of cookies Blair brought us when we moved in and head to the baked goods section.

Scanning the chintzy options on display, I realize I should have gone to a proper bakery and head back out. Luckily, there is one in the same shopping center—a small, upscale place where I buy a box of assorted cookies. I even have the presence of mind to ask the teenager behind the counter to switch out the red ribbon for a black one. By the time I get home, Elena is feeding Caleb lunch while expertly holding a contented Carter in her arms. I tell her I'm going to drop off some food for the neighbor whose husband died and will be right back.

She says sure, as she usually does. Officer Bryan had returned to our house a couple of days after his original visit to interview her in Spanish with a translator, as promised. I had briefly worried that they might ask about her working conditions but convinced myself that murder detectives, or whatever they are, wouldn't be interested in labor violations and immigration status. Their interview was short and ended with Elena asking them to join her in prayer for poor Teddy's departed soul. They'd awkwardly obliged, holding hands and bowing their heads, which had made me smile.

I grab a pair of sunglasses and hurry across the street. The box in my arms feels too light, the ribbon too thin—I should have gone for something more substantive. But this was nearly $50, which already seemed like a generous amount to spend. Now I am on the spotless brick walkway leading to Blair and Teddy's front door, and my pulse starts throbbing in my ears. I realize that I forgot to write a note. I should have bought a card at the grocery store. I don't even have decent stationery, so it's pointless to turn back. I can feel the blood rushing behind my eyes now. But I am only a few yards from the front door, and someone inside might be watching me already. I keep going, and reluctantly ring the doorbell.

I can't hear any movement on the other side. "High-quality construction," I say to myself and look up to admire the elaborate window trimmings above. A few seconds go by, and I decide to count slowly to ten before ringing one more time. I wish I could leave the basket here, but that would be idiotic to do without a note. I am at five when the door suddenly swings open.

Blair is blinking in the bright sunshine and doesn't speak right away, so I start. "Hi Blair, it's Alexis, from across the street," I say as if I'm calling on the phone instead of standing right in front of her. I'm sure that I sound nervous. "We're so sorry about what happened to your husband, and we—Sam and I—wanted to just drop off a few sweets and express our condolences." I practiced this on the drive home from the shopping center and think it doesn't sound half bad. I hold out the box stiffly and repeat, unplanned, "We're so sorry."

Blair's eyes have adjusted to the sunshine, and she is looking at me intently. Even in mourning, she looks impeccable. Her hair is pulled back into a chignon at the nape of her neck, and she is wearing a plain black shift dress. The blackness of the dress makes her blue-gray eyes look like steel. No jewelry beyond her wedding rings, and no obvious makeup. She looks miserable, but beautiful.

A moment goes by. My arms are frozen in this extended position, gripping the box of cookies, and afraid that she might laugh in my face. I don't know what else to say and feel a wave of panic starting to crest in my chest. Just as I prepare to repeat my rehearsed condolences, Blair covers her mouth and begins to cry.

"Oh my God, thank you Alexis," she says as she takes a breath and regains her composure. She accepts the box and deftly steps backward to put it down on a large circular foyer table behind her. She's done this before.

Then she comes out of the door and wraps her arms around my shoulders. She is hugging me. This catches me so off guard that I don't manage to lift my arms from my sides before Blair pulls back and says, "Alexis, this is so kind of you. Please, come in."

I did not anticipate this reaction and have no polite excuse ready. "Are you sure?" I ask. "I really don't want to disturb you. I'm sure you must be . . ."

But Blair has already gone into the house. She interrupts, "No, no, you've got to come in," and looks back at me expectantly, as if I can't say no.

Inside, her house is just as beautiful as I'd imagined it. The foyer is open to the story above, with a classic black-and-white checkered floor leading to a wide staircase. The furniture is clean-lined and expensive-looking, and there is a massive bouquet of white roses on the table, towering over my humble cookie box. I remember what I am wearing—a wrinkled T-shirt, maternity shorts, plastic flip-flops—and feel terribly out of place.

Blair leads me past the staircase, past the large formal rooms flanking the foyer, and toward the back of the house. We are in her kitchen—twice the size of mine, and far more expensive—and she pulls out a designer rattan stool at the island for me. "Alexis, God, I can't tell you how much I appreciate you coming by. I'll make us spritzers? It's so damn hot already," she smiles at me from the far side of the continent-sizesland.

"Oh sure," I answer tentatively, "but please don't go out of your way, you must have so much to do. Water would be fine, too, if that's easier . . ." I trail off, uncertain.

"I do have a lot to do, but I don't want to do any of it. I'd much prefer to have a drink," she laughs at herself, her bright voice echoing in the quiet house.

I try to casually look around as she pulls glasses out of cabinets and bottles out of fridges. There are at least two: a massive double-door refrigerator that looks like it could swallow Blair if she isn't careful, plus a full-size wine fridge. I suspect she also has refrigerated drawers in here. I wanted one to use for the kids' drinks and snacks, but it was too expensive and our remodel was already over budget. Her kitchen opens onto a large family room, the one I have seen before. Blair notices me gazing at the sofa, and offers, "My kids are staying at my mom's near Philadelphia for a few days. She took them back after the funeral. I thought it would be good for them to be out of the house."

I nod silently, not sure how to respond.

"Or maybe it's good for me, for some time to deal with all the bureaucratic crap, and scream and cry without them here to see it. And drink," she comes around the island to hand me a glass, with two slices of lime floating on top, and we just smile at each other instead of toasting.

"So how have you all been settling in? How's the baby? God I remember those first few horrible months, it's a slog," Blair goes on as she settles herself on the stool next to mine.

"Definitely a slog, but the baby's good-natured, and our nanny helps a lot." I pause, but see that she is expecting more. "We've settled in okay. Our kitchen remodel is done, but there's so much more—the bathrooms, the windows, the patio—I'm not sure what to do next, and anyway we can't afford anything else for a while." I stop short here. Blair doesn't need to know about our financial problems.

"Renovations are such a headache. I'm impressed that you've been doing them at all. You already have your hands full," she responds reassuringly. And then, "Wait, are you breastfeeding?"

I feel the heat rising up in my cheeks. I hate this question. "No," I say slowly, looking for the words. "I tried, with Caleb, but it didn't work. We went to three different lactation consultants, and a pediatric ENT, but he was losing so much weight. It was a nightmare. After a few months, I gave up." Really, it had only been three weeks, but I can never bring myself to say that. It's too embarrassing.

"Well, look at the bright side—after breastfeeding my kids, I deflated like balloons on a cold day. Thank God for modern medicine," she says with a wink.

Our conversation continues like this for half an hour—Blair asking friendly questions, me offering stilted responses and failing to find a way to ask about how she is doing. She is charming, gracious, and seems grateful for my company, as poor as it is. But I am exhausted from the effort, and when she pauses for long enough, I see my opportunity. "Blair, I'm so sorry, but I really should be getting back. The children . . ."

She jumps up right away. "Of course, I'm babbling on and you've got two tiny kids at home, what am I thinking!"

As we walk through her foyer, I look into a sitting room on my left. Everything is tasteful, coordinated, and expensive—the dark gray and white coffered ceiling, the leather armchairs, the richly patterned rug. I know how ridiculous it sounds before I say it, but the spritzer has loosened my lips. "Blair, your house is absolutely gorgeous. Every room is just perfect."

"Oh thanks for saying that," she says, patting me gently on the shoulder.

"No, it's true. I'm just so impressed. Did you . . . you and Teddy redo the house when you bought it?" I continue.

"In fact we did. We bought this house fifteen years ago. It was already huge—the previous owners built it as their dream home. The bones were good but their decorating tastes ran terribly tacky, so we had to touch every room, the whole house really."

This is a favorite topic of conversation for me, since I've been following designers online, imagining what our house could be one day, eventually, when we can afford it. But even my aspirational collections of pictures don't look as good as this actual house. "Wow. Do you mind if I ask, did you hire a decorator? I struggled even just trying to do one room myself. I started with the living room . . ."

"I'm an interior designer," she says with a small laugh. "Very part-time. I had my own little business until our youngest was born. Teddy was working all the time and there was so much to manage here, it just didn't make sense anymore. I still design for a friend or two every year, but it's not quite the same."

I think I can hear wistfulness in her voice, but it might be the alcohol. We're at her front door now, so even though I'm finally feeling comfortable, I know it's time to go.

"It was so nice to talk to you, thank you," I offer.

"I'll see you soon," she says, and before I realize it, she is hugging me again.

As I slowly walk back to my house, I feel a strange mix of happiness and pity. I've been avoiding and then simply tolerating women like Blair for as long as I can remember. But, to my surprise, my initial impression about Blair seems to have been right. We've just had a prolonged and very pleasant conversation, and she was moved to tears by my kind gesture. She had even asked for my cell phone number before I left. Blair is clearly in a terrible place, and maybe she doesn't have as much support as I assumed. Maybe she could use a friend.

Blair

Alexis seems a little afraid of me. I'm probably flattering myself, but when she came by a couple of days ago, she was so nervous. The poor girl was acting like she'd shown up to a gala wearing a paper bag. She could have pulled herself together a little more, but not a big deal, it was only coming by a neighbor's. She's more of a mess than I am, and I'm the one whose husband just died. Still, I liked her. Her condolences seemed more genuine than any of the others around here. She's also very pretty, in a way that used to be called exotic, and slim for having had a baby a month ago. That takes a lot of self-discipline, and I respect that.

Emily, on the other hand, had the nerve and bad taste to send a group text last night as if we're all best buddies. Her message announced that they are back in town and so shocked about Teddy. As if I care about Emily and Dylan's reaction. She's insisting that we all come over for a drink to help me take my mind off things. I can barely stand her, but it's better than drinking alone, so I wrote back and said sure. I also said I'd bring our lovely new neighbor Alexis.

We come out of our front doors at almost the same moment. The warm evening air presses in from every direction like rushing water, and I have to take a long, deep breath to remind myself that I'm not drowning, before raising my hand to wave. Alexis definitely tried harder today. She's got a loose, flower-print dress on, and it looks like she put gel in her hair. Those bloody, swollen postpartum weeks were miserable for me every time, and I feel a small pang of sympathy as she walks toward me smiling and waving back.

"Hi! So glad you could make it!" I open my arms for a hug as she comes up the front walk. Her body is soft and yielding, and I hang on for a few seconds longer than I probably should. One of my earrings gets caught in her glossy black curls, and it takes us a few seconds to untangle ourselves. The whole thing is a bit awkward, and we both try to laugh it off.

"Tonight's going to be a blast," I say sarcastically and start walking her back out toward the street.

"It's so nice of you, and of Emily, to invite me. I haven't even met her yet," Alexis says as she nervously adjusts the straps of her dress. "What is her husband's name again?"

"Dylan. They're basically children, flush from a tech start-up they came up with together in college. Emily's some kind of brilliant coder. It went public a couple of years ago, and the money went straight to their heads," I answer. I can't help but be honest, sometimes.

"I actually thought their house was empty. I've never seen any cars in their driveway or lights on inside."

I scoff, "They own half a dozen houses. I'm sure they'll tell you all about it, they always do. The one good thing about that is they're gone a lot."

"So you really like them then?" Alexis smiles.

"Well, they're closer to your age than mine, so maybe they'll make a better impression on you. But probably not. Dylan thinks he's God's gift to women, which is so off the mark that it's pathetic. He's a slimy bastard. Emily thinks that she's a brilliant star surrounded by dim suburban moms. She literally name-drops women who work in Silicon Valley like we're all supposed to be impressed."

We're walking up their steps now, made of a stone similar to their house's façade, so I finish up whispering, "Success and wealth just don't suit some people."

"I think they would suit me just fine," Alexis whispers back, and we are both laughing when Emily opens the front door.

She still looks like a prepubescent boy, skinny limbs and an overgrown blunt cut. I don't even think she's wearing a bra under her ironic T-shirt.

"Hi, Blair, I'm so sorry for your loss," Emily starts unconvincingly.

As I introduce Alexis, Emily steps over the threshold and closes the front door behind her, forcing us to step backward. "Nice to meet you, the other ladies are already here, so let's go around the side of the house."

She won't let us in the front door and is making us take the long way around. What in the hell is she hiding in there? Maybe she just gets off on treating us like the help. I want to roll my eyes at Alexis but restrain myself.

Emily leads us around the side of her house that runs parallel to the trail. I can't believe this woman.

"It's so awful that Teddy was murdered out on our beautiful trail. I don't think I can go out there anymore." Emily turns her head to watch my reaction as she says this.

I meet her eyes and am almost overwhelmed by the desire to push her, hard, onto the ground. I don't answer.

We come around into her backyard. It's a nicely landscaped space, but that was all the work of the previous owners. Dylan and Emily would probably have installed an amphitheater and hosted concerts, or some other childish idea, but the house came complete with manicured gardens, a large sport court, and a pool, of course. Dylan must have just come off the court. He's standing shirtless on the deck, a basketball cradled in one arm, talking to Laura and Jennifer.

After a tangle of greetings, condolences, and repeated introductions—Alexis has met everyone except Dylan before—Emily goes inside to grab a corkscrew, leaving the rest of us waiting in an awkward arc around Dylan. The sheen of sweat on his muscular torso is too much of a distraction for too many of the women here, and I know he's enjoying it.

"Blair," he reaches toward me with his free arm and palms my elbow with a hot, moist hand, "if you need anything, anything at all, we're here for you."

"The obituary was nicely written," Laura interjects before I can respond, and Dylan lets go just as Emily swings open her patio door.

She pulls the cork out of a slippery bottle of cold white wine and asks Dylan if he plans to have a glass with us. "No thanks babe," he winks at her and gives the rest of us a little wave. "I'll take that as my cue to exit. Good night ladies, have fun."

Silence reigns only for a moment as we settle into a semicircle of uncomfortable wrought iron chairs with filled glasses in hand. Then Emily jumps right in. "How've you been doing, since Teddy's passing?"

I take a sip from my glass before responding. "Well, I'm pretty awful, to be honest. I think I'm still in shock that he's gone. Just like that. We were together for twenty years."

"I really don't know what to say Blair, it's too awful for words," offers Jennifer. Her pale skin is glowing in the blue evening. I notice that she has a blowout and a full face of makeup on. A bit much for this crowd, and a little obvious. I'll have to mention it, gently, next time we're alone.

"I can't imagine—" Jennifer tries to go on, but Emily cuts her off. "Have the police come up with any strong leads?"

"God no, can you believe it? It's been nearly three weeks, and the best they've got is some complicated business deal Teddy was working on. Like maybe some foreign goons decided to kill him, instead of seeing through the negotiations. It makes no sense so I'm sure they'll drop it soon. But really, the police have been very thorough, and I can't blame them for not having answers."

This is the truth. The detectives come to see me every few days, and their latest round of questions focused on details of Teddy's work that I had almost no idea about. But Emily seems strangely dissatisfied with my answer. She's leaning back in her seat, as if to relax, but the bitten-down fingertips of her right hand can't stop drumming against her bony knee. "They really think that's what happened?"

"Well, they have very little to go on. As luck would have it, it rained all that morning. There weren't any footprints, no fingerprints or bits of anything or anybody else on him. They've been going through his emails and his phone, and this is the best they've come up with." My glass is empty now, but Emily doesn't seem to notice.

"What do you think could have happened? What does your

family think?" Laura probes. She's always been a humorless woman, with a stout, unenviable figure that belies her Brazilian origins. Lucky for her she's got the same luminous golden skin as Alexis. It makes her look at least five years younger than me, even though I think we're about the same age. Her ghost of an accent is only noticeable if you're listening for it, but she's always eager to talk about her home country, unlike other aspects of her biography.

"What can I think?" I turn slightly toward Laura so I can meet her dark eyes. "It was such a regular weekend. We drove up to my mom's Friday after the kids got out of school and talked to Teddy that night. He told me that he was going to go for a run the next morning and that he had some work to catch up on. The usual."

"We were out of town too," Emily cuts in. "We were in Boston for some investment meetings, and, well, Dylan went down to New York for a few days . . ." She trails off.

Now I think I see what's going on. Poor Emily, she's a dog hot on the wrong scent.

"Emily, sweetie, I hate to be a lush, but what do you think about opening another bottle?" Jennifer holds up her empty glass with a smile. I don't blame her. Emily is the one who invited us here, but she hasn't even bothered to turn on some music or put out a few snacks.

"Sure." Emily reluctantly extricates herself from her seat and heads inside, leaving the four of us in silence again.

"Did you grow up near Philadelphia?" Alexis asks timidly.

"I did, and we go up there a lot because my mom's alone. My dad died a few years ago. She could move to Naples or Palm Beach or wherever life would be warmer and easier. But she won't. She's a difficult woman."

We go on like this, making small talk, until Emily comes back out gripping the neck of an open bottle of the same white in each fist. She hands one bottle to Alexis and another to Jennifer, then sits back down as the two of them lean over to refill outstretched glasses. I'm not surprised that Emily's a lazy hostess. Laura seems to take her return as an excuse to jump back to everybody's favorite subject.

"You know, that weekend we were upgrading our security system, and none of our cameras were working. I think we're the only ones on this block who could have gotten a shot of anyone who came by that morning. Such terrible timing."

"What about all the footage from your drones?" Alexis asks, her eyes on Laura, as if this is a normal question.

"Did you just say drones?" Emily asks, half laughing.

Alexis nods, still looking at Laura. "Shawn told us—Sam and me—about your collection. We saw him in the wooded lot next to our house late last Friday, looking for his night-vision drone that crashed."

Laura is a piece of work, I can't believe she's never once said anything to me about this. We are all looking at her now, expecting an explanation, but she sips her wine slowly, as if she was out here alone.

"Is that true Laura? What the hell have you and Shawn been recording?" Jennifer asks, knowing that it must be true and not happy about it.

Laura is unperturbed. "Collection? That's absurd. Shawn's got one or two drones, he just flies them for fun with our kids. They don't record anything."

Jennifer wraps her pale arms around herself as if she's just gotten a chill. "That's a damn strange hobby. I really hope they aren't peering into anyone's windows with those things."

"Of course not. That would be illegal," Laura says calmly before turning her gaze on me. "Blair, what was Teddy doing out there anyway?" she asks as if she has a right to know.

The others are too intimidated by her to unchange the subject, and I don't feel like arguing. "He always runs on Saturday morning at dawn, rain or shine. Mostly on that trail." I pause to take a long sip from my overfilled glass.

"Surprising you didn't know that already, with how many cameras you and Shawn have trained on all of us." I couldn't let her off the hook so easily. The delicate ironwork screeches in protest as everyone shifts uncomfortably in their seats, except for Laura, who doesn't even blink.

I go on. "When I didn't hear from him, I just figured he got busy with emails or doing something in the yard and hadn't had time to call. I was so wrapped up with cleaning out my mom's attic, I didn't even notice the day going by, until the police called." Emily is serving us a cheap Chardonnay, but at least it's cold, and I'd rather be drunk for this anyway.

"Maybe it was a political hit. He was in the state legislature for a long time," Laura speculates. No one acknowledges her. Their eyes are on me.

"I think Teddy went out for his run and crossed paths with someone evil. Maybe a drug deal in progress, or a gang ritual, or Lord knows what. It's ridiculous. And horrific. They bashed his head in and threw him over the edge. Like trash." I have to pause to wipe away the tears that I wish would stop coming every time I think of him. "Horrible, horrible luck. And how will the police find them?"

"I don't know what to say Blair, that is beyond awful," Jennifer repeats herself. "I really hope they can track down the bastard, whoever it was."

Emily's glass slips out of her hand and into her lap, wine dribbling down her thin legs and onto the decking, but she doesn't move. "I didn't realize, is that how he died? He was . . . beaten to death?"

I give them all a weak smile, as Jennifer jumps up to get some napkins. "No, no, I'm not supposed to be going around telling people that, but you're not everyone, right?"

"They fractured his skull, in multiple places, probably with a large rock. That's what the police said. But they didn't want to publish that. I think they're still hoping they might stumble across a bloody rock somewhere. Maybe they'll find it in a homeless person's tent. Like a fucking souvenir."

"That's outrageous," Laura announces. "Crime crossing over from D.C. is a serious problem, and this would be the worst example of it yet."

I have to indulge her self-importance, but I hate to. "It just feels so random and senseless. Scary, really. They would never have done it if they'd known him."

Laura ignores me and goes on, "If we can't safely enjoy our natural spaces, then what's the point of having them? We can't let this go."

"I need another drink," I say to myself and reach for one of the wine bottles before anyone can offer to pour it for me.

Alexis

Sam and I fought last night. We've been in a bad place for a while, I know, but we don't usually fight outright, not with yelling and accusations like we did last night. Displeased looks, cutting comments, silence—those are our usual weapons. But Sam is increasingly on edge, ready to hurl insults my way as soon as I open my mouth to point something out. He's overworked and so worried about making partner, I know this, but sometimes I can't stop myself. And last night, the wine at Emily's had really gotten to me.

I think we ended up drinking at least four bottles, and I may have had more than anybody else. I just felt so uncomfortable, with Laura blatantly contradicting Shawn's story about the drones and then interrogating Blair about Teddy's murder. Emily too, walking us around by the trail—even I recognized that was beyond rude and meant to provoke. I wonder what Dylan sees in her. Blair made him out to seem like the court jester, but he was strikingly handsome, just as tall as Sam and with black, almost-curly hair and amber eyes. I'd found myself playing the old guessing game—one parent from Latin America? grandparents from Asia? which part?—the one I avoided playing with those neighbors. I'm glad Dylan hadn't stayed to drink with us. I would have ended up asking out loud, and then had to answer for myself when he inevitably reciprocated.

By the time everyone finally went home, all I'd wanted to do was crawl into bed and sleep it off. But Carter woke up after I'd already texted Elena that I was back, so she'd turned off the monitor she keeps with her in the basement and didn't come running up to help. I had to bounce Carter around for nearly an hour before putting her back down. Around 1:00 a.m., just as I was finally drifting off to sleep, Sam had come home from work and started to rattle around in our bathroom. I couldn't help myself. I'd muttered into the pillow that he was the most inconsiderate person I'd ever met. He hadn't heard me and asked me to repeat what I'd said, so I had, raising my voice and adding some expletives about how noise carries through the house.

This really set him off. He said something along the lines of *"What the fuck is wrong with you? You got everything you wanted, but all you do is bitch. You think the house has issues—can you get up and take a look in the mirror? You got an easier job and now you're on a six-month vacation, why don't you use some of that time to pull yourself together? We're burning through money, and I'm working my ass off. I'm under an insane amount of pressure. The last thing I need is you coming up with new shit to complain about."*

I should have left it alone—we were both exhausted—but I didn't. Instead, I let loose a torrent of frustrations, exaggerated by an angry mix of wine and sleep deprivation. *"Some of the women there tonight don't even work, did you know that? I've got a very real job and just had two babies, and I wash your goddamn under-*

wear myself. What else do you want from me? Do you know they all have vacation homes? Like multiple vacation homes? We can't even fix the only house we have."

I've never seen Sam angrier. He actually punched a hole in the hollow-core bathroom door installed by the previous owner who has revealed himself, in absentia, to be extremely cheap. The punch caught me off guard and I gasped reflexively. Sam just gave me a look uncomfortably close to disgusted and stalked out of the room, slamming the door behind him.

This morning, I was feeding Caleb breakfast in the kitchen when he left for work, and I apologized. I usually do. Having him, or anyone else really, displeased with me feels like a guillotine hanging over my head. I'd rather grovel for forgiveness than let the blade fall. He'd put his briefcase down on the counter and walked over to kiss the top of my head, joking that he's going to bill his clients to fix our bathroom door since they're the reason he's not sleeping enough and snapped like that.

Despite our fight, and the tension at Emily's, I'm glad I went yesterday. They'd all asked to exchange contact info, so now I have multiple neighbors' numbers, not just Blair's. But I won't tell Sam about it, at least not yet. I don't think he means to, but whenever we talk about friends the condescension is thick in his voice, as if I were a child trying something for the first time and he an encouraging parent. I can't stand it.

I'm also keeping my worries about what Blair told us to myself. If Teddy really was murdered by wandering delinquents, wouldn't there be some history of criminal activity in the woods? And why would the murderer risk breaking his own neck instead of following the trail back out? In which case, how could none of the neighbors have seen anything? We're at least a mile from the nearest bus stop, and a muddy druggie—or a whole gang of them—walking by on a Saturday morning would have had to attract someone's attention.

This is really none of my business. But I am in the laundry room folding what feels like a thousand tiny pieces of clothing, with the steady hum of the washer and dryer blocking everything else out. I can't help but let my mind come back to the murder. The police must have thought through all of this already. I guess that's why Blair said they're focusing on a connection with his business dealings. But that also seems far-fetched to me—why not find some less dramatic and dirty way to do it, like poison?

Sam would call me ridiculous if I said any of this out loud, and he'd be right. I know nothing about murder. I should leave it alone. But still, somebody killed Teddy Bard within walking distance of my own house, and the neighbors—Laura and Shawn, and maybe Emily too—somehow seem too interested. Maybe I missed the clues, and blindly bought into a neighborhood on the decline. If I had parents with their own decades of real estate experience, or if Sam had cared more about our house search and helped, maybe we wouldn't have made this stupid mistake. It feels like after all this time I'm right back where I started, in that complex with my mother, and I take a deep breath to push down the panic I feel rising yet again in my stomach.

SUNDAY / JUNE 22 / 2:00 AM

It's Saturday night. Technically, it's Sunday morning. Regardless, it's 2:00 a.m. on a weekend, and I am at the kitchen sink washing bottles. My eyes ache from constantly looking at my phone screen while holding Carter, and I've turned off all the lights except the under-cabinet ones I'd insisted on having installed. Tonight,

the waning moon is blocked by clouds and my view is of blackness, interrupted only by the neighbors' restrained landscape
lighting and a faint pool of white cast by a lonely streetlamp at
the right edge of our property, on the side bordering Jeff and
Jennifer's Tudor. Out of recently formed habit, my eyes go to
Blair's house—her driveway is empty. She hasn't had any visitors this week besides the detectives, and the light but steady
trail traffic has slowly resumed—early morning runners, weekend hikers, the occasional sturdy dog walker. Unnervingly back
to normal.

Carter has been getting fussier, and I've worn a path into the
hardwood between the only two places I've been in the last three
days—her nursery and the kitchen. If this were five years ago,
Sam and I would be at a great bar with friends of his or passed
out after an amazing dinner. But we're parents now, suburban
homeowners with burdens too heavy to put down for an evening out, certainly not with each other. I'd suggested to Sam that
we watch TV together after the children went to bed, but he's
preparing for a trial and then Carter woke up anyway. Sam's still
up working now, in the office, which is also our fourth bedroom.
I hadn't managed to convince him to put his office in the den,
on the main floor—he said he needed a place where he could
lock himself away from the rest of us. So we turned that fourth
room into a combination guest room and office, complete with a
custom Murphy bed that cost more than all the furniture in our
first apartment combined.

I did have one point of contact with the outside world today—I texted Blair. I haven't heard from her since Emily's. We'd
walked out together that night, and she'd been very quiet, lost in
thought it seemed, and I imagine she's been just like that, alone
in her house, for the past few days. My text asked if she'd like

to go for a walk, because I don't want to get drunk and fight with Sam again. She'd written back right away, and we're going tomorrow afternoon—today, technically—before her mother and children arrive. I'm looking forward to it, enough to have already picked out my cutest athletic clothes. Unfortunately, they're athletic maternity. Six weeks out, and I still have a lot of weight left to lose. A walk will also be good exercise.

I am putting the last nipple on the drying rack when something catches my eye outside. A dark mass, at the very edge of the pool of streetlight. Not a fox or a raccoon or a deer—the upright shape of a person. I blink, and the shape is gone. I lean over the sink on my tiptoes, my hip bones rubbing against the cold marble, my eyes squinting to focus on the blackness around the streetlight. I think I see the trees between us and Jeff and Jennifer's rustling, but it's so dark. I'd have a better view from our sunroom. I run across the house, the floors creaking wildly under my feet, through the dining room and living room, straight into the sunroom. In here, I am only about twenty feet away from the trees.

Shawn is the person I'm expecting to see, creeping around again, this time on the opposite side of our house—self-appointed neighborhood surveillance, or something worse. If I tell Sam he might go out there and get into a fight, which would be mortifying. But I don't like it either. The idea of Shawn out in the darkness makes me feel even less safe. We barely know him and Laura, what they're watching for, or what they're lying about.

Everything outside is perfectly still. I stay where I am for about ten minutes, standing motionless in the sunroom and barely breathing, waiting to see his flashlight click on. But nothing happens, and the need to sleep drags me away from my vigil.

I walk through the house slowly, checking all the locks and making sure the new alarm is on. I was too slow to catch him. Or maybe I'm imagining things.

SUNDAY / JUNE 22 / 4:00 PM

Blair and I meet in front of my house in the late afternoon. I am standing at the end of my driveway, pushing and pulling Carter's stroller in a gentle rhythm. She's in the bassinet attachment, flat on her back and fast asleep.

"Hi! I'm sorry, do you mind if I bring her?" I point down at the stroller. Sam was supposed to watch both of them, but he'd snapped at me that he's too busy, and locked himself back up in the office. Elena spends most of her Sunday at church, and she's worked too much overtime lately anyway. So I've got to bring Carter with me, but at least Caleb is still napping.

Blair just laughs and says, "As long as we don't go walking anywhere near that trail, I don't mind who comes along, especially cute little babies."

She comes around the stroller to give me a hug. Her body feels slim and slippery in high-end Lycra. Even her large breasts feel firm against my soft and sloppy fat.

I hadn't thought about that—maybe suggesting a walk was insensitive. But I suppose everything in the neighborhood must remind her of Teddy, most of all the inside of their house, so this can't be so bad. We are walking slowly toward the intersection with Sunrise, away from the trailhead. "How are you doing?" Blair asks me. She sounds sincere, and interested.

"Me? Well other than the sleep deprivation and lack of exposure to sunlight, I'm not bad." I'm laughing, but assessing in my mind how I must look to her. Bags under my eyes, my hair more frizzy than curly and pulled into a halfhearted ponytail, pudge poking out everywhere. A wreck.

She laughs too, and compliments my leggings, just to be nice I'm sure. We turn right on Sunrise and then left on Bright Drive, making our way slowly along the winding, shaded streets of River Forest. Clouds are keeping the heat tolerable, and children are out playing. Most of them are tucked away in their expansive backyards, out of sight, but we can hear their peals of laughter. A few teenagers are shooting hoops on an extra-wide driveway, and over the rhythmic thumping of basketball on asphalt, in the far distance, I think I can make out the rushing river.

This is the soundtrack of affluence and calm that I've been waiting to hear all my life. The one I'd imagined in my mind falling asleep as a child, the nights when a nasty argument or brazen sex in a nearby apartment wasn't muffled by the thin drywall. I still can't accept that all of this is a façade—that even in a place like this, someone can get murdered next door and everyone else goes on living as if nothing happened. I ask Blair why she and Teddy first moved here. She looks around for a few long seconds before answering.

"For the first couple of years, it felt like a collection of private country estates. It was so green and so quiet. We planned to have at least three kids, and three big dogs, one for each kid. Neither of our parents had let us have pets growing up, so it was high on our priority list. Well we both turned out to be allergic, so no dogs. But it was still the right place for us. They've been subdividing lots and building more houses, so now it really feels like a neighborhood. Even if some of the neighbors are questionable." She gives me a sideways glance and a smile.

I'm not sure what she means but decide to take a risk. "This may sound weird, but you know the other night at Emily's? I don't think Laura was being totally honest about the drone thing. Shawn really did tell us he's got a bunch of them."

"I know," Blair laughs as one of her manicured hands lands lightly on the fingers I have curled around the stroller bar. "Laura's a damn pest, don't worry about her."

I hadn't expected this reaction. "Are she and Shawn the questionable neighbors you were talking about?"

"Ha! There are so many of them. You see this house up here?" she is gesturing discreetly toward an immense French Provincial on our left and is clearly excited to share. "A couple of years ago it sold for a bargain. The former owner died on a fishing trip with his business partner, and it came out that he would've been indicted on securities fraud charges. Even worse, his wife and daughter were in this weird sex thing with the business partner and ended up moving away. The whole story barely got any press coverage though, so at least someone was willing to buy the place."

"That sounds awful," I say. "I wouldn't touch that house with a ten-foot pole."

"Alexis, don't be so naïve! Every house has skeletons in the coat closet. Maybe in every closet. In this neighborhood that's for sure." She looks over and catches the skeptical face I'm making. Her eyes are sparkling, more blue than gray, with amusement. I bristle over being called naïve. Blair is probably eight or ten years older than me, but I know without having to ask that I have seen a thousand things she never has. A thousand difficult, awful things. But I let it pass.

"Oh you can't just say that without any specifics!" The whole point of this walk, of these repeated encounters with Blair, is to try and be neighborly, friendly even, because she's going through a hard time.

Blair looks over her shoulder before moving closer to me. "You know the farmhouse next door to me, across from you?"

"Of course, Mack—"

"Well I'm sure you think he's a nice grandfather type, but remember this. Don't ever go into his house, or invite him into yours, or have anything to do with him if you can help it. He's not actually nice at all."

"What does that mean?"

"He was the business partner, is what that means," she says as she glances back again at the still empty street. I wait for her to go on, to share more disturbing details, but she doesn't. It almost seems like she's scared of Mack, so I don't push, and after a few seconds our conversation moves on.

Blair tells me about her most demanding and ridiculous design clients, about the never-ending process of decorating her own house, and about how supportive Teddy had always been of her work. We compare notes on the houses that we pass, mocking the occasional excesses—five-car garages that stick out like snouts, overcommitment to columns, and other expensive but poor choices. We have similar tastes, which is no surprise given how much I like her house.

We are nearing the intersection with Dappled Walk when a Lexus sedan pulls up slowly next to us. The passenger-side window rolls down, and a woman leans over from the driver's seat. She looks like she's in her seventies, with shoulder-length silver hair and a good deal of large jewelry on. I am standing closest to her car, but she looks right through me. "Blair! Blair, I'm so sorry about Teddy. We just got back from Italy the other night, and we missed the funeral. I need to come by and visit you!"

"Hi Nancy. Thank you, yes, it would be lovely to see you," Blair answers as she steps forward, next to me. "This is our new neighbor, Alexis Crawford. She and her husband bought the Robinsons' old house," she adds as her hand lands lightly on the small of my back.

Nancy blinks as she processes Blair's words, then says to me in a less enthusiastic tone, "Nice to meet you."

I give her a small smile and wave, "You too," and start pushing the stroller forward. Blair says something else to Nancy that I don't make out and takes a few big steps to catch up with me as the Lexus slowly pulls away and passes us. I plan to say that I kept moving to keep Carter asleep, but instead I blurt out, "I'd bet you $100 that that woman thought I was a nanny."

"Oh God," Blair groans and puts a hand over her face. "Nancy is an old-fashioned bore if I ever met one." She looks uncomfortable.

"No, I'm sorry, it's not a big deal. Nothing's wrong with being a nanny anyway."

We keep walking, the silence between us an expanse of moments like these.

"Does Nancy live nearby?" I ask after a few minutes.

"She does, just over on Cliffside Drive, maybe four blocks from here. But let me give you some more advice. Don't ever accept an invitation to her house. She's not like Mack of course, but the river view from her yard would drive you nuts with jealousy. Trust me, I learned that the hard way."

We both find this funny enough to laugh out loud.

"But why does she have Maryland license plates?" I ask as I wipe a small tear from the corner of my eye.

"Oh, haven't you heard about the state car tax here? She must have some rentals or other property, and just registers her car over there to avoid it."

Of course I've heard about it. We received our first tax bill a few weeks ago—nothing for the Honda, but over a thousand for the new BMW. Sam had cursed, and I had waited to put a check in the mail until the due date, to put off paying as long as possible. It had never occurred to us that there was a way to avoid the tax altogether. In reality, we don't own any other property so we couldn't even if we wanted to. But it still makes me feel like a fool.

I don't want to dwell on this, so I change the subject to the aggressive landscaping choices of the house we are passing. After a few more blocks, we circle back toward Shadow Road, and it is nearing 5:30 as we walk up to the end of my driveway. I realize it's a good moment to make a friendly gesture. "Would you like to come in for a drink, just some water even?" I ask.

"Thanks so much, but I'd better get home. My mom and the kids will be here any minute," Blair says as she looks toward her house.

"Of course!" I've forgotten that she is about to be surrounded by loved ones again, and probably won't need me to pass the time with anymore. "Okay, hope to see you soon," I say, and this time I lean in for the hug first.

I watch Blair cross the street back to her house, then slowly push the stroller toward our front door. I am watching Carter starting to stir from her nap, her tiny, perfect lips twitching, when a large black Mercedes sedan drives by too quickly and turns abruptly into Blair's driveway. Her three children jump out of the car right away, followed by an older woman with a chic platinum blond bob and dark sunglasses. Blair is still out on her front steps and turns to watch them with her arms folded tightly across her chest. They each grab their luggage from the sedan's trunk and file grimly past her into the house. She reaches out and touches each of them as they go by, but when her mother comes up after them, her own small suitcase in hand, Blair folds her arms again and looks away. Then her head shifts slightly, and I think that she knows I'm watching.

Blair

"Listen, Blair, we went back and forth on this for a while. In the end, Teddy agreed to do it. He must have told you."

Mack's not a big man. He's much shorter than Teddy, and only a couple of inches taller than me. But I always feel like I have to be on guard around him, even with the liver spots and Mister Rogersesque pullover. With his hands on his hips and feet stepped apart, he looks like he expects me, and everyone else, to do what he says.

"Honestly I don't know what you're talking about. He never said anything to me about this. And anyway, I don't understand, why would you want this hedge to come down?" I put my own hands on my hips, to show him I'm not intimidated.

We are standing in my side yard, shaded from the evening sun by the long row of evergreen privet that separates our properties. Teddy and I had these bushes planted when we first moved in, and now they tower over us.

"You're misunderstanding, Blair, we weren't talking about ripping them out. I simply asked Teddy to have them trimmed.

They've grown too deep into my yard." He steps his feet out wider, as if to emphasize his point.

I'm not misunderstanding anything, of course. Teddy told me about Mack's absurd request. He'd been emailing for weeks about the hedge, demanding we pay to cut them back on his side. Teddy was so annoyed that he was planning on just having our landscapers do it as part of fall cleanup. But I'm not as nice as Teddy. Mack's house sits on nearly two acres, one of the largest lots in River Forest. A hundred feet of rolling lawn separate his house from this hedge, and without it, we'd be looking straight into each other's family rooms. Even at a distance, there would be no privacy. He should be thanking us for having had the foresight to plant them, not asking us to foot the bill to cut them back a few feet.

"Mack, if it bothers you, you're welcome to trim them as much as you want on your side. I really don't see what this has to do with me." I'd like to add, "You inconsiderate jackass," but instead play it safe with my pity card.

"You know, I've had so much on my mind since Teddy died, it's really overwhelming. I haven't even found the contact information for all our maintenance people and contractors in his files yet. Our pool's probably going to turn green soon." I let my shoulders droop.

Mack is a founding partner at a successful private equity firm and has more money than he can reasonably spend in what remains of his lifetime. He owns multiple lots in the neighborhood, including the acre next to Alexis, and I don't know how many vacation homes. He even owns an island for God's sake. But here he is, acting as if it's difficult to cough up a few hundred dollars to solve his own problem.

He sighs heavily, and lets his arms drop to his side. "Look, fine, I'll take care of it this time. But if it becomes an issue again, we'll need to discuss."

This conversation should end soon, before I say something I'll regret. Mack has a low tolerance for nuisance. When his business partner's widow realized that he'd forced himself on her eighteen-year-old daughter and confronted him, he didn't hold back. He broke her nose, then made financial problems and nasty rumors rain down until she drowned. People even started saying that she'd been having an affair with Mack herself and was involved in her husband's death. The poor woman eventually gave up on legal action and moved to one of the Dakotas. I need to be careful and avoid a fight I can't win.

"Sure, I really appreciate that," I give him a tight smile and turn to walk toward the street. He follows, walking quickly to stay right behind me. As we near the curb, he says my name and puts a hand on my lower back, grazing the top of my butt, and I turn sharply to push him off.

"Didn't mean to scare you," he says, but seems pleased. "You know that couple that moved into the Robinsons' old house?" He points a bony finger toward Alexis and Sam's house.

"What about them?"

"The wife, where's she from, do you know?" he asks, his eyes still on their house.

"Alexis? I think she grew up somewhere around Baltimore. Why?" I start walking again.

"Ah, I thought it might be somewhere overseas. She's got that tropical look to her," he adds, and I can hear the subtle drop in his voice.

"You know she just had her second baby last month. I think she's older than she looks, probably close to forty." I'm not sure why I'm saying this, but decide that it's to protect Alexis.

"Hmm," he grunts dismissively as he steps off the curb into the street.

"Have you met them yet?" I know he has but ask anyway, trying to gauge if he's really interested.

"Of course. I brought them a bottle of champagne," he says without turning around. I don't bother to say goodbye, but stay at the curb, watching him walk slowly back to his front door.

Everything is ablaze now as the sun falls lower and casts its orange glow over the street. The landscaping crews are hurrying back to their pickup trucks, eager to get out of here after a long day of pulling weeds and mowing lawns. I never noticed them before, because I never sat around staring at the street like a shut-in. But these past few weeks, it's like I can feel them. Window washers and duct cleaners, dog walkers and mobile groomers, painters and stonemasons. A legion of worker ants surging through the quiet streets and into the big houses during daylight hours, only to drain the life away and leave us to our own devices at night. Eventually I turn to head back inside and pay our cleaning ladies so they can get on their way and join the exodus. They've been tiptoeing around me since Teddy died. But what I really want is for them to turn up the pulsing Latin music they play on their headphones. Blast it on our speaker system, actually, so I can drown out my own thoughts.

Alexis

I've taken up gardening. Not with the aim of growing anything, but of culling the flock—ripping out what doesn't belong, cutting back what's withered. It isn't entirely by choice, but it is surprisingly satisfying work. The day we came home from the hospital with Carter, I noticed a profusion of new green growth all over our property that's only become uglier and more aggressive since. Our lawn service does a desultory weeding every few weeks, but it's not enough to keep this growth at bay. When I complained to Sam about it, he'd said something sharp about how he has enough to deal with besides my bullshit complaints, so I'd decided to just figure it out myself.

I'm home, after all, and prefer not to be inside with Elena if she's not watching the children. Usually, when they nap, she makes herself a big mug of tea and walks slowly through the rooms of the main floor, as if looking for me to talk to, instead of finding other ways to make herself useful. She is always looking for a pretext, even if I have my face obviously buried in a book or my laptop open. *"Miss Alexis, did I tell you about my cousin with the throat cancer?"* she'll start, eager to share her tragic stories. Or even worse, sometimes she'll ask, *"Tell me more about your mother. In another life, we could have been friends."* So I am forced into hiding outside my own house, trying to avoid her.

Gardening like this also helps to take my mind off last night. I woke up with Carter at midnight and again at 2:00. Sam is in New York all week for depositions, but anyway he's begged off night feedings until promotions are announced. After putting her back down the second time, I went to the kitchen to do dishes, instead of going back to sleep like a sane person. As I alternated between wiping down the counter and glancing out the window, I thought I saw Shawn move in and out of the streetlamp's pool of light, just like Saturday night. I dropped the dish towel in my hand and ran to the sunroom, but again, I was too slow. I fell asleep there, on our old futon from grad school that I want to get rid of but Sam has made me keep until we can afford to buy more furniture. Elena found me, curled up on the old futon, and I must have been a pitiful sight, because she put a blanket on me, did Carter's early morning feeding, and kept Caleb from waking me up until nearly 9:00 a.m.

After coffee, I'd put on shorts and one of Sam's old T-shirts, not bothering with a shower, and have been on my knees hacking away in the front yard since. I can't make sense of what's been going on. If it's Shawn out there, could he really know something the police don't? But if it's not him? This makes my heart pick up speed, as that spot is only a vantage point for a few houses, mine included. I know this is ridiculous. I'm not even sure I've seen someone at all. I know this rationally.

It's almost 11:00 now, and the thick midday air is already slowing me down as I pull the last few weeds from the base of some large hydrangeas near the end of our driveway. The early summer heat has already browned the edges of the pale blue flower clusters, and, as I work my way deeper into the bushes, the stiff, hand-sized leaves start gently scratching at the backs of my legs like spiders. I bat at them—at nothing—and quickly disentangle myself. I need some cold water, and a back massage. As I carefully stretch over to the left, my right hand high in the air, I see Laura moving down her front walk toward the street. She holds up a hand, thinking I am waving at her. I smile back like a reflex, and right myself quickly.

Laura is one of the only other nonwhite homeowners I've identified in the neighborhood, but the two times we've spoken – once when she and Shawn brought us a cheese board a few days after we'd moved in, and then again that night at Emily's – quickly disabused me of the idea that I might ask about her experience living here. Her hair is ironed too straight, her face is set too firm, to admit any weakness, and although she's several inches shorter than me and at least one hundred pounds heavier, I find her even more intimidating than her husband.

The first time we met, she had been polite but businesslike, handing over the cheese board while requesting background information as if we were in a job interview. She'd volunteered that she and Shawn are semiretired from the human resource company they cofounded, having achieved enough success for one lifetime, and that their two kids are incredibly talented athletes with schedules whose management is a job in itself. She'd asked Sam about his law firm and his prospects for making partner, all while looking us each over, as if inspecting cuts of meat at the butcher's. The second time, at Emily's, I'd gotten the feeling that she's accustomed to having things her way, she'd been completely unfazed lying about the drones and so brazen with her questions to Blair.

Watching her in the late morning sunshine, standing barely taller than her mailbox and calmly flipping through the contents she's just extracted, it seems absurd to imagine that she and Shawn are connected to Teddy's murder. Maybe I've been too quick to suspect, and they actually are just trying to help keep us all safe. Maybe that's why Shawn is out at night. Or maybe not. I decide to make my way toward her and see if I can learn anything by talking to her directly.

"Hi Laura!" I say in my friendliest voice.

"Oh hi, Alexis. It looks like you've been hard at work." Her eyes are slowly scanning the length of me.

"Yup, just trying to clean up the garden, I've never seen weeds so big."

She takes a step sideways to see behind me, her plump arms holding the thick stack of envelopes and catalogues close to her chest.

"Neither have I," she says, straight-faced. "I've been meaning to ask, what are you planning on doing with that house anyway?"

"With my house?" I ask, turning my head to see what she is looking at.

"What other house would I be talking about? It's been run-down for years. The Robinsons couldn't maintain it properly in the end. I'm surprised it didn't just get torn down."

Walking over here may have been a stupid idea. I want to defend our house, to tell her that if any house on this block should be torn down, it's her 1990s mega mansion. But instead, I just meekly offer, "We're renovating it in stages. We already did the kitchen."

"Hmm," she says, still looking past me. "I guess it will be a long process."

With this personality, I wonder how she has managed to be as successful as she seems to be. I thought being a jerk was only a viable strategy for certain types of people—not people like Laura and me. I may have been wrong all this time. Either that, or she just doesn't think I'm worth being polite to. I try to redirect the conversation, toward where I need it to go. "I can't believe it's almost July already, I've been hoping for a chance to invite you all over for a little housewarming party."

Laura sighs. "You know, Blair and Teddy would throw parties all the time and invite the whole neighborhood, all the houses on Sunset too, and we'd drink all night. She's kind of a bitch, but she knows how to throw a party. Not like some people. Now, obviously, it will be a while."

I assume she means to disparage Emily's hosting skills but don't want to get off track by asking for clarification. "Oh definitely, it's way too soon, that's why we haven't planned anything I mean, it's much too soon for a party." I am stumbling, but in the right direction. "It's so awful about Teddy's murder, I would never have expected something like that to happen here. And poor Blair."

Laura raises her eyebrows at me. "Anything can happen anywhere. Don't let the big houses fool you." She closes her mailbox and looks toward her front door. "And Blair will be fine. She's not the kind of person to dwell."

"Do you and Shawn have any theories about who killed Teddy?" I ask quickly, trying to cut through her vague comments before she leaves. It's more obvious than I'd hoped to be, but I want any information I can get, more than I'd even realized walking over here.

Instead of answering, Laura takes a step toward me and looks around before asking, "Where are you from Alexis?"

"Around Baltimore."

"What did your parents do?"

"Um, I grew up with my mom. She was a secretary," I answer, too confused to be embarrassed.

"Well, comparatively this must seem like paradise to you. But do you see how many people are swarming around here every day? All the help? All the people taking advantage of the free trail?"

I look around, ignoring this latest slight. Our street is empty, except for a couple of guys climbing into their pool service truck in Mack's driveway and an organic butcher delivery van at Emily and Dylan's. But I know what she means—it's a quiet neighborhood, of course, but all kinds of different people come through each day.

"You think it was somebody who's been here before but doesn't live here?"

"That's my theory. I hope you keep your doors locked. Anyway, you should get back to your work."

"Wait, one more question, Shawn—" A woman's scream slices through the humid air and cuts me off. We look at each other but both our bodies are already turning toward my house. Laura follows me in a slow jog—neither of us is really capable of going faster—and as we come into my backyard, I see Elena on the patio, gripping our outdoor broom like a shield.

When she looks up and sees us coming, Elena shouts, "Miss Alexis, watch out! It's a snake!" which is enough to stop Laura and me where we stand, our eyes turning to the grass.

"Where? Where did it go?" I yell toward Elena.

"I didn't see. Be careful!" she calls back unhelpfully.

Only once Laura and I finally reach the patio does Elena lower the broom and drop her shoulders in relief. "Hola señora," she offers to Laura, assuming—I assume—that she is Hispanic.

Laura ignores the greeting. "What kind of snake was it?"

"Oh it was at least six feet long, a big black snake," Elena answers, holding her arms out wide. "I came out to sweep, too much pollen that's not good for the babies. The snake almost came across my feet, and I screamed and hit it with the broom," she reenacts this for us.

Laura looks bored now, still holding all her mail and sweating. "That's just a rat snake. They aren't dangerous to people. They're attracted by rodents." This last part she says as if she knows something about our house.

"It went into the grass, away from the house," Elena continues, defensively. Then, looking at me, "You know, back home there are so many snakes, all different colors. You'll see when you go. I shouldn't be so scared, but I hate them. Just like the Book of Genesis says."

I can already see the questions on Laura's face—we hadn't gotten past Baltimore—but I'm not interested in answering. What sensible explanation could I give, anyway? I hired a nanny from the same country as my dead mother, not on purpose, at least not consciously. I also told her about it within a month of starting with us, without her asking and without meaning to. The truth just slipped out one day when we were talking about her family, as if it had been waiting for its opportunity. Since then, she's treated me like an awkward hybrid of employer, adopted daughter, and cultural education project. Before Laura can open her mouth to ask, I apologize for the scare and tell her we've got to check on the children, closing the patio door behind me and leaving her out in the yard with the snake.

Sometimes it feels like hiring Elena was a way of punishing

myself, of resurrecting my mother after both of her deaths—right into the heart of my own family. Like when she asked and I told her the truth, that my mother's name was Raisa, and she'd excitedly reminded me that *raíz* means "root" in Spanish, a sure sign that I should go to Honduras and find mine. Instead of ignoring her, I'd said that names can be very wrong—my mother named me Florencia Maria Alexis, and it had felt great to shed the heavy mouthful when I legally changed it at nineteen. Elena had looked at me with so much pity for days after that, I'd started to think about firing her. But sometimes—a lot of the time, really—I love her for it, in a way I'd never want to explain to Laura, or anyone else.

/ 8:30 PM

My phone screen lights up just as I am sitting down in the den with a souvenir cup full of ice cubes to watch TV. It's Sam. I want to ignore it, but we haven't spoken since Monday night—he's only had time to check in by text and ask for pictures of the children.

"Hey, how's it going up there?" I try to sound happy to hear from him.

"Hey old lady. I'm good. We're on a quick dinner break, our takeout's about to get here. The kids asleep?" There's noise behind him, his colleagues chatting and shuffling papers around.

"Of course they are. I'm ready to pass out too—I spent three hours weeding today. And you'll never believe this, but Elena crossed paths with a giant black snake on the back patio."

"Whoa, did it bite her?"

"No, she scared it into the grass with a broom, and Laura said it's some kind of snake that only eats rodents. So embarrassing."

"Why? There must be mice living in the woods all around us. I'm sure we aren't the only ones who've had a snake in the yard."

I still haven't told him about possibly spotting Shawn out at night again, or about Laura's lie—I don't want him to make a scene with neighbors who already don't think much of us. "I never thought I'd say this, but I kind of wish we had a smaller lot."

Sam laughs quietly, "I don't believe you."

"This place is just overwhelming sometimes. It feels like we need an estate manager. There's so much to fix, and even things that aren't broken need upkeep." These words drain my last bit of energy, and I let myself fall back onto the couch's firm leather cushions. We'd gotten it at a Veterans Day sale at one of those warehouse furniture stores with cheesy commercials, but its restrained lines make it look higher end.

"Why don't you see if Elena wants to expand her scope of work to include pest control and home maintenance?"

"Please, I'm too tired to think you're funny." As I say this, my eyes scan the ceiling and land on a large cobweb in one corner, intricately detailed like the crown molding it's clinging to. Our cleaning ladies are getting lazy. We probably shouldn't have kept the same ones from our city rowhouse, they aren't used to so much square footage.

"I've got to go in a minute anyway, but I wanted to tell you, I scheduled a couple of pool contractors to come out on Saturday."

I blink at the cobweb a few times before responding. "Are you joking?"

"No, I'm not." The background chatter fades, and he is whispering now. I guess he's moved to another room. "We talked about this when we were buying, Alexis. I said we needed a pool from the beginning. And we're the only house without one probably in all of River Forest. That's embarrassing."

"Seriously? Our house is falling apart. We've got lead paint. And a warped front door. And moldy shower tile." Reinvigorated by annoyance, I keep going. "And that damn snake was probably after more mice we don't even know about. That all seems much more embarrassing than not having a pool."

"Bitching about minor stuff again, I'm so sick of this. You're just picking apart the house like you do with everything. No one needs to know about that stupid shit you're mentioning. But the empty backyard is so obvious." He's straining to keep his voice quiet, but the disdain comes through loud and clear.

"So what do you have in mind, a brand-new pool and some loungers on our crappy old brick patio?" I throw back at him.

"Don't be an idiot. We'd redo the whole backyard. A big bluestone patio and a rectangular pool. Look up pictures online, you'll love it."

"I'm sure I would, but with the kids—"

"Automatic safety cover," he interrupts.

"Sam, you know this makes no sense. We have to prioritize other things. A pool is a luxury. It has to wait."

It stings when he acts like this—mocking, dismissive—but telling him that now won't help. We shouldn't even be having this conversation. All the money from the sale of our rowhouse went into our down payment, and renovations have already burned through most of our nonretirement savings. We've exceeded our joint credit card's limit twice since January and had to pay it down before the due date. If we go much further, I'm afraid we'll be living paycheck to paycheck.

"No, it doesn't have to wait. Do you know how long it takes

to get permits for a pool? If we don't start now there's no way it'll be done by next summer. I haven't been working my ass off just for paint and tiles. And I'm pretty sure that having a pool is a prerequisite for being a partner at my firm. They may even want to see the permits before the final sign-off on my promotion."

"Sam, you're being ridiculous." I can't help but laugh at this. "Do you know how much pools cost? We can't afford it."

"We're wasting money on so much crap right now. We could afford a lot more if you'd just stop."

"What are you talking about? Like what?" I ask defensively.

"If you just stopped buying furniture and the rest of it. And fired the cleaning ladies. Give me five minutes and I'll come up with ten other things, probably enough to pay for half the pool."

"Are you serious? And what, we'll live in a half-empty, dirty house? Just to have a pool?" I can't believe that Sam is serious.

"It doesn't have to be dirty. You're home. Elena's home," he says, as if it's obvious.

"Oh my God, Sam, I'm on maternity leave. And Elena does clean, it's just a big house. Anyway, even cutting off our utilities wouldn't be enough to pay for your precious pool."

"It would be much easier with two partner salaries instead of one, you know that don't you? And what's your real issue with the pool? You don't want to be seen in a bathing suit. That's it, right?" He doesn't pause for an answer. "Takeout's here, gotta go."

By way of goodbye, I toss my phone to the far side of the couch. He's gotten disturbingly good at homing in on the comments that shut me up immediately, that leave me exposed and ashamed of myself. I guess he's realized it's the most reliable way to win a fight.

Sam had pushed me hard to stay at my old job, on the partner track at a top-tier consulting firm. Even when I was on the floor of our cramped rowhouse bedroom, crying over my packed carry-on for yet another weekend business trip. Even when I drank a bottle of bourbon after hearing at the office head's holiday party, in that beautiful Georgetown mansion, that half my cohort—the male and/or childless half—was getting promoted. He'd said we should hire a second nanny, a meal delivery service, whatever we needed to make things less stressful. But that I shouldn't willingly get on the slow track when I'd been doing so well at work, that I should just focus on figuring out how to do that well again.

He refused to see that everything had changed with Caleb and accused me of just giving up. We discussed it ad nauseam, with him countering every justification I could come up with—

I wanted to spend more time with our children, because my own mother was never around—radically different situation, and I shouldn't let my own past weigh so much on the present.

I could still be successful, it's not like I suggested staying home full-time—but a tiny firm would never pay as well, or lead to as many opportunities, no matter what.

Eventually, I went ahead anyway, and he still hasn't forgiven me for it. Worse, he sees me differently now. In college, he used to joke that he was hitching a ride on the star of his multiple-box-checking, top honors girlfriend. I won academic prizes and got paying internships, and Sam was always there to tell me I'd end up in *Forbes,* especially if I could just loosen up and make some friends. I'd laugh him off but loved hearing it. By his senior year, when we were clearly pretty serious, we'd let ourselves daydream wildly about where we'd end up. Sometimes it was living in an airy flat in a European capital, multinational work during the day and drinking in atmospheric bars at night. Sometimes it was raising a big family on a massive, Kennedy-style compound. But it was never this—fighting over an old house, stressed about money, despising me for the weaknesses I can't hide from him—not even when we talked about how things might go wrong.

My stomach starts to grumble, and I reach for my souvenir cup. The ice cubes have melted together into a large, watery block that I'll need a knife to break up. I decide it's not worth it and reach for the remote. But in a few minutes, without some-thing to chew on, I'll be too tempted to eat. So I change my mind and slowly push myself off the couch to lock up and go to bed. It's early—not quite 9:00—but I'm tired of thinking about how mean Sam just was on the phone. Anyway, I'll have to be up with Carter again in a few hours.

Blair

The salon's air-conditioning hits each individual pore on my face like icy cold air being blown through a sieve. I love this feeling, so much that I'm lingering by the product display before paying, just to enjoy it a little longer. I don't care who sees my shiny, pink-red skin. Anyway, it's Friday afternoon, there's a line to check out, and I'm not in any rush. There's no cocktail party or dinner date to run home and get ready for. The social life of a new widow, after the first couple of weeks, is nonexistent. At least it leaves plenty of time to wallow in the few pleasures I can find these days. I'm reading the back of a color-preserving conditioner bottle when she calls out from the far side of the shampoo stations.

"Blair, is that you?" Laura practically barks in my direction, already knowing the answer. She's sitting in the lounge area, her hair tarred up in black dye, with a black robe tied tight around her middle and puddling on the floor. I'd forgotten that we go to the same salon.

She waves me over, as if I work here. It takes me nearly a

minute to decide to acknowledge her. Laura is far from my favorite person, and now that Teddy's gone, there's no need to even be nice. She's paying close attention though, so I need to be careful. I make my way past the bent-over twentysomethings, each scrubbing a middle-aged head, and force a small smile onto my face.

"Hi Laura, I didn't know you dyed your hair."

She leans her head back carefully to not disturb the mound on her head, and gestures at the matching armchair next to her. I stay standing.

"Of course I do, I'm fifty-one," she laughs. Annoyingly, that means she's six years older than me despite looking younger. "Is your face bleeding?"

"No, it's part of the facial, with the tiny needles. I'm sure you've heard of it."

She's giving me a blank stare that I don't buy for a second. She probably does these facials all the time to get that glow.

"So it is blood? What's it for, antiaging?"

I nod slightly.

"I'm surprised they have a license to do that. How was it?"

"Totally worth it—I'm trying to be nicer to myself these days." This is not quite a lie, but I've been getting one of these facials every few months since they started offering them last year.

"Hmm," she says as she stares intently up at my raw, exposed skin. "Listen Blair, I've been thinking about safety in our community. We should seriously consider a video surveillance system and private security guards. I'm going to propose it to the River Forest email list."

The nerve of this woman, I'm sure she will offer her company's services to the homeowners at a very minor discount. She and Shawn like to use bullshit euphemisms, but I know exactly what kind of company they have because Teddy spent nearly all of last year trying to acquire it. Guards, guns, surveillance, all for hire anywhere in the world. Laura's father was a Brazilian general, or something like that. Shawn was in the military here, and when they met, they put two and two together and parlayed their connections into a very successful business. Teddy called it private security and kept talking about phenomenal growth, but the acquisition didn't go through in the end because of an intercontinental scandal.

Something awful about an assassination in Africa and soldiers-for-hire that was all over the news for a couple of days last December. I'd brought it up at a neighborhood holiday drinks, and Laura had looked me straight in the face and said, "That's really none of your business, is it?" As if that's ever stopped her. I used it as a reason to ignore her for a few months after that but wasn't actually surprised by her reaction. She must have been in a particularly sour mood thinking about all the money she would have made in the acquisition. But things will work out just fine for her. A few days before he died, Teddy told me one of his competitors had jumped in, ready to snatch up her company, scandal and all.

"Don't you think that's going a little overboard? We don't want people to think we live in a dangerous neighborhood," I finally answer.

"It *is* dangerous Blair. Your husband was murdered there," she says matter-of-factly. "We should also consider asking the neighbors to identify anyone they've seen who might be suspicious."

"Laura, the police went around and spoke to someone in every single house already."

"I know that. But some people may not be comfortable naming their suspicions so formally. I'm sure there's someone within a couple of blocks who has a gardener with a record."

Her expression is impassive, but her dark eyes are gleaming. She enjoys this kind of thing. I'd kick her in the shins if we were little kids, right through her too-long robe, and tell her to stop. I hadn't anticipated that she'd be so interested in Teddy's death since she's already caught up in her own neighborhood drama.

I probably should have known she would be, given her line of work, and all I can do now is protest. "Laura, we don't live in a planned community. It's not an HOA. We can't gate it off. And nobody wants your scary ex-army guys patrolling River Forest and interrogating people. It's not a Third World war zone either."

Now she looks annoyed, so I add, "Just leave it to the police, please," and move toward the front desk before she can answer. Mercifully, there's no more line and I manage a smile as I hand the silver-haired girl behind the counter my credit card. She must truly loathe herself to have picked out such an old-lady hair color.

"Mrs. Bard?" she looks at me shyly, holding the card between her thumb and forefinger.

"Hmm?" If she tells me my card is expired or their reader is broken, I'm going to scream. I need to get out of here.

"Jean-Paul and all of the staff are very sorry for your loss. Your service today is complimentary," she squeaks.

I hadn't expected this kindness and my eyes start to burn. "That's very sweet, thank you," I manage without my voice breaking. I snatch my credit card back from her and walk as quickly as I can out of the salon, ignoring Laura calling out my name behind me.

I take the winding way home, my foot heavy on the gas pedal and Imagine Dragons blasting on the stereo. The kids introduced me to their first album a couple of years ago. But they'd immediately regretted it when I dragged the whole family to a concert and embarrassed the hell out of them, dancing and singing at the top of my lungs. Teddy had just laughed and bounced in place awkwardly, then bought us all ice cream afterward at a dingy little shop next to the theater. I'd give anything to be back there now, with my happy, normal family eating soft serve out of stale cake cones.

The passenger sideview mirror brushes against the blur of undergrowth that crowds right up to the narrow road. Sun and shadow strobe through the windshield too quickly for my eyes to keep up, and my tires briefly trespass across the double yellow line. I feel like I could lose control any second. But I'm just kidding myself. I know exactly what I'm doing. This is Teddy's Porsche, there are no speed cameras on these back roads, and the school buses aren't out anymore, it's already summer. I turn the volume to the maximum and let myself go even faster.

Alexis

In the dream, I am trapped in a cavernous room filled with flies, the air thick with vibrating masses of glittering green and black bodies. I'm frantically batting them away, spitting them out of my mouth, kicking my legs as they try to crawl into my clothes, my ears, my eyes. Through the roar of their buzzing, I hear knocking. The knocking gets louder, and now I am awake, spitting and coughing out flies that don't exist. It is pitch-black, and someone is knocking hard at the front door. It takes me a few seconds to realize that I am on the futon again. I grab for my phone and find it against my heart. It's 3:30 a.m.

The knocking is loud and keeps coming. I get up and walk as quietly as I can to the door. Just as I reach it, Sam comes pounding down the creaky stairs. He got home from New York late Friday night, and we spent most of Saturday fighting about the pool. I put a finger to my lips, angrily, but I don't think he can see me in the dark. He steps in front of me and looks through the peephole.

"What the fuck. . . ." he whispers.

I push him out of the way and look myself. A woman is standing on our front steps, completely naked and clutching a pair of black stilettos under one arm. Our porch light is on, and she looks like she's had a bad night—raccoon eyes from running mascara, remnants of red lipstick, or maybe blood, smeared on her cheek, and tousled dark blond hair. She knocks again, hard, and I can hear her saying what sounds like, "Please, please."

Sam and I look at each other. Before he can say anything, I disarm the security system, unlock the door, and open it just wide enough to show the woman my face.

"Oh my God, please, please help me! He's trying to kill me!" she begs as she looks over her shoulder toward the street.

I open the door enough to let her slip in past me, shut it, and lock it.

"Sam, grab my bathrobe. I'll call the police."

I dial 911 and explain the situation to the operator, who promises that the police will be there shortly. The words coming out of my mouth sound so bizarre, I have to stop myself from laughing. The operator asks if we also need an ambulance. Sam has come back with the robe and is trying to help the woman put it on, but her whole body is shivering hard, and she can't seem to let go of the stilettos. I say yes to the operator and put him on speakerphone while we wait for the police.

Sam and I gently pry the shoes from under the woman's arm and manage to get the robe on her. I switch on the foyer light, and we all wince at the sudden brightness. I can see now that she is quite young, probably no more than twenty-five, and very good-looking under the mess on her face. Sam is staring, his mouth slightly open, and I wonder if he is thinking about how attractive she is, or how bad she looks right now.

"Who hurt you? Are you hurt?" Sleep mixes up the questions as they come out of my mouth.

"Bill. Bill. He asked me to come back to his house tonight, I don't usually do that, but he's been so nice," she manages between shivers. "So I did, but he got really weird and scary. I know he likes it rough, but I told him to stop and he wouldn't . . . I had to fight him off, and then he got his gun, so I just ran out." She is crying now, heaving and shivering at the same time.

"Who's Bill? Which house did you come from?" I ask, confused.

"Across the street. Bill lives there, in the big house right across the street from you," she says between sobs, gesturing vaguely at the door.

I look at Sam, who shrugs his shoulders uselessly.

"You mean Mack? The yellow house right across the street from here?"

"He told me his name's Bill. Ya, that house. I saw your porch lights on, that's why I came here."

She starts swaying slightly, and I worry she might faint. We are still in the foyer, and I guide her to the new bench I bought a few weeks ago. I'm silently grateful my bathrobe is a barrier between her skin and the seat of the bench. The robe I can just throw out.

I sit down next to her and ask again, "Did he hurt you?"

"He was choking me. I couldn't breathe. He wouldn't stop, I think he was trying to kill me, seriously." Through her sobbing, I can hear the high-pitched whine of sirens closing in. Sam looks incredulous, and just a little bit amused. I want to slap him.

"The police are almost here," I say and pat her very lightly on the shoulder. Now the sirens are deafening, and Sam unlocks and opens the front door as if to greet them. The woman and

I get up and follow, and I peer around Sam to see that they've come out in force—four police cars and an ambulance.

The next few minutes are surreal. Sudden silence as the sirens stop, slamming car doors, heavy footsteps. The police officers, serious and alert, asking the three of us questions out on the front steps. As soon as they have the story, they seem to automatically kick into another gear, all their attention turned to Mack's house across the street. The emergency technicians quietly pull the woman to the back of the ambulance, wrapping some kind of sheeting over my bathrobe, and ask her their own questions. Sam and I just stand on our front steps, watching the spectacle play out.

It takes me a minute to realize what is going on. The officers have arrayed themselves in a semicircle around the front and sides of Mack's house. There may be more of them in the back. A dead-serious voice on a loudspeaker is demanding that he put his weapon down and come out of the house with his hands in the air. I can see, out of the corner of my eye, lights coming on in our neighbors' houses and front doors opening. Elena comes up from the basement and to the doorway behind us, gripping the fabric of her floral nightgown.

"It's okay," I say. "It's just the man across the street. Listen for the kids please, in case all this noise wakes them up. We'll be out here for a few minutes."

She nods and slips back into the house, closing the front door behind her. I glance down the street and see a handful of people standing in the middle of the cul-de-sac, lit up every few seconds by the silently spinning blue and red lights. "We'd better go over there, I don't want them thinking we're criminals," I say to Sam.

"Where?" he asks, fully focused on Mack's house.

"To where all the neighbors are standing. To explain what's going on."

"Sure. But not till this is over. Definitely don't want to miss the ending."

I can tell he is really amused now, as if this is somehow funny.

"What is wrong with you Sam?" I hiss at him. "Our block is a permanent crime scene. We shouldn't have moved here."

He opens his mouth to answer me, just as Mack's front door swings open. Mack's shape fills his doorway for a moment, then he steps out with his hands raised just up to his ears. He is only wearing boxer shorts, and his sagging old man body looks pathetic even from here. The officers rush toward him, but he maintains his meek stance. The danger seems to have passed. The officers break up into three groups—one group occupies itself with handcuffing and speaking to Mack, a second goes into his house, and a third fans out to speak to the gawking neighbors. The emergency technicians are packing the woman into the back of the ambulance, slamming the doors behind them.

Two officers in the third group head straight for us. We recount the same story we'd given at first, and as soon as they are satisfied, I grab Sam's hand and hurry toward the neighbors on the cul-de-sac. The officers have finished with them too, and they are standing awkwardly, as if unsure of what to do next. Tonight's moon is too dim to see anything more than shadows and outlines, but I catch glimpses of each person as the lights of the emergency vehicles continue their silent rotations.

Jeff and Jennifer are standing slightly apart from the others, and speaking to each other in tense whispers. Jeff looks upset and sloppy as usual, and more so next to his wife, whose pajamas are borderline lingerie—a silky black top, cut low enough to expose impressive cleavage, and matching, hip-hugging shorts trimmed in lace. I've only spoken directly to Jeff once, when they brought us a dozen beautifully frosted cupcakes after we moved in. Even then, Jennifer had done most of the talking, and Jeff had grunted awkwardly before pulling out his phone and stepping away to take a call. He must be very wealthy to make this worth her while.

A few feet away, the strobing lights catch Laura and Shawn with their arms wrapped around each other, talking to Emily and Dylan, who are both in T-shirts and shorts that could be pajamas, or not. I think Laura's and Shawn's pajamas are a matching plaid, which is absurd, but then I remember what I must look like right now.

"Alexis, what the hell happened? Is Mack all right?" Laura asks as we walk up.

Sam laughs, and answers before I can. "Mack's under arrest, but I think he's just fine."

"What are you talking about?" Shawn asks.

"Mack attacked a woman, but she escaped and knocked on our door," I jump in before Sam can, but he adds right away in an almost gleeful voice, "A naked prostitute!"

This grabs everyone's attention. Jeff and Jennifer come back to the group, and everyone starts talking at once. It's hard to make out their individual reactions, but I can hear the mix of surprise, confusion, and smugness.

"Welcome to the neighborhood," Dylan says over the chatter, then takes a long sip from what looks like an extra-large plastic sports drink bottle. He turns and offers the bottle to Emily, but she pushes his hand away. I wonder why he's drinking something like that in the middle of the night, but before I can even consider asking about it, Laura takes command of the group questioning.

"Why did the prostitute knock on your door in particular? Has something like this happened before?"

"I don't know!" I say defensively, without thinking. "She said she saw our porch lights on. You know we've only lived here for a few months. I have no idea what Mack's been doing."

"You all would be in a better position to tell us if it's a new thing," Sam chimes in. "No drone footage of this, Shawn?" I can hear the smugness in his voice.

"Damn sure it is a new thing," Shawn says, sounding angry. "This is the first year we've ever even had a police car on this street, and now two crimes in a month." The lights pass over his muscular jaw, and I believe the worry pulling at his face is genuine.

"Where's Blair?" Emily asks suddenly, her thin arms crossed tightly around her, and everyone's gaze turns toward Blair's house. Light shines from multiple first-floor windows, so it seems like someone is up.

"You know Blair wouldn't be caught dead nosing around out here," Jennifer offers. Jeff grunts after she talks, as if annoyed by the sound of her voice, and steps to the side of the group to spit. He seems slightly unsteady on his feet, and I wonder if he's drunk.

"Well this obviously concerns us all, regardless of what Blair thinks," Laura says dismissively. "Alexis, what did the prostitute seem like?"

"She may not even be a prostitute, Sam just assumed that. She was really scared, and I guess she looked pretty young." I don't mention that she looked beat up.

"How young? Do you think she could be a minor?" Laura asks.

"Oh no, I don't think so. I mean, maybe, she was wearing a lot of makeup, it was hard to tell." It hadn't occurred to me the poor girl could be that young.

"Whoa, is Mack such a complete pervert?" Sam adds, a question directed to no one in particular.

"There are rumors, but that doesn't mean much. There are rumors about everybody," Emily says. This is the only answer we get.

We stand like this, huddled awkwardly together in the middle of the street as a group, for another few minutes watching the emergency response wrap up. Our conversation has faltered, but it doesn't matter as the air fills with the whine of sirens being switched back on. The ambulance is first to slowly curve around the cul-de-sac and drive away, followed by the police cars. As the sirens fade, we all say good night and turn to walk back to our houses.

The lights are still on at Blair's. I wonder if she watched the whole scene unfold, and why she didn't come out.

Blair

Mack is a blight on this neighborhood, even if he owns a quarter of it. His wife killed herself a decade ago, his kids haven't shown their faces since, and he's ruined more lives than he can probably count. But he still can't stop his predation. Worse yet, at his age he's probably popping pills to make it happen. Goes to show how strong our basest impulses can be. The police were swarming all over his property the day after, and I bet my two favorite detectives gave him hell before letting him go. But they let him go, of course, and at this rate, our street might end up being a fixture on the nightly news, like those blighted blocks in D.C. where people are always getting shot.

I've got my own problems though. Beryl and the kids have been here for almost two weeks, and we can barely sit at the dinner table together, we're all so angry. The kids desperately miss Teddy, I know it, and I do too. But it's more than that. They're also mad at me, and I'm not sure why. We were always careful about our fights, and in the weeks before he died, we never argued or said anything in front of them. Maybe I'm getting my own bad energy reflected back to me. That's what my Pilates instructor would say (she also teaches yoga). And I've got plenty of bad energy these days. I've come to hate Beryl, with a passion I didn't know I was capable of.

We've never been particularly close. Maybe because the very fact of me ruined her plans, she always seemed to take a perverse joy in my disappointments. When I'd cry over a failed test or a bad boyfriend, she'd tell me to stop being hysterical and to learn from what went wrong. Once when I fell off my bike and broke my arm, she had a housekeeper drive me to the doctor's (not the hospital) in that poor woman's sputtering old car instead of taking me herself. I think she was hoping the car would break down and prolong my agony. In all my lowest moments, before this, it's as if she could barely hide her satisfaction. I stupidly told her about the miscarriages before and between my miraculously perfect kids. Each time, she would tell me to keep things in perspective, that it could always be worse. Worse!

It's not as if she's incapable of empathy. Brad got plenty of it growing up. He's always been her golden boy, even if he got Dad's swarthy looks. My kids too—she's been coddling them for the past few weeks as if she were their mother. But she can't even be bothered to offer a kind word to me, her only daughter who ended up in this miserable position because of her. After so many years I didn't expect it would bother me so much, but it does. Even now that I know the whole story, I can't forgive her. More than once, I've found myself fingering a steak knife in the kitchen and imagining the look that would come across her face if I slid it into her stomach. I guess it's a slippery slope.

But they'll all be out of the house again in a few days. The kids are going to their sleepaway camp in Vermont, and I'm sending Beryl back to Philadelphia right after Brad's party. He offered to cancel it, out of respect for Teddy, but I told him not to. Teddy loved being out on the river for the 4th, and besides I think I've been through enough to deserve a night out.

Most of the guests, as usual, will be Brad's friends and clients. But he always lets me invite a handful of my friends. A small brotherly kindness. Last year I had to waste two of those spots on Laura and Shawn, for Teddy's sake. They might be interesting if they weren't so hell-bent on the wholesome average couple act. I don't know who's buying it anyway. Shawn looks like G.I. Joe on steroids, and Laura eyes everyone like they're a potential perp. I need to remember that and not let her get under my skin like she did at the salon. She doesn't know anything, but she loves inserting herself into other people's lives.

She doesn't do it with good intentions, just vindictiveness. When Dylan and Emily moved in two years ago, I could tell right away that she had a thing for Dylan and those amber eyes. He was the only person I've ever seen her flirt with, and she would actually laugh out loud when he made bad jokes. He flirted back, of course, like he does with everyone, and she eagerly lapped it up for a long time. But all that changed once she realized she'd never get more than the occasional suggestive pat of her bra fat. After that, she became fixated on exposing who he was sleeping with instead of her. I used to wish she'd give it up, but now I want her to go back to focusing on her obsession, not on Teddy's murder. It would certainly make me feel better.

I'm sitting at the kitchen island and half listening to Beryl criticize me for shortcomings in the funeral arrangements, when I decide that this year, I'm going to give those spots to

Alexis and Sam. There's something about spending time with Alexis that I really enjoy. Maybe it's because we have similar tastes, as ridiculous as that sounds. Plus, I doubt they have plans. I pick up my phone and walk out of the kitchen without saying anything to my mother. Upstairs in my room, I close the door behind me. It's looking even more gray and tired in here than I realized a few months ago. I need to start planning for the redesign soon. It should probably include a smaller bed. I'll also have to deal with Teddy's closet. But not now.

I look down at my phone and quickly text Alexis, "Hey! Got plans for the 4th? You and Sam are invited to our family party."

I stare at the screen waiting for a reply, then think better of it and just dial her number. She answers on the second ring.

"Hi Alexis, I should have called you in the first place. Delivering an invitation via text is very high school."

"I'll trust you on that, there were no texts when I was in high school," she laughs.

"Stop, I feel old enough already. Look, my little brother has a boat, and we always go out on it for the 4th to watch the fireworks and get drunk. You guys should come, it's a good time."

"Oh wow. Thanks so much for inviting us. Are you sure there's enough room?"

I smile to myself. "Of course, plenty of room. We can drive over to the marina together. It's adults-only, so my mom's my date."

For just a moment, there's silence. Alexis is probably wondering why I've invited them. Maybe this is too much.

"Okay sure, sounds great!" she says, and we agree to meet in my driveway at a quarter past seven.

Alexis

I spend an embarrassingly long time picking an outfit for tonight. Nothing fits—my maternity clothes are too big, my normal clothes are too tight, and my body is a lumpy mess. Finally, I settle on a navy blue T-shirt dress that I've never had a chance to wear, with my size ballooning and shrinking over the past three years with two pregnancies. It's made of thin cotton, so I try to dress it up with big earrings and metallic flats. In the aggressive humidity of D.C. summer my hair stands on end, forming a frizzy halo that would have been a dead giveaway if it were the nineteenth century and I were trying to pass for Southern European. As it is, I slick it back into a ponytail with palmfuls of gel and hope for the best.

I look away from my unhappy reflection and out of the floor-to-ceiling picture window to the towering green trees at the edge of our backyard. It's a beautiful view that floods our bedroom with light, but the glass is single-paned and the window frame is rotting. When we did the home inspection—

for our information only, since we had already agreed to buy the house—our jolly, Santa-like inspector had suddenly turned serious and warned us that the window was a real safety hazard.

Like so many things in the house, Sam and I have had multiple tedious arguments about how to deal with it. I am petrified Caleb will push through the glass, and I want to replace it now, or at least cover it up with shutters. Sam thinks I am being dramatic and doesn't want to spend the money—he claims that putting a chair in front of it should be enough to protect Caleb. We finally agreed that Sam would build a makeshift railing across the window, but of course he hasn't done it yet. So now, every time I look out at that beautiful view, it makes me more resentful.

I hadn't been sure if Sam would be willing to go to Blair's brother's party, but I should have known he'd love the idea of an exclusive event. No one else we know in D.C. has a boat. It's also a chance for us to celebrate. He had called me from work about an hour after Blair, to tell me he got the partner promotion. I suggested we celebrate by going to this party, and he'd said "You two are really friends, huh? Sure, why not. Let's go." I could hear the condescension in his voice but decided to ignore it.

I can tell that Sam is looking forward to tonight—he spent a long time getting ready in the bathroom and emerges wearing a new polo shirt and crisp Bermuda shorts. He's smoothed back his red hair in a way I've never seen before.

"That's what you're wearing?" he asks as he slides his expensive watch onto his thick, freckled wrist.

I look down at my dress, embarrassed. "What's wrong with it?"

He sighs, considering how to respond. "It's obviously too big. And it looks cheap. We're not so strapped for cash that you can't buy nicer clothes."

I stand there stupidly, not sure of what to do. If I try to change now, we'll be late meeting Blair, and besides, there is nothing better in my closet.

"Forget about it, let's go," Sam says as he walks out of our bedroom.

The children are already asleep, and we leave Elena watching Spanish-language news on the playroom TV. Outside, a light breeze cuts through the heat and carries off the shame of Sam's latest insults. I'm hoping we have a good time at this party.

As we cross the street, I try to grab Sam's hand, but he shakes it off without even looking at me. There's no time to react. Blair and her mother are already waiting for us in her driveway, standing next to Blair's white Range Rover. Blair is wearing a cherry-red sundress, short enough to show off her lean legs. Her mother is wearing a white shift dress, nearly the same creamy shade as the Range Rover, and the biggest diamond earrings I've ever seen in real life. Blair walks toward us and gives me a big hug before I reach the car. "I'm so glad you guys could make it!" she says as she turns to shake Sam's hand. "Hop in, and buckle your seatbelts, I'm a fast driver. Oh, and this is my mother, Beryl." Her mother gives us a cold "hello" and climbs into the passenger seat.

The drive to the marina is about twenty minutes, but the stilted conversation in the car makes it feel endless. I try to fill the silence by asking Blair how she's been and mentioning Sam's promotion. Blair seems just as excited for the evening as I am and answers me eagerly, but her mother's mood is taciturn at best. She is an attractive woman, and with her platinum hair looks young enough to pass for Blair's older sister. But from the backseat I can see that the profile of her face is set in a displeased mask, and she says nothing for the entire ride.

She may have a good reason—she and Blair are not getting along, or she is still devastated about the murder of her son-in-law. Yet I can't help but feel offended. It's quite possible that she thinks I am not worth making an effort for, and I feel the heat rising in my cheeks. Maybe accepting this invitation was a bad idea. We finally turn into the marina and pull up to a valet station in front of a towering white yacht. As we climb out of the car, Sam whispers to me, "If the rest of the guests are this rude, we'll have to swim back to shore." I poke him in the ribs and try to suppress a laugh.

When Blair said her "younger brother's boat," this is not what had come to mind. I should know better by now. Even after so many years living among them, my imagination is still sometimes too poor to conjure up aspects of regular life for the wealthy. The river's murky water laps at the long, sleek hull, and I count at least thirty people milling around on the deck above me as strains of upbeat jazz music float toward us.

Her mother quickly walks ahead, straight onto the yacht, and hugs a man in white shorts and a navy polo shirt waiting for her at the end of the gangway. I assume he is Blair's brother, but his dark hair and soft features look nothing like hers. Blair grabs my hand and grins at Sam and me. "Let's get the introductions out of the way, then head to the bar."

Her mother has already disappeared, but her brother is waiting to greet us. "Brad, these are my new neighbors I was telling you about, Alexis and Sam," Blair says as she reaches out to hug him.

Brad gives us vigorous handshakes. "Welcome aboard! It's gonna be a great night, always is. The only rule we've got is no shoes."

Blair sees the confusion on my face and quickly adds, "It's a boat thing. The decks are fragile."

"Of course, thanks so much for inviting us," I reply awkwardly, and follow Blair and Sam past Brad, to a tuxedoed valet who silently accepts our shoes. I hand my ballet flats over with deep regret for not having bothered to get a pedicure yet this summer.

"Drinks!" Blair announces as soon as the valet gives us our tickets. Sam gives me a big smile and a shrug, and I reach up and kiss him on the cheek. We haven't had a fun night out in forever, and after all the stress of making partner, he deserves to get blackout drunk, if he wants to. In the glowing evening light, I notice new streaks of silver that look almost painted on the red hair at his temples. The past few months have really drained him.

We obediently follow Blair, who stops every few feet to hug fellow guests—Brad's business partners, two congressmen and their wives, a few cousins. Each time, she graciously turns and introduces us too, as her "wonderful new neighbors." I cringe at this—I wish she'd say something like "my friend and her husband" instead. It's ridiculous, but calling us her neighbors makes it seem like we are just tagging along thanks to proximity. Plus, she's barely ever talked to Sam. I'm the reason we are here.

When we finally get to the bar, Sam shouts "Shots!" and we all laugh. Blair asks the two tuxedoed bartenders to open a new bottle of champagne for us, and we take our glasses out on the top deck. The sun is setting, and the yacht is slowly pulling out onto the wide brown river. We toast to the 4th of July and to

Sam's promotion. I am about to add something about Blair being so nice to invite us, when Sam spots a law school classmate on the deck below. I suggest he go down and talk to him—I know how much he misses socializing, and I want to talk to Blair alone. He takes off eagerly, and Blair and I turn to look out at the low-slung city skyline. The fireworks won't start for another hour or so.

"This is quite a boat," I say.

She smiles. "Brad's got a lobbying shop on K Street. He's been pretty successful."

I nod, curious, but not wanting to seem nosy. "I'm sorry to ask, but is your mother okay? She seemed upset in the car."

"She's just fine. Her problem is that she's as stubborn as a mule, and so am I. It can get tough when we don't see eye to eye."

I assume this oblique answer means she doesn't want to discuss it, so I change the subject. "Oh, I almost forgot, did you hear about what happened with Mack last week?"

Blair almost snorts her champagne, and says, "Of course I did. Did the poor girl really come knocking on your door? Naked?"

"She did. Weirdest night of my life. But you know what's really strange? Mack was back on his front porch this morning. I saw him when I went out to pick up a package, because that damn delivery guy is so lazy and leaves them at the end of the driveway. He was out there reading the paper as if nothing had happened!" I continue, the disbelief obvious in my voice, "I can't even find anything about his arrest in the news, or in on-line police records. I don't even know if they're really going to press charges."

"Don't waste your time. There won't be any charges. And there certainly won't be any news coverage." Blair is smiling at me from behind her champagne glass.

"What do you mean?"

"Mack is a very well-connected guy. He has friends in the right places, including on this boat. Nothing's going to happen to him just because some poor little escort freaked out when he got too rough." She sighs, as if she's just had to explain something obvious to a child.

"They're just going to cover it up? If that's how the police work, how can they ever solve any cases? What if Mack's done worse things?" My voice is too shrill and the implication too obvious. Blair gives me an impatient look, and I gulp down the rest of my champagne.

"Remember what I told you about him? He's *definitely* done worse things. But he didn't murder Teddy if that's what you mean."

"I'm sorry, I'm just surprised I guess. I didn't mean to bring up . . ."

"Teddy. I know."

"Have the police made any more progress?" I ask quietly.

"Not that I know of." She drains her glass too. "They keep telling me they've got leads, but the weeks are going by. I think they're spinning in circles. Let's get another drink."

We go back to the bar, and from there the rest of the night starts running together. The music gets louder, we have more drinks, and Sam makes his way back to us. All the guests crowd together to watch the sky turn deep purple, then black, and then explode with starbursts and spheres in a dozen colors, reflected on the black mirror-glass surface of the river. We are surrounded by other yachts, and strains of the clapping and cheering and music from dozens of other parties merge with ours into an exuberant soundtrack.

After the fireworks, I can't find Blair or Sam, and a spark of suspicion flickers across my alcohol-addled mind. I probably drank too fast, and since I've barely been sleeping, or drinking, it's hit me all at once. The music and the laughing and the beauty of it all is overwhelming. Instead of looking for them, I decide to find a relatively quiet spot where I can sit down, just for a few minutes.

Sam is shaking my shoulder, hard. "Alexis, Alexis. Wake up old lady."

I fell asleep. We are back at the marina, under the glaring lights of the docks. Sam is looking down at me, and with the glare I can't tell if he's smiling or grimacing.

"Oh my God, I'm sorry. I didn't mean to . . ."

"Don't worry, we just got back, you didn't miss anything," Blair says from over Sam's shoulder.

Sam helps me stand up with a look of distaste. I can't blame him really. My dress is damp and badly wrinkled, and when I touch my fingers to my face, I feel a thick crust of drool trailing from the right side of my mouth down to my chin. We don't speak as we make our way to the shoe valet, off the yacht, and back to Blair's car. Her mother is already buckled into the passenger seat, wearing the same look of displeasure. I wonder if she looked that way during the whole party, or only put it back on for us.

No one tries to make conversation on the drive home. Blair plays smooth jazz on the radio, and after texting Elena that we are on our way, I close my eyes and lean on Sam's shoulder. My head is pounding now. When we pull onto our street, Blair stops in front of our house, and I thank her again for inviting us, pointedly ignoring her mother. The house is dark and quiet, and we don't turn on any lights.

Without talking, Sam and I kick into our usual night routine.

He walks around and checks all the locks, and I go to the kitchen to clean up. When we first moved in, we had mice. I came into the kitchen early one morning to find it full of metallic green flies spreading their filth all over our new countertops and custom paneled appliances. The cause ended up being a rotting mouse, entombed behind our dishwasher. Besides desperately demanding that our contractor close up every possible access point, we committed to never leaving dirty dishes in the sink or food out on the counter. Since Sam is too lazy to ever proactively clean up, and Elena hasn't rinsed a single utensil since I took over Carter's bottle washing and offended her, the responsibility falls to me. I wipe down the counters and then go to the sink. Reflexively, I scan the street as I work my way through the bottles and dishes piled up inside.

Blair and her mother are standing in her driveway, in front of Blair's mother's Mercedes, faintly illuminated by the light from her open garage. It's too far to make out their faces, but by the way they are facing each other, tensely holding their bodies, I'm convinced they are fighting and trying not to look like it. It goes on for maybe four or five more minutes, then Blair's mother stalks around to the driver's side of her car and peels out of the driveway and past my house.

My head is still aching, and a swell of nausea pushes into the back of my throat as I watch her taillights disappear. Her mother must really be heartless, to fight with her newly widowed daughter and then abandon her in the middle of the night. Blair is still standing in her driveway, alone and probably miserable. An unwelcome feeling of familiarity cuts through the nausea, and I look away.

Blair

I don't bother to turn on the lights and just head straight for the sitting room to pour myself a drink. Teddy was the family bartender. But I know where everything is, because I designed every detail. A quartzite tray, with half a dozen cut crystal highball glasses, and a hammered-gold metal ice bucket sit on top of a lacquered wood cabinet that hides an icemaker. Teddy used to love this little parlor trick, opening up the cabinet to fill the ice bucket. Our guests would always exclaim in surprise, and then everyone would laugh at Teddy's goofiness. Tonight nobody's laughing. I just grab a fistful of ice cubes with my bare hand and pour some whiskey over it. A finger, a fifth, I never paid much attention. That part was Teddy's job. But the bottle arrangement on the bar cart was mine. I always checked every few days, to make sure it looked right. When it didn't, I'd switch out from the rest of our liquor collection in the butler's pantry. I haven't thought about this since Teddy died, and now I see that many of the bottles are nearly drained. Beryl's been drinking again, and I was too distracted to notice.

She was at her finest tonight, icy and dismissive. I could have let it go. She was planning on leaving tomorrow anyway. But the way she treated my friends, and me, just made me so angry. It was as if I were in high school again and brought home the wrong sort of people. The second Sam slammed the car door behind him, I'd had to say something.

"You never cease to hit on new ways to insult me," I sighed as we pulled into my driveway. I left the garage door open behind us, because I could feel the fight coming on and didn't want to go into the house in case one of the kids was still up.

She waited until I parked and turned the car off before answering.

"Blair, I know exactly what you're doing, and I'm ashamed of you," she said leaning toward me, almost whispering it into my ear. Then she unbuckled her seatbelt, got out of the car, and walked out of the garage.

I watched her in the rearview mirror, standing there in my driveway staring up at the sky, as if she were expecting another round of fireworks. I knew she was waiting for me to react. I could have just reached up and pressed the remote, gone inside, and locked all the doors. Shut her out. But I didn't. I followed her out onto the driveway, trying to keep my voice down.

"Mother, come inside. What the hell are you doing?"

She didn't bother to look at me. "Didn't you hear me Blair? I saw you tonight. This is disgusting. Aren't you ashamed of yourself?"

Her words are like fingers around my neck, tightening their grip. "I'm disgusting? Really?" I spit back. "I wonder where I get it from? If it weren't for you—"

"No, don't you dare. This is all your fault, Blair. You brought all of this on yourself. How do you expect—"

"My fault? Like everything else, it's always my fault? You can tell yourself whatever you need to sleep at night, but you can't twist the truth around this time. We are here because of you."

"You can't begin to imagine the things I've swallowed for you Blair. Choked down. And only for you to act like this. I almost talked to Brad about it tonight."

"You already told me about those things, remember? And don't mock me, you'd never break his heart. You love him too much for that."

We went on like this, two lunatics hissing at each other in the moonlight, until Beryl finally drove off in a fury. She hadn't even bothered to go inside and pack her belongings.

I assume she's sober enough to make it home, but I don't care if she's not. The ice is watering down my whiskey, so I get up to top it off. A soft knock at the front door comes through as I finish pouring. It's not like my mother to turn back, much less meekly ask for permission to enter. Anyway, I don't keep my doors locked. Maybe Alexis forgot something in my car. I set down the whiskey bottle and walk slowly to the peephole.

Emily is standing on my front steps, deep half-moon shadows under her eyes and a ridiculous tinsel headband wobbling on her mousy brown head. She is swaying unsteadily in the porch light. I open the door quickly, before she decides to ring the bell.

"Why are you here Emily? It's after midnight."

She takes a few seconds to form a sentence. "Is Dylan in there? Tell him to get out here now," she finally manages to say.

"Why would your husband be at my house?"

"I'm not stupid!" she yells at me. "We were at a party tonight and he just disappeared. He's said things. I know what's going on. I'm not stupid," she says again, now on the verge of tears.

"What has he said?"

"I know he's not happy with me. Satisfied. I mean, unsatisfied. I know all about the sex." She leans forward to support herself with a hand on the doorframe, and the stench of liquor on her breath is nauseating.

Poor, pathetic Emily, groveling for the return of her faithless husband. I think about helping her, bringing her inside to sober up and talk through all the pain she's been living. But then I think better of it. The first time we met, at a cocktail party, Teddy had introduced me as his brilliant interior designer wife. Emily had laughed and said, *"That line of work seems to be in vogue. It must be fun to spend all day shopping, I envy you!"*

If she's half as smart as she thinks she is, she should be able to figure this out for herself.

"He's not a bad guy, I don't know what you got him to—" Emily continues, slurring her words.

Before she can finish, I wrap my fingers around her wrist and push her arm off the doorframe. She staggers slightly but manages to steady herself. She is blinking at me, expecting an answer. I smile and slam the door in her face.

Alexis

The sun has set and Sam is nowhere near coming home from work, so I head outside to drag our trash and recycling bins back to their positions along the back wall of the garage. Each bin is enormous, five feet tall and hard to maneuver even when empty, but if I leave them out into the night, the equally enormous raccoons that live in the woods all around us will pull them into the middle of the street, scratch up the thick plastic with their long claws, and defecate inside as a warning that next time there had better be food inside. We learned this the hard way.

I have to push each bin one at a time, tipping it back onto its two little wheels and leaning my body into it. Just as I cross from the street into our driveway with the first one, someone touches the small of my back, and I jump forward, letting the bin thud heavily back to the ground, before turning around to look.

"Hi Alexis. It's Alexis, right?" Mack says from two feet away.

"Oh gosh, I didn't see you coming in the dark." My heart is racing but I try to keep my voice calm.

"Ah, I was just out for the same reason as you. But shouldn't your husband be doing the heavy lifting? You're not much bigger than these bins," he chuckles.

Mack himself is not much bigger than me, but I still hesitate to tell him Sam's not home. "It's good exercise," I offer, keeping one hand on the lid and rotating my body to the far side of the bin, so that it stands between me and him.

He keeps chuckling to himself as he goes on, "Listen Alexis, I wanted to apologize for all that ruckus a couple of weeks ago. It was a misunderstanding, but the police got out of hand. What with Teddy's murder, I think they're too eager to jump on any little thing. The whole episode was just ridiculous."

I don't know if he expects me to agree and tell him it's okay. If that's why he chose this moment, when we are alone in the dark, to approach me. I let a few seconds pass before answering. "I hope that young woman is all right." I'm too scared to be more direct.

"Of course she is. She's just fine," he says dismissively. "She feels terrible for having woken you all up for nothing."

"It's good to hear she's okay. We were happy to help." I wonder what it took to reshape what happened into Mack's version of events, how much money or intimidation or who knows what he had to pummel that poor girl with to change her story.

"It would've been more helpful to call me," he says as he drops a dry, bony hand onto the bin, rubbing his fingers against mine. "Just keep that in mind, okay?"

I flinch at the feeling, but he pulls away and turns to leave before I can answer. "Good night Alexis," he adds without looking back, confident that he got his message across.

I hurry to finish my chore, ignoring the hot mixture of fear and anger belatedly accelerating my pulse, so I can get inside and wash my hands.

Saturday / July 12 / 8:00 AM

The last communication I had with Blair was a pathetic text I sent last Saturday, the day after the 4th, to apologize for passing out on her brother's boat and to thank her again for having invited us. I probably used too many exclamation points and came across as desperate. Desperate for what exactly, I'm not sure. But I know my message didn't go over well, because I sent it a week ago today and Blair still hasn't replied. I haven't seen many signs of life at her house for the past few days either, so maybe she's out of town. That doesn't explain the lack of response though.

"Alexis, are you listening?" Sam says suddenly.

I haven't been paying attention. We are sitting around the breakfast table, and I am encouraging Caleb to try and use his thumb and pointer finger to pick up blueberries instead of squishing them by the fistful. Sam is giving Carter a bottle and trying to explain something to me about his new responsibilities as a partner. But I was thinking about Blair.

"Sorry, I got distracted. I forgot how much not sleeping wrecks my brain. Can you start again? From the part about L.A.?" I ask sheepishly.

Sam gives me an exasperated grunt. "I was telling you that the firm is targeting new clients in L.A., so I'll have to start going out there in a few weeks. Probably Sunday night, back on the Friday morning red-eye."

"Ugh, that'll be hard. Every week? For how long?"

"That's what I just said. At least six months. Longer if things go well."

Now I am paying attention. "Sam, what—" I stop myself because of the children. "You know I'm going back to work in November. They talked about promoting me to senior manager in the next cycle if things go well. If you're gone every week, how can I go on any business trips? It's not fair to them."

Even I hate the strain in my voice, but I can't help it. Sam and I used to talk about this, before we had children—we each need to take turns, both of our careers are important, family matters for both of us. I hadn't anticipated that it would all be contingent on me making as much money as him.

"Hey, calm down, okay? What did you think would happen, I'd become a partner and just play golf every day? You're the one who wanted to slow down, not me." He gruffly pulls the tiny bottle from Carter's mouth and starts burping her against his shoulder, his hand nearly the length of her entire body.

"Anyway, at your little firm you'll still outperform. Just ask them for more local clients. You don't even want to travel, do you?"

I bite the inside of my cheek to stop myself from saying something accusatory. "Gently, please? You don't need to slap her back like that."

I know what this means. I'll push my own promotion out another year, or two, and maybe out beyond my reach. Even if I say it—this wasn't the deal, it's not fair—what would be the point? I wanted a big house, and of course a partner at a prestigious law firm makes far more than a senior manager at a small consulting boutique. I don't get to have everything. I don't need Sam to tell me that.

The rest of breakfast is quiet, except for the sounds of Caleb's babbling and Carter's steady sucking. As Caleb starts to motion that he wants to get out of his highchair I ask Sam, "Can you play with them for a little while? I need to do some weeding." I am still angry and need to take it out on something.

"Fine. I'll walk them over to the park before it gets too hot," he says in a tone that implies great sacrifice.

I pack up the diaper bag and help Sam load the double stroller before going around to the side of the house. My arsenal of gardening equipment has grown exponentially in the past few weeks, even though my main task is still weeding. Besides gloves, I am now the proud owner of a kneeling pad, a pair of hedge shears, a lopper, a combination knife-shovel called a hori hori, three watering cans, a pruning saw, a pair of pruning shears, and a large pack of slate labels on metal rods that I stick in front of every tree and plant on our property whose name I learn. I also have a wide-brimmed, khaki-colored hat.

Sam has found no end of amusement in this collection. He calls it hard evidence of my old-ladyness. But these tools, neatly arrayed on a purpose-bought plastic shelving unit tucked against the side of our house under an awning, make me feel wholesome and productive. Just a normal suburban woman taking good care of her property. Silently ripping aggressive weeds out by their roots, cutting off dead growths, swatting away wasps and flies and squeezing the life out of giant ants— all of it helps quiet my mind and briefly forget about how unhappy we are here.

This house is ruining our lives. We should have stayed where we were and avoided all of these problems—the ever-lengthening list of renovations, the fights about money and the children, the creepy things going on right outside our door. If we were still downtown, Sam could have walked over to the coffee shop that puts on kids' puppet shows, instead of the same park we go to every weekend. If our mortgage weren't so much, maybe Sam wouldn't be so hell-bent on being a rainmaker and actually take on some child care, so I could do more at work.

But here we are, all those decisions already made, living in our dream home for six months without having had sex once.

Last weekend, the night of the 4th, I'd actually tried. After we'd cleaned, locked up, and I'd thrown up discreetly in the powder room, I'd brushed my teeth, put on more deodorant, and crawled into bed. I'd started kissing his neck and whispering into his ear that I was so proud of him for getting promoted. He pushed me away, hard, and told me I was still drunk and needed to sleep it off. I thought it must be my body, lumpy and deflating, and started to say something about getting a personal trainer. He'd cut me off coldly—*"Alexis, sometimes you're really pathetic, you know that?"*—then gotten up and walked out of the room.

Sam was right, I probably was still drunk. I fell asleep quickly after he left, but all this week I haven't been able to stop thinking about his words. The only other person who's ever called me pathetic to my face was the chubby girl who lived next door my sophomore year of college, on a hallway of singles. For months, I'd find her hovering silently outside my bathroom stall, a snarl of displeasure contorting her pretty face, until finally one day she confronted me at the sinks. She'd told me that it was a pathetic thing to do, that if I didn't stop she would tell our dorm supervisors. Then another girl walked in, and I remember wishing I could dissolve into the dingy tiled walls. I couldn't even make eye contact—I just pushed past her and left the bathroom.

That was the last time I threw up on purpose in college. The thought of being shuttled off to counseling by the sloppy-looking grad students who were our only adult supervision was more than I could stand. A few months later I learned why my neighbor had taken such an interest in me. I was at a party, standing with a drunk friend—Sam's friend, really—who spotted her across the room.

"Look! It's the girl Sam used to hook up with," he'd laughed, as if we were in on some joke together.

"Her?" the shock on my face erased the grin on his immediately.

"Umm, yeah, it was before you guys got serious I think. Don't worry, he was only into her because her parents are loaded and she kept promising to take him to all these fancy places. But when they went to St. Barts for winter break, he said it was awful because he had to see her in a bikini every day."

I never said anything to Sam about that girl, because it was never relevant. We've had so many good years together since then. But the way he talked to me the other night—the way he's been talking to me more and more lately—took me back to that dorm bathroom, and to the realization that it was his fault she'd humiliated me like that. Now, I'm not sure what I'm doing wrong, or why I deserve to be humiliated again, even if Sam is under a lot of pressure. He could have said no to this house, to me, but he didn't. So here we are, pushing away from each other, and it feels too late to change course.

Hat and gloves on, I start picking up the equipment to attack an overgrown thicket of pink-blooming azalea bushes that's taken over a far corner of the backyard. I reach for the pruning saw on the second shelf, but my hand lands on a wide swath of empty. My eyes slowly scan over all three shelves, in case it got misplaced, but it's too large to be overlooked. I already know it's not here. Maybe our landscapers used it and forgot to put it back.

I'll ask Sam about it later, but for now I take the rest of my tools to the shade of a maple tree, then kneel down on the pad to dig out the roots of the weeds snaking their way through the azaleas' branches. It's not yet 10:00, but the July sun is beating intensely and the air is so thick that even the sparrows' occasional twittering sounds muffled. Within a few minutes, I am sweating through my clothes. I sit back on my heels and start to pull myself up to go inside for a glass of water, when my phone vibrates in my pocket. I yank the glove off my right hand and pull it out. It's a text from Blair. I lean over and squint to read the message in the bright sunlight. "Kids are finally at camp for the rest of the summer! Come by for a drink tonight?"

Why didn't she write sooner? She could have told me she was taking her kids to camp. Why do I care? I'm still in a crouch, squinting at my phone and thinking about how to respond, when a branch cracks behind me. I don't turn around immediately, glued in position by the heat and fear. The crack was a sharp, distinct sound—the kind a branch makes when a person steps on it. An unmistakable sound that even the humid air couldn't muffle. I realize I'm holding my breath and force myself to let it go and look.

Nothing. There is nothing behind me but the wide expanse of our backyard. Green grass baking yellow, shimmering trees, our crumbling back patio. Squirrels and bugs and birds that I can't make out in the dazzling sunshine. My mind reaches for a reassuring explanation, and I quickly decide it was just an animal. Sometimes we see deer walking delicately through our yard, on their way down to the river. It was probably one of them, holding so still now that I can't even make it out.

I keep scanning the yard for another minute or so, and then turn back to my phone. Being upset with Blair makes no sense. I quickly write back, "Sure! Can I come by around eight?" and slide the phone into my pocket. The nape of my neck is tingling, but I ignore the feeling and get back to work on the weeds until I fall into a steady, silent rhythm. After about thirty minutes, I stand up to stretch.

Some of the azaleas have bare branches that I assume are

dead and should be cut off, a job perfect for my missing pruning saw. I'd been overly eager and bought a heavy-duty model with a curved fourteen-inch blade. When it came in the mail, Sam had asked, *"Who are you planning to hack to pieces with that thing?"* I'd laughed and explained to him that the saw was for trimming branches that our landscapers are too lazy to notice. It hadn't occurred to me that it really might have other uses.

/ 7:45 PM

I haven't told Sam about the missing saw. They'd returned from the park just as I finished searching for it and started slowly placing my other tools back on the shelving unit, as if I could make the saw reappear with enough patient staring. Sam had come around the corner suddenly, pushing the stroller with both children fast asleep inside. I'd started to say it, but then I'd looked at him, and instead of the familiar warmth that usually looks back at me, I'd felt a cold, hard sense of distrust. Panic gripped me momentarily as I considered whether it had even been a good idea to send him off to the park alone with our children. So instead of telling him, I'd smiled weakly and said thank you for the alone time.

Could I have imagined what happened this morning? My heart starts to race every time I think about that branch cracking, and I am afraid. Afraid that this is real—that Shawn is in the trees when I look out the window at night, that Mack is committing sex crimes across the street, that one of them—or worse yet, Teddy's murderer—was just in my backyard a few feet away from my oblivious, crouching body. But also afraid that it's not—that my tired mind is manufacturing dangers that don't exist. Maybe Sam's right, and I'm just looking for excuses

to second-guess our decisions and to blame him for my unhap-
piness. Every neighborhood has its characters, every house has
its challenges.

But by the time we eat dinner—pizza for the boys, formula
for Carter, nothing for me—and get the children to bed, my head
aches from the gnawing possibility that my saw really has been
stolen. I'm not sure whether I should tell someone or not. Sam
probably won't believe me, and I can't swallow another dismissive insult from him. It's nearly 8:00, so I take two aspirin,
vigorously rub on deodorant, and change into another T-shirt
dress. This one has an unflattering kangaroo pocket, but at least
it helps to hide my postpartum belly bulge. I know Sam always
does this himself, but before leaving I walk through the house to
make sure all the doors and windows are locked. The children
are fast asleep, and Elena is quiet in the basement. On the main
floor, Sam is sprawled out on the couch in the den with his laptop on his stomach, watching a baseball game on the muted TV.
I am trying to fix my hair in the foyer mirror when he calls out to
me. "Aren't you going to bring a bottle of wine or something?"

I hadn't thought of this, of how graceless it looks to show up
empty-handed. Why has Sam waited until now to point this
out? Before I can reply, he adds, "I left a bottle of red on the
counter."

I hate being caught in another social stumble but make a
point of going into the den and putting a hand on his shoulder.
"Thanks for thinking of it." He covers my hand with his and
looks away from the TV long enough to smile up at me. "Have
fun. You'll be back before the baby's up right?" I force myself to
nod and smile back at him. Pointing out that it's a weekend, that
he's already made partner, and that he should be able to feed her
himself, will only start a fight.

Walking toward Blair's is a relief, and I almost skip across the street in the deep pink twilight, cradling the wine in my arms. I decide that I will tell her about the saw, if there's a good moment. I'll bring it up casually and see what she says. Her reaction will tell me whether it's a regular occurrence around here—forgetful landscapers, neighbors who don't think anything of borrowing each other's things—or if it sounds suspicious. And if this has anything to do with Teddy's murder, I'm sure she'd want to know.

Blair is sitting on her front steps, in a pale gray romper and gold jewelry that glints off her taut, tanned skin. Everything she is wearing, which isn't much, probably cost more than half my wardrobe. I wish I'd spent more time picking out an outfit. She is scrolling through her phone and only looks up as I get close.

"Hi Lex! Does anybody call you Lex?"

"Not anymore," I laugh and present the bottle to her, awkwardly cradling it in both my hands. No one's ever called me Lex.

"Perfect! I was still worrying over what cocktail to make tonight. Nothing felt right." She pauses to examine the wine's label. "Pinot noir. I've got an amazing cheese and fruit tray that will go perfectly with this!"

She grabs my elbow to pull herself up as I fumble with the bottle, and we go into the house. Through the elegant foyer and back into her family's personal space. I haven't been inside Blair's house when anyone else was here, but I can imagine what she must be aching for now that Teddy is gone. The golden-haired family laughing in their magazine-ready kitchen, the sparkling couple hosting chic cocktail parties across all these formal rooms, the intimate moments with him that she can never get back.

"Let me just grab our supplies and we can go sit on the

patio," Blair says and starts opening drawers in the kitchen. With her back to me, she starts telling a story about a laughably complicated effort to source her cabinet pulls from Italy.

As I listen, I walk slowly into the adjacent family room, toward a wall of artfully hung photographs. The photos document the evolution of the Bards, from the beautiful young couple to the beautiful babies and onward—a growing, prosperous family. One of the oldest pictures is an 8x10 Sears-style portrait of Blair and Teddy from what must be the late 1990s. Even the tasteful mounting can't elevate their haircuts and the neon laser lights in the background, and I smile to myself as I lean in for a closer look. The picture is almost a close-up, their torsos cut off unflatteringly in the middle. They look so happy, Teddy's arms wrapped around Blair and their heads touching. I'm not sure if it's their smiles or the shape of their faces or the matching sweaters they are wearing, but they share an unsettling resemblance in this photo.

Lots of couples look alike, and to many people, our family pictures are probably a more jarring sight—Sam's pale, freckled skin next to my brown one, and the fine, red hair around his temples just touching the top of my black curly head. Even in college, some of his friends used to say that Sam had jungle fever, and everyone would laugh, because it was supposed to be a joke. I never thought it was funny but of course I always laughed along, not wanting to make a thing of it. For some reason, looking at this picture of Blair and Teddy makes me wish I'd just told them all to go to hell when I'd had the chance.

"Lex?" Blair asks. She is holding up two excessively full wineglasses and looking like she expects an answer to a question.

"Oh gosh, I'm sorry Blair, I was looking at all these beautiful photos. I missed what you just said."

"Ah, our life in pictures. You know our friends used to call us 'Teddy Blair'? I thought it was the cutest thing in the world," she sighs as she walks over to where I am standing. "Don't think I'll be adding too many more to that wall. Let's go outside."

I follow her through one of three sets of French doors, out onto an expansive bluestone patio that steps down to a nearly Olympic-size rectangular gunite pool, the kind Sam wants to get, and a thick, towering row of evergreens beyond. A soft reggae beat is playing on speakers built somewhere into the patio. I'm surprised to recognize a UB40 song—I wouldn't have guessed Blair's musical tastes crossed any borders.

We sit on teak lounge chairs with thick cream-colored pillows, a low teak table loaded with grapes, strawberries, hard and soft cheeses, and three types of crackers between us. The chairs are large enough for curling up, and I sink in and take a sip of my wine. Its cool, tart taste makes me take a second sip immediately. I'm relieved that Sam picked a good bottle.

"I'm so glad you could come tonight. Honestly these empty evenings are the worst now that my mom and the kids are gone again," Blair sighs as she settles into her lounge chair. "Have some of the goat cheese, it's incredible."

"Oh no thank you, I'm trying not to eat at night. I'm sorry you went to all the trouble of putting this out."

"Ah, you mean not snacking after dinner? I know, it's such a bad habit. I shouldn't do it either but it makes the alcohol go down easier," she laughs.

I hesitate before going on but decide it's not extreme enough to hide. I also don't want to have to awkwardly turn down any dinner invitations in the future. "No, I'm trying to only eat once a day, and usually that's lunch. I have so much baby weight to lose, and this one-meal strategy worked for me after I had Caleb."

"Once a day? Lex, that's pretty tough. And you already look great. I mean, I don't think anybody could even tell that you had a baby, what, only two months ago?"

"That's because I hide it well. I mean, that's what all the shapeless dresses are for," I joke, patting my kangaroo pocket.

"I'm serious Lex. You're gorgeous, you don't need to torture yourself like that. Trust me, it took until well into my forties for me to realize. So I'm trying to save you some time." She grabs a cracker and pops it into her mouth, expecting me to answer.

I don't. There's no way I'm going to tell her that keeping one meal down is much better than throwing three up.

Once she's finished chewing, she goes on. "Just to be clear, I'm not delusional. Of course looks matter. But loving yourself matters much more. When my daughter tried skipping meals and whatnot, telling me she was fat and all these things that were wrong with her body, I started dragging her to yoga night for this self-love stuff. Watch out or I'll drag you there too," she winks at me.

I hadn't thought about my daughter. Carter is so tiny, it's almost incomprehensible to think of her as a little girl, entering the painfully self-critical years of adolescence with nothing but my bad example as reference. I can't do that to her. For now, though, she has no idea, so I'll stick to my lunch-only strategy.

"How is your mother? Did she leave right after the 4th?" I ask, tired of this topic. Blair can't know that I saw them fighting after the party. I'd been doing the dishes in the dark.

She takes a slow slip of her wine, gazing steadily at me over the rim of her glass, before answering. "My mom and I are not in a good place right now. I know her mood did not escape you that night. She really can be a bitch."

"I'm sorry. That's probably the last thing you need right now," I say quietly.

"Hmm. She's always been like that. Once she takes a stance, she'll never change her mind or admit she was wrong, no matter how obvious it is."

"That must not have been easy when you were growing up."

"It certainly was not!" Blair smiles at me. "You know, the thing is, she's always blamed me for everything that's gone wrong in her life."

"Sounds familiar," I say without meaning to, and quickly add, "When did you start sabotaging things for her? Before or after you were born?"

Blair laughs, "Definitely before. You can't tell from looking at her, but she was a complete nerd when she was young. A science prodigy. She was at the top of her class at Cornell, all set to break glass ceilings, but her boyfriend knocked her up." She pauses and raises her eyebrows in my direction. "With me!"

"Oh wow. What did she do?" I ask, genuinely surprised. I would never have guessed that kind of disappointment could be behind Blair's mother's steely composure.

"It was the late 1960s. God I'm old. She did what most of them did I suppose. She dropped out her senior year and married the boyfriend. My dear old dad. I don't see that she has so much to complain about though, he was well-off to begin with and ended up being very successful. But no, it's like I forced her into this unbearable life. I think she's always resented me more than she's loved me."

The way Blair describes her mother's feelings sounds uncomfortably familiar, even though the particulars of the story are wildly different. I'm afraid to say anything. We both take long, slow sips and sit in silence for a minute, staring out over

Blair's lush backyard. It's nearly dark now, and her landscape lighting is starting to automatically flicker on. I realize that we aren't listening to a stock playlist, it's actually the full *Labour of Love* album.

"What about you? Are you close with your parents?" she finally asks.

The heat starts to rise in my cheeks, and I wish I hadn't started us down this line of conversation. How to give an answer that doesn't elicit pity and suspicion? Usually, I just say both of my parents are dead and turn to a different topic. But I feel like I shouldn't completely evade the question, when she's just been so candid with me.

"What about my parents?" I parrot back slowly, looking for the words. "They're both dead. My mother and I were never close. It was like she couldn't quite love me, or at least she couldn't show it, but without ever explaining to me why. To be honest, it was like psychological torture, growing up and feeling like I'd done something horrible, or that I *was* something horrible. But not having any clue how to fix it. She died before my senior year of college."

I pause to finish off the wine in my glass. "It was a relief at first, but the past few years I've been thinking about her a lot."

"I don't think they ever stop tormenting you, dead or alive," Blair offers, then adds, "Refill time!" She goes inside before I can say anything. I take a few deep breaths while she is gone, pushing away the memories, and manage to smile up at her as she comes back out with the rest of the bottle I'd brought, plus one of her own tucked under her arm.

She refills our glasses before resuming her position in the oversized chair across from me. "A belated toast," she smiles. "To difficult mothers!"

"May they rest in peace, and leave us be," I smile back and reach out to tap her glass with mine.

"You know, sometimes I think the definition of my life's success will be if my kids never make a toast like that," Blair starts laughing, so hard that she spills some of her wine on the bluestone and has to put her glass down on the table between us. I laugh too, and the evening starts to glimmer and blur as we work our way through the second bottle. She tells me about her brother—born five years after her, the spitting image of their father, the favorite—and a panoply of cousins and assorted relatives scattered across the patrician enclaves of the continental United States. I tell her I have no siblings, which is the truth, as far as I know.

The invisible speakers move on to *Promises and Lies,* and we both sink further down into the lounge chairs, draping our legs over the thick arms. Blair has so much she apparently wants to tell me, and I relax to the clear rhythm of her voice against the soft music. After our laughter over a story about her daughter stealing a pair of her mother's earrings trails off, I remember that I also have things to tell her. As gently as I can manage with my heavy, boozy tongue, I ask about the investigation.

Blair purses her lips and blows air out, almost scornfully. "I'm thinking of hiring my own private investigator. The police have gotten exactly nowhere."

"God I'm sorry," I mumble, and pull myself upright. It sounds like her patience has run out.

"You know, if I'd had any clue how hard it would be to get answers, I would have done this from the beginning. By now whoever did this could be on the other side of the world."

"He might still be around," I add feebly. This isn't how I wanted to tell her, but I'm too tipsy to do it right.

"What?" She's still sunken down into her seat, but her head has snapped up. Her face is caught in a soft wash of light coming through the patio doors, making her eyes gleam silver. She is staring at me intently.

"Blair, I need to tell you about something that happened to me today," I start again. She is still staring at me, without blinking, and it takes me a few seconds to pull together the words. I walk her through my morning, from noticing the saw was missing through to hearing the branch crack, keeping my voice as even as possible.

Her stare is unrelenting, and I realize as I speak that we are no longer in the realm of candid girlfriend conversation. Blair is assessing every word that I say, weighing it for meaning. I can tell from the stillness in her face she believes that I am serious.

"Have you called the police?" she asks as I conclude with a shrug.

"No, I haven't, not yet," I answer sheepishly. Wine starts burning its way back up into my throat. Teddy's murderer is out there, and I'm not sure if I've been too slow to recognize relevant clues or hallucinating from exhaustion. I decide not to say anything about seeing—maybe, possibly, probably not—a person under the streetlight.

Her eyes narrow slightly. "Why not?"

"I, I wanted to tell you about it first. I don't know, I wasn't sure if it was real. So many weird things have been going on, I didn't want to overreact."

"What did Sam say?" she asks, with no warmth in her voice.

"Sam?" It would be normal to have discussed this with my husband first. "No, I haven't told him. He has no idea. Like I said, I wanted to tell you first."

Blair holds my gaze, and I hold my breath. After a few seconds, she says, "Lex, are you doing okay? You know, all the hormone changes and everything can really mess with your head. Have you been getting enough sleep?"

"You're right, my mind's been kind of foggy lately. Speaking of which, I should really try and get a couple of hours of sleep before the baby wakes up," I answer meekly. This is true, but ten minutes ago I would have happily stayed where I am, curled up in this expensive seat, laughing and drinking, until guilt dragged me home in anticipation of Carter's tiny cries.

Blair smiles at me now, warmly again, and nods, "God I remember those early days are so tough. Shame on me for keeping you out this late in the first place. Thanks for coming over."

We each slowly get up and carry the empty glasses and bottles back into the kitchen. Blair walks me to the front door, and we hug. Unprompted, I promise to let her know once I figure out what happened with the saw. She reaches out and grabs both my hands in hers and says, "Why don't you start by talking to Sam about it? Maybe he's storing it away for one of those reno projects you said he's got to do." We both laugh as I walk out toward the street.

It's pitch-black out tonight, no moon or stars, and I use the single streetlight as a guidepost to make my way home. The warm air has eyes—I tell myself it's Blair watching me from inside her house. Still, I can't gather up the courage to do anything but stare straight ahead and move as quickly as my unsteady legs will go. Blair is right. I'll ask Sam. If he hasn't seen it, then the landscapers will be back to mow in a few days, and they must have it.

My cell phone buzzes in my kangaroo pocket as soon as our warped front door closes behind me, askew in its frame from the rising summer humidity. When I stand on my toes and reach my fingertips toward the top edge, I can feel the warm air streaming in, but the contractor who did our kitchen thought it would be at least $7,000 to replace. The quotes we get for everything seem to include an extra zero as a penalty for living in this neighborhood.

I assume the buzz is Blair, and don't pull my phone out to confirm until after double-checking all the main floor locks and activating the alarm. When I finally do, I'm surprised to see it's a text from Emily. Her message asks if I'm free to join her for lunch at her club this upcoming week. I have no idea what kind of club she belongs to, or why she's asking me to lunch, but I have no reason not to go. And getting out of the house more often is probably a good idea. So I quickly write back, "Sure, how about Tuesday or Wednesday?" Only later, as I'm trying to fall asleep with the wine sloshing around uncomfortably in my stomach, does it occur to me that the timing of Emily's message was strange. As if she's the one who watched me come home from Blair's tonight.

Blair

The outside of Jennifer's house is lovely. I truly don't mind this type of reinterpretation for a Tudor. Crisp colors, big windows that let in lots of light—some aspects are superior to the original. It's the inside of Jennifer's house that gets under my skin. Really it's Jeff's house, since he's the one who paid for the place and everything in it. But she's the one responsible for how it looks. Making my way up the modern walk of oversized gray flagstone, I remind myself not to make faces when I go in.

Jennifer is waiting for me in the doorway, the generous curves of her body encased in charcoal leggings and a blush tank top knotted just under her large breasts. Her thick black hair gleams nearly the same color as the open round top door behind her. She's a beautiful woman, and the idea of Jeff's big, droopy body on top of hers makes me shudder.

"Hi!" she waves almost frantically as I walk up. "Blair, are you sure about this? I really don't want to be a bother."

"Don't be silly Jen, you're doing me a favor. I need

distractions." I follow her into the wide foyer. This is where the trouble begins. Instead of tastefully transitional, appropriately period, or thoughtfully modern, Jennifer's house is splashed with a migraine-inducing mix of aggressive primary colors. Plus bizarre furniture shapes. It feels like she grabbed on to an idea of what a stylish interior should look like from certain 1980s TV shows and held tight. I've been trying for a while to steer her in a more sophisticated direction, but she won't let the tackiness go.

She and Jeff bought this house from a developer who built it on spec, and when they moved in four years ago I'd just assumed she was a second wife and kept my distance. But it turned out she isn't. Jeff is a second husband, just one of those guys who stayed suspiciously single into his early fifties, plodding away until he was promoted to CFO of a massive logistics company. At that point, he became an attractive life partner. At least in financial terms.

"You want something to drink?" she asks gesturing toward the kitchen. Luckily, the builder had already selected all the finishes in there before Jennifer could get her hands on it.

"I'm good, just eager to see what you've got."

Jennifer grins and leads me into her dining room where four paintings are propped up against one wall. They are so large that she's had to push the table (a gray-speckled laminate top with chrome legs, God help us) out of the way. We lean our bottoms against the offending table and take in the paintings.

The day they moved in, only one tiny truck showed up. Later, Jennifer told me it was filled with the contents of Jeff's bachelor condo, because she'd left everything with her ex-husband. I'd watched in the weeks after for furniture deliveries, but nothing came. So when we ran into each other at the clothing boutique she manages (and now owns, thank you Jeff), I'd struck up a conversation about decorating. She'd latched on to me like a lost puppy, and I've been stuck with her as a client ever since. If I'd known what she'd gravitate toward, I would have run screaming. At least I like her as a friend.

"I got these paintings at that gallery in Milan I told you about. It took forever to get them shipped and framed. What do you think about putting this one in the master and these two in Jeff's office? What about this last one?" she asks pensively.

All four look like bad Picasso knockoffs, but I know how much Jennifer paid so I've kept my opinions to myself.

"Maybe a couple of them could go downstairs, in the basement?" I offer.

"Hmm, I think Jeff would lose it. I made such a big deal about buying these, and we've still got empty walls up here."

"I like your idea for Jeff's office. You can treat them like two pairs, and do the other two in your master—these two would work right above the chaises in your sitting area." At least this way, I won't have to see them when I come over.

"Oh that's brilliant! We've been talking about going back to Italy next spring actually, so maybe I'll just wait on more art and visit that gallery again."

I want to tell her not to, but that would be pointless. "Do you think your son might come with you this time?"

Jennifer groans lightly and pushes herself off the edge of the table. "I'll invite him, but I doubt it. Do you want some coffee or anything? I could make mimosas?"

"I don't like to drink on the job. A sparkling water would be great," I laugh and follow her into the kitchen. "Is he doing better though?"

Jennifer's first husband was her high school sweetheart. The captain of the football team, her prom date, the guy she lost her virginity to and had a baby with at eighteen. All very "Jack and Diane." Except Jennifer stayed beautiful, while her ex-husband lost his hair, grew a beer belly, and never got promoted from his low-level desk job at a logistics company. So I don't blame her at all for going for it when Jeff fell hard for her at a company event.

"Yup. At least, I think so. He switched majors when he transferred, and his dad says he's much happier," Jennifer answers as she hands me a little glass bottle of Perrier. "I keep calling him every week. One of these days, he's got to answer, right?"

Back then, she thought getting together with Jeff was a great opportunity for her and her fifteen-year-old son too. She couldn't have known that her son would treat it as a betrayal and not only refuse to move in with her, but stop talking to her altogether. They haven't spoken directly in nearly four years, but she keeps paying his college tuition and inviting him on every trip she and Jeff take.

"Before he graduates, I'm sure. These things take time."

"Time? It's been four years already. That damn kid . . ." She stops herself and shakes her head.

Teenagers are complicated. Shake up their world at your own (possibly permanent) peril. That's what I tried to tell Teddy, but he wouldn't listen. He thought I was exaggerating. I would never say this, but Jennifer may have lost her son forever. I feel for her. Jeff is uninteresting, unattractive, and so jealous that he prefers to act as if her son and her ex don't exist, and yells when she brings them up. There's nowhere for her to go, and she's getting reckless in her desperation. But Jennifer's not the first person to take a risk and end up disappointed.

"What else did you want to show me?" I backtrack to happier

territory, because there's no point in wallowing. Regret is like quicksand, and I don't want either of us to get sucked under.

"Oh! I'm so glad you reminded me, I got this great catalogue in the mail the other day, and I wanted to show you a few of the accent chairs in there. Also, they've got some amazing coffee tables."

"Sure," I smile at her, and brace myself.

Alexis

Emily's club is of the urban, social kind—taking up multiple floors of a glass-clad building in a new development with the ambitious goal of making downtown D.C. hip. There are three restaurants, a gym, a pool, meeting rooms, and a whole lot of other amenities that Emily rattles off with her back to me as we wind our way up two sleek escalators. Today's the first day I've felt well-dressed in a long time, having managed to squeeze myself into slacks and a sleeveless blouse. Emily is wearing a thin cotton maxi dress in an unflattering shade of faded olive green. It's long enough to cover the chipped purple nail polish on her toes, but only when she's standing still.

After the hostess seats us, Emily continues her monologue, telling me that she and Dylan are both on the board of the company they founded, and that their house and this club membership are all in service of making political connections. Too much regulation of artificial intelligence would be terrible for the company, and really for society as a whole. But if it were up to her, she'd spend most of her time in Southern California. She actually hates this city.

Our waiter comes over to take drink orders while she is still talking, and she just redirects her monologue at him.

"Actually, we'll go ahead and order. Hope you don't mind." She makes a face at the waiter and then at me, by way of apology, I think. "I've got a 2:30 meeting and I don't want to be running late."

"Sure," I agree and quickly scan the menu, while she orders a summer veggie farm salad and organic lemonade. I ask for a club sandwich and Diet Coke. It's the only time I'll eat today, and I'm hungry. Once the waiter walks away, Emily seems to have suddenly run out of things to say and we're left staring at each other across the table.

I still have no idea why she asked me to meet her here. An alarming thought comes to mind as I watch Emily nudge her flatware. This might be related to work. That night at her house, I did mention that I'm a manager at a boutique consultancy. Laura had forced me to be awkwardly specific by asking if I was a partner yet. My heart starts to race a little faster because I'm totally unprepared for that type of conversation. Normally, I would have already been scanning emails and joining some calls without being asked, but with the house and everything that's happened, I've barely thought about my job since the day Carter was born.

Emily is looking around the restaurant now, her eyes scanning the small groups of professionals filtering in for a weekday lunch. I quickly mine my memory for a handful of basic questions I can ask if this invitation does turn out to be about a consulting project.

"So Alexis, where are you from originally?" she asks as she finally turns her eyes back to me.

"Around Baltimore. How about you? Are you from California?" Out of habit, I reflect the question to avoid continuing about myself.

"No, a small town in Indiana. I met Dylan at Caltech, that's where everything started. But it must be so nice for you to be this close to home."

"It's not really home anymore. I haven't lived there since high school." I take a long sip of water in the hopes that we can move on.

"I know how you feel. I hate having to go back to Indiana, but my parents refuse to move. It's so annoying. Are your parents still in Baltimore?" She's undeterred, blinking at me as I keep sipping.

Finally, I have to stop and answer. "My parents are dead, and I was an only child. I don't have any other family."

I see the knot of pity starting to form between her eyebrows, but luckily the waiter shows up with our drinks.

"The club is really nice." I take the opportunity to change the subject.

"It's not bad for D.C. But anyway, how are you guys settling in? To your house?" she asks as we both reach for our drinks.

I'm not sure why Emily is asking, but it's better than talking about our families. "There's a lot that we love about the house, but the work it needs is just unbelievable."

"I know what you mean, our house is ancient, so we've got lots of crazy stories," she laughs. "What fun surprises have come up at yours?"

I hesitate for a moment before deciding to go ahead and tell her. "At breakfast today, our poor nanny almost lost her right foot. She's a tiny woman, but she just stepped straight through the floor in our breakfast room."

"That just happened today? Do you know why?"

"It turns out that the subfloor is rotting. Something about the crawl space underneath the breakfast room not properly draining. I think it'll take a lot of work to fix."

I don't mention that we had the breakfast room retiled as part of our kitchen remodel a few months ago, or that I'd been sending Sam long text messages in all capitals asking him how he could have let our contractor do such a poor job. I also don't mention that Sam hasn't even responded.

Our waiter is approaching with our food, but I can't stop myself before adding, "The contractor I talked to on my drive here told me to tape Saran Wrap over the hole in the floor, so that animals don't come in from the crawl space. Like insects and snakes. Can you imagine?"

Now Emily's face looks ashen. "Oh that's really bad," she says quietly. I guess this particular story is a bit crazier than what she was expecting.

"I'm so sorry, that was way too much information."

Neither of us touches our food for an awkwardly long time. Finally, Emily reaches for her fork and knife, and smiles at me. "So, the neighborhood's also got some nasty surprises, huh? We haven't talked since that night Mack got arrested. Can you believe him? I hope he gets jail time."

"Ugh," I shudder. "I wish he would, but apparently nothing's going to happen. Blair told me—"

"Speaking of which, a friend told me that you were at Blair's brother's 4th of July party," she interrupts.

"Oh yes, Sam and I were there, Blair invited us to go with her—" I stop. "Who's your friend?"

"No one that you know, she just said she saw you on the yacht. It seems like you and Blair have become really close already." She smiles again, while her forked fist stabs at her salad.

I want to ask how her friend recognized me—had Emily mentioned her new, brown-skinned neighbor and this person easily spotted me in a mostly white sea of partygoers? But there's no reason for Emily to be talking about me, we barely know each other. Had her friend described each person of color in attendance with such detail that Emily just happened to recognize me in her words?

"Next time your friend should introduce herself," I try to sound displeased, but she just keeps eating, so I go on. "But really, everyone in the neighborhood has been very welcoming. I've just gotten to know Blair because I reached out to her after Teddy died, and it seems like she appreciates having company."

"How well do you know her?" Emily asks between bites.

"Blair? I mean, obviously not that well. I met her when we moved in. She's just been super friendly and welcoming, like everyone else." I know this isn't quite true—Blair grabbed on and pulled me close as if she'd been waiting for me, as if we were always meant to be friends. The rest of our neighbors just brought us expensive housewarming gifts.

"Listen, Blair isn't someone you should trust. She doesn't respect boundaries, and she only cares about herself."

I'm not sure where this is going, but my appetite is quickly fading. "Why are you telling me this?"

The waiter approaches to check on us, but Emily waves him

off with her fork. "I'm doing you a favor Alexis. I'm warning you to be careful with her."

"I'm sorry, I'm not following," I say, trying to smile. I can't imagine she is just doing this to help me.

"Well, I also need to ask you something." She puts her utensils down and glances around before asking. "Has she said anything to you about Dylan?"

I remember the night we went to Emily's how dismissive Blair was, mocking Dylan for thinking of himself as a ladies' man. I'm not sure what to say. "Nothing in particular. Not that I can think of."

"Has she said anything about sleeping with Dylan?" She's leaning into the table now, not believing me.

"What? No! Why would you ask that? Her husband just died," I answer without thinking. I feel offended for Blair, and wish I could add that not everyone wants to sleep with Dylan.

"I know he did, that's exactly why I'm asking. Dylan's brilliant in certain ways, but in others, he's an idiot. If you put a pair of big tits in front of him, he'll do anything to get at them."

Involuntarily, my eyes go to Emily's modest chest. She sounds like she's speaking from bitter experience.

"Look, I have no idea what Dylan is doing, but I don't have any reason to think Blair is sleeping with him. She's never said anything to me remotely hinting at that."

"Well you just said you don't know her that well, but I've seen them. Dylan couldn't keep his eyes off her when we first moved here. He chatted her up at every social hour with no shame. But after a while he started ignoring her completely. That's what he always does. To try to cover it up."

She pauses to suck down the rest of her lemonade. "But it's not fooling me anymore. I'm sure they're fucking each other.

And now that Teddy's gone, it's oh so convenient . . ." She trails off, and starts rubbing her eye sockets with the heels of her hands. I think it's meant to hold back tears.

Accusing Blair of sleeping with her husband is awful, but it seems like she is pushing even further. I don't really want to hear more. "Emily, I'm not sure what you mean. But are you all right? Do you want me to go grab some tissues?"

"No. I don't mean anything, okay? Dylan and I were out of town when Teddy died. He couldn't have been involved. But I don't know what Blair's capable of, and I can't let her drag Dylan into it. I have to protect him. Us. Our company."

I barely manage to suppress a nervous laugh at how ridiculous Emily sounds. "I'm sorry, I really have no idea about any of this."

"Just promise that you'll tell me if she says anything about him." She pulls her hands out of her eyes, and now I can see a nasty flush of pink running from her chest, up her neck to her nose, as if she's having an allergic reaction.

I want this conversation to end, so I nod. "We'd better finish up, I know you've got a meeting soon."

While Emily signs the check, I look down at my plate and realize I've only eaten one small wedge of my sandwich. The thought of asking for a to-go box crosses my mind, but that would be ridiculous. I'm disappointed by the missed opportunity for a big meal, and console myself with ideas of what I can have for lunch tomorrow.

/ 8:15 PM

Only now, as I'm swaddling Carter, does the wave of recognition crest and crash over me. I hadn't asked Emily why she was talking to me—why she didn't just confront Dylan—because I know. He'd never admit it. Until the very last possible second, when presented and pushed with solid proof, he'd deny absurdly. That's why she came to me, to collect her evidence. The first time, when Sam's drunk friend told me about the rich girl on my floor, I'd realized right away that he had dated us both simultaneously for weeks. We'd started dating near the end of the semester, and he'd told me he was going to Jamaica with high school friends for winter break and would be too high the whole time to call or write.

I never said anything, because we were young, boundaries were fluid, and he was the only boyfriend I'd ever had. I was scared of being alone again, and it's not as if we were married. But the second time, I left him. During his third year of law school, I'd already finished business school and was out of town at client sites most weekdays. That time, it was the flirtatious emails on his desktop that gave him away. She was the editor of the law review, and in his study group, and wasn't this overreacting, it was just a few messages? I was traveling so much now and, besides, I was always pushing him away and not sharing, just holding grudges. He wasn't sleeping enough and made a bad decision, and would never do it again. That's what he'd said.

I pointed out that it wasn't technically his first bad decision and threw one of his casebooks at his face. He'd needed a few stitches, and after taking him to the twenty-four-hour urgent care, I went back to our apartment, packed most of my clothes, and went to a hotel. A few days later, I rented a furnished studio and decided we were done for good. But Sam wouldn't leave me alone—he sent flowers every week, timed to arrive on Friday nights just as I got home from the airport, and long voicemails about his days, and little gifts in the mail—it was all so desperate that it reminded me of my mother, and after six months I finally answered the phone when he called. Since then we'd moved on, mostly. It's been more than a decade but sometimes, for no apparent reason, doubt crystallizes like icicles in the pit of my stomach and I wonder if I'm being made a fool.

Maybe Emily isn't crazy. I don't know Blair that well, or what might have happened before we moved in. Really, Emily is right. I don't know what Blair is capable of. After Carter finishes her bottle, I watch her tiny pink lips tremble in sleep for a long while. Then I put her down in her crib and text Emily, to thank her for lunch and ask her over for a drink. She writes back right away to say yes. I guess I shouldn't be surprised—after what I said about the breakfast room floor—that she suggests I come to her house instead.

Blair

It's been over six weeks, and those two detectives keep show-ing up. They came by again this morning. I always ask them to come into the kitchen and serve them coffee while they sit at the island, side by side. It's a little ritual we have going. And just like every other time, this morning they told me that, basically, they've got nothing.

Detective Kim did most of the talking, per usual, explain-ing that they've followed every lead to its dead end. Nothing at Teddy's work had uncovered international intrigue after all, or financial misdeeds, and all his colleagues had solid alibis. The detectives have been to the country club, to the kids' schools, and down to the state capitol in Richmond. They'd tracked down and spoken to every single homeowner in River Forest. They'd posted officers along the trail on two Saturdays, to ask passersby if they'd seen anything, and staffed the tip hotline twenty-four hours a day. But all for naught. Everyone who knew Teddy loved him, and no credible tips had come in. When Mack got arrested a few weeks ago they'd even questioned him, but he'd gotten off a private plane only a couple of hours before Teddy's body was found.

They told me all this while I stood across from them at the island, my palms pressing into the ridges of the thick, French-coved stone. I know they're suspicious—there aren't many other options left. As Detective Kim talked and in the long silence that followed, I could feel their eyes watching me, intent on reactions. *"What do we do now?"* I'd finally asked. *"There must be something else we can do?"* They'd promised to keep working and to keep me updated, but asked me to be patient.

I'd nodded slowly and thanked the detectives for their perseverance. They'd lingered five minutes longer than I could really stand, sipping their coffee, but I bit my tongue. I even offered them refills as they stood up to go. When their black sedan finally pulled away from the curb and down the street, I'd grabbed my car keys and nearly run to the garage. It felt like all seven thousand square feet of my house were closing in on me, and I needed room to breathe. The muggy heat outside would have made for a miserable walk, so I drove to the only place I knew could calm me down. West, to the light industrial zones of the outer suburbs and their steely sea of warehouses.

I know the best ones, and less than an hour after the detectives left this morning, I was pulling back a deeply tinted swinging door to reveal the brightly lit paradise of my favorite kitchen and bath showroom. Over an acre of the world's most fashionable and expensive metals and stones, gleaming in wide aisle after aisle. The managers know me well, and their staff didn't ask questions, they just politely smiled as I passed each tasteful display. I walked through the whole warehouse a few times, reminding myself that there had been no other way, and that everything is and will be fine. After two hours, I felt much calmer and started driving home.

Now, I am stuck behind a little Honda hatchback that's stalled at the four-way stop at the entrance to River Forest. I lean hard on my horn. It's obnoxious, but the last thing I need right now is somebody's babysitter or cleaning lady to break down and block my way home. The Honda finally shudders and lurches forward, and as it turns left into my neighborhood I realize it's Alexis.

"Oops," I say to myself and try to wave, but she is hunched over the steering wheel and staring straight ahead. I follow behind and stop in front of her house, expecting her to park in the driveway. But the Honda chugs straight into their tiny garage, and the door rolls down immediately behind it. I wait a few seconds, thinking she might come out of her side door, or reopen the garage, but the house is still. I guess she didn't realize I was the jerk who honked. But she really should get rid of that car. It doesn't seem fair that Sam's got a BMW while she's stuck with a piece of junk.

Alexis

Replacement window contractors may end up being my least favorite. This is what I decide as I lead one named Tom through the house, over an hour into what increasingly feels like a complete waste of time. But I didn't know what else to do besides schedule this appointment—Sam hasn't even pretended to start working on the safety railing for the picture window in our bedroom, and the air-conditioning units are running constantly, never managing to cool down all the rooms to a tolerable temperature. Our June electricity bill was more than $500. I knew this appointment would be useless though as soon as Tom arrived and asked in a slightly annoyed tone where my husband was. He said their company "strongly prefers" to meet with both homeowners at once, and I'd bitten the inside of my cheek to stop myself from telling him to leave. Since then, he's been measuring every single window and external door, and punching the dimensions into his tablet, while extolling the virtues of triple-pane glass and ignoring my attempts to move things along.

He is following me up the stairs to the second floor now, and I try again. "Really, all we need right now is a rough estimate of what it would cost to replace everything. Maybe you could just count the windows and doors on the other floors, since you got all the main floor measurements?"

Tom chuckles to himself as we reach the narrow second floor hallway. "That's not how it works, Mrs. Crawford. There are so many variables, and your house isn't standard at all, practically each window is a different size, it's kind of wacky honestly. Also there are options to decide on and specials we run, so I can't give you a number until I input all the information. You understand don't you?"

I've realized, after probably two dozen of these sorts of appointments, that contractors fall into a handful of types. I've made the joke to Sam that I could do a market analysis in my sleep, and if my firm has any clients in the home renovation business, I'll ask to work with them after my maternity leave. There are the self-important types, who seem to think I have nothing better to do than spend an afternoon listening to them belittle my intelligence and my house. Like Tom. There are the old, weary types who decide as soon as they walk in that whatever I've asked is more work than they really want to do, like the carpenter I had over for built-in bookshelves in the den. They spend our few minutes together sighing doubtfully as they take notes and, I assume, thinking about how to inflate their quotes high enough to dissuade me. My favorite types are the charming ones who try to ingratiate themselves by complimenting the house and telling me about their own children. At least those conversations are pleasant.

"Look, this is the one I told you about. It feels like an accident waiting to happen, I mean our son is almost two and just wants to touch everything." We are in my bedroom, and I demonstrate for him how placing my hand on the glass makes the old picture window shift in its frame.

"Whoa, watch out for that," Tom reaches out an arm as if he were going to grab on to me for safety, but then thinks better of it. "You really need to get this replaced. It's dangerous."

I know it is, but I still think he's just feigning concern as part of his sales pitch.

"Can I record you saying that for my husband?" I joke. "He thinks I'm overreacting."

Regardless of the type, I prefer to meet contractors during the week, while Elena is taking care of the children, so I can focus and filter for Sam. Some of them I don't even bother to tell him about, like the $15,000 quote for built-ins from the carpenter. Others I reframe, like the lead abatement guys who'd mentioned that the cheapest thing to do would be some selective repainting ourselves—Sam didn't need to hear about that option.

It's past 3:00 when Tom finishes measuring the last window in the house, and we sit at the dining room table for the big reveal. "So, with everything we talked about, in terms of going with the double pane and some of the more budget-friendly options, plus all of our applicable promotions right now, your total is right around $120,000."

I barely manage to suppress a laugh. "Wow, that's really a lot. And that's with all the special discounts you mentioned?"

"Quality is what you're paying for here and remember what they say—you get what you pay for. Also, you've got to remember that you have a whole lot of windows in this house, and this kind of investment will really save you on energy bills."

Yes, window contractors are the worst, this confirms it. No

one else has managed to make me feel simultaneously ashamed for having made an appointment without any intention of spending that kind of money, angry for wasting so much of my time, and insulted for assuming I can't do math. He must have seen, as soon as he drove up, that this would be a six-figure estimate. That's all I would have needed to know.

"Okay, and what about just the picture window in the master? Like I said, that is really our top priority right now. How much would it be?"

Tom sighs as if I've already made a big mistake. "Well, if you just did that window, you wouldn't get any of the discounts. You'd be looking at around $12,000, maybe a little more."

He turns his tablet toward me on the dining table, to show me the breakdown. The doors and the biggest windows each have a five-figure number next to them. I thank Tom for his time, disingenuously, and say I'll discuss it with my husband. Before he can drag things out any longer, I stand up from the table to show him out.

As soon as I've shut the door behind him, I call Sam.

He doesn't pick up until the last ring before voicemail. "Hey, what's up? I've got a meeting in a few minutes."

"Nothing, that window contractor just left. Replacing everything would be $120,000." Full transparency is not my usual strategy, but I don't see a better option.

"What, are they gold-plated? Who's crazy enough to spend that kind of money on windows?" He's annoyed. The two pool contractors who came a few weekends ago both sent us estimates in the low six figures, and I'd told Sam to stop dreaming — we'd have to and dip deep into our retirement accounts for a project that big, and I'd never let him do that. The idea of doing it for windows is more ridiculous, even to me.

"I know, I know. But if we just do the window in our bedroom, it would only be around $10,000. That one is worth it."

He grunts dismissively, "Sounds like a real bargain. No way are we doing that."

"I can get a few more estimates," I offer.

"Please, you know they'll all be outrageous," he counters.

"Sam, our house is dangerous. This whole neighborhood is dangerous. I don't know, maybe we should think about just fixing up the worst parts and moving."

"Okay, I'm not going to listen to this garbage again. The window's fine. The house is fine. I've got to go."

"No, at least the window—" I start to say, but then realize he's already hung up.

Saturday / July 19 / 11:15 PM

I am outside my house, staring at the front door. The dark red paint looks streaky and faded under the bright portico light, and flecks of dirt give a grimy tinge to the detailed white molding of the pilasters. It makes me think a replacement might deserve moving up our renovation list, even if it costs more than we could get for our awful old hatchback. Before I can make my key fit in the lock, I remember the poor girl who stood here naked and petrified, and feel embarrassed that this was her view.

All the lights are off inside the house, and I focus on trying to tread lightly. I must be drunk again, because I'm failing miserably. The floor creaks and groans against my every step as I lock the door, take off my shoes, and walk into the kitchen. Our contractor assured us that the old wood could take a refinishing, but the top layer of the narrow boards is starting to peel off in spots, like a scab.

Emily and I just spent more than two hours in her sitting room, drinking gin and tonics while she told me in uncomfortable detail about her marital problems. When I arrived, she'd opened the door with such an expectant look on her face, I almost felt guilty for not having a signed confession from Blair to hand over. She led me directly to the front sitting room, where she had the drinks already prepared on a coffee table, but even in the few seconds it took to get from the foyer to my seat on a small couch, I'd seen that the interior of her house was a disappointment. The history and charm promised by the exterior stone and detailing must have been ripped out of the house at some point in the past—most recently in the 1990s, judging by the blank, molding-free drywall and cherry-red wood floors. Emily's overstuffed beige furniture and heavy area rugs make it even worse. My best guess is that they came straight from her parents' house in Indiana.

Despite the setting and the tough topic of conversation, it wasn't a bad time. The gin and tonics were just strong enough, and even though I feel ridiculous thinking so, Emily's lack of style made me slightly prouder of my own house. Dylan wasn't home—out with some friends she said—and Emily hadn't wasted any time, asking me as we both settled into our seats if since our lunch I'd remembered anything relevant with Blair. I hadn't of course, and as she slumped back into the matching couch across from me, she'd sighed deeply before launching into her past unprompted. She and Dylan met in a computer science class during their sophomore year at Caltech. She had already known who he was—a legend for being so handsome, and not just by nerdy college standards—but he completely ignored her until accidentally knocking her over with his bike. She should have known better—a plain, mousy girl from the middle of nowhere with a campus demigod—how long could it really last? But she'd been dazzled, and when she shared her ideas with him and they started their company, it seemed like their fates were blessedly and permanently intertwined. He became the charismatic face of the business, she the brains better kept behind the scenes. Emily didn't exactly put it this way, but this is what I surmised from her telling.

Her words had started to slur around the time she got to his proposal. They'd grown the company so fast, she barely had time to see what was happening around her, until she walked in on him having sex in her office with a woman from their sales team. He'd begged her forgiveness on his knees with a ring, a five-carat monstrosity that she leaned over to show me. She should have said no, but she was still so young and still so taken with him and wanted to believe he really would settle down. After all, his parents had met in graduate school after his dad immigrated from India and they'd been married for decades. He said he wanted to be like them, and anyway who had ever heard of an Indian sex freak?

My own tongue had loosened up a little too much, and I'd pointed out that there were multiple flaws in her logic. Dylan is half Indian, and besides there are over a billion people in India, some of whom are inevitably freaks of different kinds. And hadn't she ever heard of tantric sex? We'd almost fallen off our respective couches laughing.

After bringing our third rounds in from the kitchen, Emily filled in the seedy details of the general idea already in my mind. Nearly a decade of marriage had yet to stop Dylan, and she put up with all of it—signing off on well-compensated nondisclosure agreements with employees, pushing down the jealous bile that would bubble up from her stomach at every cocktail party when good-looking women smiled in their direction, even being made to feel like a selfish prude when he suggested threesomes and she flat-out refused.

While she talked, there were moments I had to resist the urge to grab her by the shoulders and shake her, to tell her how incredibly ashamed she'd be if all her employees and investors knew that she was desperately clinging to Dylan like this. For a few fleeting moments, I'd even wanted to tell her about what happened with Sam so many years ago, to encourage her to walk away. But she didn't ask anything about me—she just went on and on, until my head was swimming with Emily's misery and too much gin, and I'd finally interrupted to say I had to get home for the baby. As we walked to her front door, she'd quickly come back to the point, pleading with me to let her know if I see or hear anything about Blair and Dylan. I asked if he usually likes older women before I could stop myself—Emily just scoffed at the question, saying he doesn't discriminate on anything except bra size.

I should go to sleep right now. It's not yet midnight and Carter hasn't been waking up until after 2:00 a.m. But I feel nauseous and confused, unsure of what comes next, if anything. As I walked down her front steps, Emily had called out that we should get together again soon, and I'd said absolutely, without being sure I meant it. I feel sorry for her, and I believe what she's told me, but more than wanting to help, I left her house tonight repulsed. She's pathetic, willing to tell someone she only recently met horrible things about her life in exchange for scraps of information, and for what? To extricate a man who can't seem to control himself from another mess of his own making. I think about taking a shower and forgetting that tonight, and our lunch this week, ever happened—I could ignore any messages she sends me and play dumb whenever I see her. She'd have to give up eventually. But doing that would also mean ignoring the possibility that Blair and Dylan had an interest in Teddy dying.

The espresso machine switches on with a familiar glow and hum. I need to sober up and think about what to do next, but the only thought that comes is regret for not having stayed in our rowhouse with its mundane urban dangers. Hurrying by the homeless man who predictably hassled me every night on the way home from work wasn't as scary as stumbling blind around an unsolved murder. The smell of fresh coffee makes my stomach grumble, so I fish out a mini brioche bun and a chunk of cheddar cheese from the refrigerator. This midnight breakfast will cost me tomorrow's lunch, but it tastes delicious. As I sit at the kitchen table chewing in the dark, I pull my phone out and look at the calendar to help order my thoughts. Teddy died on May 31. I remember because it was exactly two weeks after Carter was born. This means Carter turned two months old this past Thursday, and I'd forgotten. Maybe being an awful mother is genetic.

When did I see Shawn out in the dark? The first time, in the wooded lot next door, wasn't long after the murder. After that, the handful of times I saw him passing under the streetlight were random—nights when I happened to look out while washing bottles at the kitchen sink. If I'd written down the dates, I might have been able to decipher a pattern to when he goes out. That is, assuming he is the one who was out there, if there was anyone at all. I should keep waiting for a good opportunity to ask him or Laura directly for an explanation, but my gardening saw still hasn't turned up—neither Sam nor the landscapers had any idea what I was talking about when I asked. And now, with two new friends I hadn't even tried to make, it feels like I'm caught up in Teddy's death, without knowing how or why.

No woman has ever taken real interest in me before, other than my teachers. Living with my mother taught me to be quiet unless I could say something I thought she wanted to hear—this was a great way to be a teacher's pet, but not much else. At every age, the girls around me seemed to naturally be attracted to one another, easily and unselfconsciously sharing secrets, crushes, clothes, even food. But I was always at a loss, friendly with everyone, but friends—real friends—with no one. It wasn't until Sam and I got together that I realized the burdens I'd been spared—remembering the minor dramas of multiple people's lives, asking after family members, filling every weekend with plans. I tried to learn quickly from Sam how to do all this but never got very good at it. I guess that's why I don't make the cut for book clubs, and why I should suspect two sudden overtures of friendship when so few have ever come my way. At least with Emily, it's clear that she has a use for me, distasteful as it is—I have yet to figure out what Blair wants.

My chewing slows to a stop as an absurd idea forms in my mind. Shawn might be out there again tonight. If I could just get a glimpse—to know if it's really him, or just a figment of my imagination—I might be able to start putting the pieces together. The espresso is clearing my head, and I consider the practicalities of this idea. It is pitch-black, so I'd have to get absurdly close to even have a hope of making out any details. But the darkness could work in my favor. If I hide myself well among the trees, there's a good chance of going unseen. I feel almost sober now, but still a little reckless. Shawn could easily hurt me if

I catch him off guard, and I don't know for sure that he is out there with good intentions. But I may never have seen anyone at all. Besides, the espresso won't let me sleep and right now I'd rather be alone outside than tossing in bed next to Sam.

It's already past midnight. I clean up and commit to myself that I will only stay out there for one hour, so I can be back before Carter wakes up. If nothing happens during that time, I'll give up and try again another night. I pull on sneakers with no socks—too afraid of waking someone up if I go upstairs to get a pair—and decide to go out the back door. It takes my eyes a couple of minutes to adjust to the inky blackness. Even the crickets have given out, and the silent, humid air envelops me like a suffocating blanket. I cross the patio with my hands outstretched and groping, using memory to avoid stumbling over the cheap plastic chairs we got from a big-box store. By the time I get onto the grass, I can see, more or less. One step at a time, I make my way to the grove of trees that separates our property from Jeff and Jennifer's, stopping every few seconds to listen and turn my head in all directions. By the time my fingertips brush the first trunk, I feel confident that no one is out here with me.

The grove consists of about a dozen trees, broadleaf deciduous varieties at least thirty feet tall. They are in full summer leaf, but their branches don't start until about ten feet up. I have only the trunks to hide behind. I feel my way between them, assessing how far from the streetlamp to position myself. I settle on one roughly in the middle of the grove and push my back as close as possible to the trunk. The rough bark grabs at my hair, and I try to relax and lean my head slightly forward.

My chosen tree sits on our side of the property line but has an unobstructed view of the back of Jeff and Jennifer's house. It's too dark to make out now—their landscape lights aren't even on—but I've enviously peered through these trees in the daytime and remember every detail—a screened-in porch, an expansive deck, and a basement with a wall of folding glass doors that walks out to a huge, free-form pool.

I'm gripping my cell phone in one hand and quickly tap the screen to check the time: 12:41 a.m. The only time I ever sit staring into the dark is when I feed Carter, and my nipples begin to itch even though I'm not breastfeeding her. Another black mark on my parenting record. I can't even imagine how negligent I would be with a third child. Part of our family compound fantasy included dreamy talk about having four, maybe even five, children. And a perfect house filled with laughter. Those conversations took place only a few years ago, but they feel like they're from another lifetime. I close my eyes and wonder how things could have turned out differently.

When I open them again, I realize that a light has come on in Jeff and Jennifer's basement. Basement seems like the wrong word—high ceilings, large pieces of art on bright white walls, a low-slung black leather couch. From here, it looks like a modern art gallery, bathed in an after-hours glow. They really pushed the modern in modern Tudor, I think to myself, and then gasp reflexively as a woman and man emerge from behind a wall. From this distance, I can't make out her features, but I know immediately from the pale skin and flowing black hair that it is Jennifer. She starts to undress the man who followed behind her, pulling his T-shirt over his head as he pushes down his own shorts. His face is half buried in her hair now, but his naked silhouette doesn't look familiar. His own hair is too full, his body too muscular and tan, to be Jeff.

I am so focused on this scene that I don't hear him coming until it's too late. A soft rustle, and before I can even turn my head, a hand is over my mouth and an arm is pressing against my throat. I try to scream and kick and punch, but this man is much bigger than me, and in one easy motion spins me around and slams my forehead against the tree trunk.

"Shut the fuck up," he hisses into my ear.

There is liquor on his breath. Pain and panic rise up in a red wave, and I can feel my legs starting to give out. The man is still pressing against my throat, holding me up this way, and I claw at his forearm, gasping for air. My vision starts to go blacker than the night around us, and I feel myself quickly running out of fight.

He presses harder, and whispers, "I am going to let go. Sit down, or you will be very fucking sorry."

I try to nod, but his hold is so tight I can barely move my head. Slowly, excruciatingly slowly, he lets go, and allows me to slump against the tree whose bark I have embedded in my scalp. I look up and even in the dark, I know that this is not Shawn.

It's Jeff. His heavyset body is taking up most of the space around me, heaving from the effort of the attack. My knees curl up and my hands go out defensively, as I gasp for air and am forced to inhale the stink of Jeff's alcohol and sweat.

"Alexis, why the hell are you out here?"

Ridiculously, my first thought is pleasant surprise that he remembers my name. We haven't spoken many times. But quickly, I remember where I am and what he's just done to me, and shrink back toward the tree trunk for support. I have no idea what kind of man Jeff really is, why he is out here, or what he could try.

"Jeff? Is that you?" I answer, my throat burning.

"Yes. Why are you out here?" he asks again, angry.

"Oh God, you really scared me. I, I've seen shadows out here, you know I'm up a lot with the baby, and I wanted to know who it was."

I sound ridiculous. Although I'm telling the truth, I don't think I'm believable and scramble for better excuses. "Some of my gardening equipment disappeared, and I don't know, I just thought something weird was going on and came out to see if I could figure out . . ." I let my voice trail off.

Jeff's slack outline goes tense at these words, and I know he's the one who stole it. This big, wealthy man—a man who could buy nearly anything he wants—had snuck onto my property and taken a potentially lethal piece of gardening equipment from me. My mind is spinning, trying to think of reasons why. I think he is staring down at me, but I can't tell if his eyes are open. I know I won't get answers now, and instead focus on finding words that will not make him angry.

"It was a mistake. I shouldn't be out here. I'm really sorry Jeff, about what's happening to you," I say as carefully as I can.

My back is braced against the tree trunk and I can feel every rough ridge of bark through my thin shirt. Jeff takes a step forward and hawks spit inches from my left shoulder. A few drops of spittle land on my cheek, and I use my shoulder to furiously wipe them off. He puts a heavy hand on the trunk above my head and crouches down to face me.

"What the fuck do you know about what's happening to me?" he says slowly, and then, "Are you her fucking *friend*?" It sounds like a threat.

"No, no, I barely know her. I don't know really, I just, I'm just so sorry that she's doing this to you."

This makes him chuckle grimly, and he drops himself to the ground in front of me.

"Can you believe she's fucking that guy right under my

goddamn nose? In the brand-new house I bought her? Fucking the goddamn neighbor twice a week in my basement. She thinks I'm playing poker until 3:00 a.m. and just fucks her brains out until two-fucking-fifty-five," he finishes with a grunt.

Dylan. That's the man with Jennifer. Now I remember his attractive face and Blair's comments. I wonder if Jeff is unbearable, or if Jennifer is just faithless. Maybe both.

"That's awful Jeff, really I'm sorry," I whisper.

He's leaning back on his hands now, his big legs splaying out on either side of me. "They'll get what's coming to them, that's for fucking sure."

The more I hear, the less likely it seems Jeff will let me just stand up and walk back into my house. His head is turned toward his own house, consumed. This might be my last chance. I take a deep breath and slowly pull my feet under me into a crouching position, trying to make as little noise as possible. He is still staring intently at the scene playing out in his basement. I count to ten in my mind, jump up, and stomp as hard as I can on his crotch.

He makes an awful groaning sound and lurches toward me, but I take a wide step to the left, over his big leg, and take off running. I keep my hands out in front of me to avoid the trees and within seconds I am out of the woods and on the grass, running as fast as I can toward the back patio doors. All I hear is the blood pounding in my ears. I have no idea how close Jeff is, and I'm too scared to look over my shoulder.

Too frantic to find an entry point, I hurdle over the low brick wall, onto the patio, and into the house, slamming the door behind me. I lock it and hold my breath, waiting for Jeff's hulky shadow to appear. But there is no sign of him. Suddenly I realize how stupid I am being—every old window could easily be breached. I run through all the rooms on the main floor, checking each lock twice, and silently praying that Elena locked everything up in the basement. Then I position myself behind the futon in the sunroom, watching the trees through the windows but keeping my body mostly hidden. Inside and out is still and dark. After a few minutes, my heartbeat slows back to normal, and I begin to realize how much my head aches. I don't think Jeff is coming after me, at least not tonight. He was too drunk for subtlety and would have banged on a door or broken a window by now.

I let my body slip onto the bare wooden floor. How did I let this happen to me? And it isn't over. How can it be? Now that I've had a glimpse of what Jeff is thinking, I am a threat to his plans. But I'm too tired to think it through, so I push away the dread and close my eyes.

SUNDAY / JULY 20 / 7:00 AM

"Alexis, Alexis, wake UP." Sam is kneeling next to me, yelling into my ear, as if he's been at this for a while.

I open my eyes, but immediately close them against the bright sunshine.

"Why did you pass out here? And what in the hell happened to your forehead?" He sounds exasperated.

All I can manage is a moan. My mind is slowly emerging from the blackness of sleep, and grabs on to the familiar chatter of Elena and the children from the kitchen.

"Carter. Oh shit. Did you feed Carter last night?" Now I remember, where I am and why I am here. I awkwardly push up on my elbows and watch him stand up and step back, so that he can stare down at me in disapproval.

"Of course I fucking fed her, she was screaming like a banshee. Where in the hell were you?"

I grab on to the frame of the futon to pull myself up, but my legs don't feel up to the task. I sit back heavily onto the floor. Is he actually mad at me? I know I shouldn't, but I can't help myself.

"I'm so sorry you had to wake up once to feed your own child," I say with as much sarcasm as I can muster.

"What the hell Alexis? What is wrong with you?" He is wearing fresh workout clothes and must be annoyed that I am delaying his run.

If he were being kind, I might tell him and worry that he'd go looking for Jeff to punch him in the face for what he'd done to his wife. But he's not kind right now, and I am beginning to wonder if he ever was. If he ever would have defended me, even if it was my fault. That same sense of distrust is hardening in my gut again, and I decide not to tell him anything.

I reach my hand up to my forehead and wince. My fingers pull away and I see the dirt and blood. "I went for a walk last night after leaving Emily's, and it was so dark that I tripped and fell into a tree," I smile feebly up at Sam. "I'm sorry, it sounds even stupider now that I'm saying it aloud."

"Jesus, Alexis. Out colliding with trees in the middle of the night? You're forgetting that this is a dangerous neighborhood." Sam's voice has lightened, but there is still an edge to it.

"I know, I'm sorry," I say as he grabs my elbow and pulls me up roughly. When he lets go, I almost fall back into the futon, but manage to steady myself and walk slowly past him toward the kitchen. The chatter stops as soon as I step through the doorway. Elena tries to distract Caleb by singing a song, but keeps her eyes on me as I pour myself a glass of cold water and gulp it down.

"I'm sorry," I apologize to her too, embarrassed by what she must be thinking. It's Sunday morning and she should be getting ready for church. "Can you just watch them for another half hour? I'll be back." I kiss them all on the forehead, including Elena.

Every part of my body aches as I drag myself up the stairs to our master, closing the door behind me. In the floor-length mirror, I look like I've been run over by a car. Splotches of mud cover my shirt and shorts, my legs are scratched, and there is a palm-sized wound above my right eye, bloody and bruised and caked with dirt. I turn away from my reflection, and head to the bathroom to shower. I linger long past our water heater's limited capacity, letting the hot then freezing cold water drum the pain into numbness. I want to wash off the stink of Jeff's breath and every last trace of his spit.

I don't know what I stumbled into last night. Jeff could have been on his way to actually hurting them. Maybe he did after I left. He's obviously been out there before, a drunk cuckold who can't stop himself from watching. When he was choking the life out of me last night, all I could think about was my children. They wouldn't remember me, so they couldn't miss me much, but who would be here to protect them? To do what no one had done for me, and kiss the palms of their tiny hands and forgive all of the sins that led to their existence? I can't make any more stupid mistakes.

I get out of the shower and hurry to get dressed, pushing my aching body through the motions. I pull my wet, tangled hair into a bun on top of my head, and after a moment's hesitation, I go into my walk-in closet and close that door behind me too. Detective Bryan's business card is at the top of the little pile I keep in a shoebox, and I dial his cell phone number quickly, my heartbeat picking up speed with each digit. He answers on the second ring. "Rich Bryan," he says authoritatively.

"Hi, Rich, sorry, Detective Bryan, this is Alexis Crawford," I try to speak softly but clearly, so he doesn't have to ask me to repeat myself. "I'm one of Teddy Bard's neighbors, the man who was murdered in River Forest. You came by my house and spoke with my husband and me?" I'm not sure if I am expecting him to remember who I am. He must have talked to dozens of people in those first few days.

"What can I do for you Mrs. Crawford?" he answers, not coldly, but businesslike.

"Well, I'm calling because some strange things have been happening. I don't know if they have anything to do with Teddy, but I thought you should know about them. I'd really like to speak with you in person."

There's a pause long enough for me to let out the breath I've been holding since he answered the phone.

"Mrs. Crawford, unfortunately I'm out of town right now, but I'll be back on Wednesday," he continues in the same impersonal voice. "We have two options. I can send my partner Detective Kim over to your home this afternoon to speak with you, or I can come by as soon as I get back. If there is anything urgent about your concerns, I suggest we go with the first option."

All the permutations, the ones he mentioned and the ones he didn't, are running through my mind. Today won't work—Elena will leave for church soon and I don't want to have to tell Sam everything just to get him to watch the kids for me. "This afternoon I really can't. Could your partner come tomorrow morning? How early could he get here?"

"He can be there at 8:00 a.m. Are you sure there's nothing we need to discuss right now?"

"No, tomorrow morning is great. I'll see him then, thank you!" I answer lightly, as if I've just made a manicure appointment. I hang up and take a deep breath. Sam always leaves for work around 7:15, so he'll be safely out of the house. I could have asked to meet Detective Bryan's partner at a police station or a coffee shop, but I think it's a good thing if Jeff notices an unusual car in our driveway. My hope is to keep him hesitating.

Coming out of the closet, I realize someone is knocking softly on the bedroom door.

"Miss Alexis? Can I come in?" Elena's muffled voice comes through from the other side, even as the door itself starts to open slowly. I should have locked it.

"I'm done Elena, sorry to make you late for church."

"It's okay. This is for your head." She reaches up toward my forehead with some kind of herbal poultice cradled in her hands. "It will help your skin heal and not make a scar. All natural, my grandmother taught me how."

I accept her offering and should respond with a hug, but instead I snap, "Thanks for doing this, but you should be paying attention to the children, not to me, okay? Where are they right now?"

She shrinks back toward the bedroom door, offended, and I immediately regret it.

"Let's go down together," I say, poultice in hand, hurrying to follow her out. The only answer I get is the whine and groan of the steps as we descend.

/ 11:00 PM

The day passed in a blur. Sam kept looking at me sideways, silently, as if he were sizing up my story and trying to decide whether to believe it. The children were mercifully calm, and while they napped I fell into a deep, black sleep on the floor of Carter's nursery. I'd woken up with Caleb squeezing my nose and Sam standing in the doorway, staring down at me suspiciously with Carter in his arms. We'd gotten through the evening—playing in the backyard, ordering Thai for dinner as a special concession to myself, and the bedtime routine—without speaking more than a few transactional words.

After putting Carter down, I'd found Sam slipping his shoes on in the foyer. He said he was going out for a drink with a friend, some guy whose name didn't sound familiar. But I know he really went out to speed around country roads in the BMW, risking a ticket or even worse an accident for a chance to burn off his frustration. This is not uncommon for him, but around 10:00 I started to worry.

I haven't called because he has no right to be mad at me. But I can't activate the alarm until he comes home, which means I really shouldn't fall asleep. I've checked every door and window lock four times, drank three shots of espresso, and pulled two steak knives out of the butcher block. The front door seems too obvious, and Elena is in the basement, so I decide to focus my attention on the only other exterior door—to the back patio. I brew myself another espresso and curl up in an armchair facing the patio doors, with a knife carefully tucked into the cushion next to my right hand. There's nothing much to do but wait. My stomach is churning and I can't bring myself to drink this fourth shot. Next to the demitasse on the coffee table, my cell phone sits reassuringly, and I pick it up and pass some time dialing and erasing "911" over and over again.

If Jeff is going to try and hurt me tonight, I'm ready. But

what if it's not tonight? The thought of doing this every night, indefinitely, is crushing. The armchair's low barrel back makes it impossible to find a comfortable position. Finally, I settle on slumping down low enough for my head to rest on the hard side. I remember the fight Sam and I had in the store, about whether to buy the floor models, when I was so caught up in imagining how elevated our life would be here. Funny to think about that now. This house, this neighborhood, this family—it feels like more than I can handle, and just staying alive is exhausting. My eyes close, and I tell myself it's only for a moment.

His large, firm hand is on the back of my neck. The weight of it is what woke me up, but it was so subtle that I realized before opening my eyes. Thank God. My only advantage is surprise. I try to keep my breathing steady and feel for the knife. My knuckles brush against the cold metal sticking out of the cushion and slowly, slowly I take hold of the handle and count to three. I don't know which comes first—my eyes opening, my left hand grabbing his forearm and my whole body pivoting, or my right hand plunging down with the knife. It's all over in a breath, and I look up and realize it's Sam. He's yelling, but I can barely hear him over the blood in my ears.

"Alexis, what the fuck! What is wrong with you?" he says, not for the first time today.

The steak knife is deeply embedded near the top of the chair's curved back.

"Oh my God, it's you," I say quietly. "I thought you were Jeff."

"Why in the hell would I be Jeff? What is going on? You've been acting insane since last night." He's yelling at me now.

It's enough to make me confess. "I should have told you this morning, but something really bad happened."

Monday / July 21 / 7:00 AM

A siren pierces through the depths of early morning sleep to reach me. I haven't set an alarm in months, one of the few luxuries of maternity leave, and forgot how awful the default sound is. The children are still sleeping, but Sam is already downstairs. He was incredulous at my story last night. I could see the surprise sparkling in his eyes and the corners of his mouth twitching in an effort not to smile as I recounted the whole absurd series of events. His reaction made me angry, but also relieved, as if his amusement meant that it wasn't so scary after all.

When I told him that it wasn't funny, he'd said, *"Really? Are you listening to what you're saying?"* and followed me just inside the kitchen doorway, leaning against it with his arms crossed and watching me while I put the knives back in their block. *"Who would have thought this neighborhood would be chock-full of weirdos."*

We'd both started laughing, and he'd come up behind me for a hug. *"You should've told me earlier, you must have been terrified. Anyway, you did the right thing by calling that cop. If Jeff is crazy enough to do that, who the hell knows what else he's done,"* he'd said as he wrapped his long arms around me. I'd felt safe and re-laxed, and actually slept well.

But this morning the dread of having to recount the story again is heavy on my chest, and I press the snooze button and turn my body to stare out the window. The children will wake up any minute, and Detective Kim is coming at 8:00, which is the same time that Elena ascends from the basement. If I'm not dressed quickly, I risk having to talk to him with unbrushed teeth and in my ratty old T-shirt. This is enough to make me drag my-self out of bed and into the bathroom. By the time I come out, Caleb is in my room, trying to open dresser drawers, and I can hear Carter screaming in her nursery. We haven't childproofed anything in this house, besides the stupid chair in front of the window, and my heart skips a beat when I see him tugging intently at a drawer knob. The three of us manage to make it downstairs and into the kitchen for breakfast just as Elena opens the basement door.

I am halfway through giving her instructions for the week when the doorbell rings.

"I have a short meeting right now," I explain apologetically and run to open the front door.

Detective Kim is not at all like his partner. He is older, taller, and the waves of his thick black hair shine in the early morning sun. I find myself silently playing the guessing game again, this time with East Asian countries.

"Good morning, are you Mrs. Crawford?" he asks, with gravel in his deep voice.

"Hi, yes, that's me—please call me Alexis. Come in!" I answer, too brightly, and move aside to wave him in.

"Thanks so much for coming, can I get you some coffee or water?" I offer as I lead him to the living room.

"No thanks, I appreciate it though," he says as he settles in on the armchair I'd stabbed last night. He's too tall for the chair, and I offer to switch seats with him. "Don't worry, this is perfectly fine. Now, I'm here to listen, so please, go ahead." He leans forward with elbows on knees and hands clasped, holding my gaze. In this position, the short sleeves of his black T-shirt are pulled taut by his tanned biceps. Korean, that would be my first guess. I wonder what he would guess about me.

I dig my fingernails into my palms to focus. "Well, Detective, this is a pretty strange story. It's embarrassing actually, and I'm not sure it has anything at all to do with the murder. But it was scary, and my husband and I felt like the police should be informed. So, apologies in advance if this turns out to be a complete waste of your time."

Detective Kim hasn't moved. He is just looking at me intently, waiting to get past the disclaimers and to the point. I hate myself for letting this happen while Detective Bryan is out of town—I wouldn't have cared if he were the one here, listening to my idiocy. But he's not, so I take another deep breath to summon my courage and walk Detective Kim through how I spent this last Saturday. Listening to my own story makes me cringe. I sound desperate and impulsive—looking for trouble, like a teenager.

I get through it all quickly, and end with more excuses. "I know how ridiculous this all sounds. I don't know what I was thinking, channeling my inner Nancy Drew was a bad idea I guess." I try to laugh, but it comes out more like a cough.

Detective Kim gives me a small smile and leans back awkwardly to consider what I've just said. These chairs were such a bad choice. I make a mental note to start looking for replacements.

"Mrs. Crawford, well that must have been quite a shock to you. Do you mind if I ask a few questions?" he asks as he pulls a small notebook out of his jeans pocket. This is the first sign I've seen that he and Bryan are really partners.

"Of course not, please, ask me anything."

"Can you tell me, have you ever interacted with this neighbor, Jeff, before?" he asks.

"Very little actually, we barely know each other."

"And do you have any specific reason to think this may be connected to Theodore Bard's case?" he continues, pen poised over a blank page. My eyes stay on his hands as he starts scribbling. He is left-handed, and not wearing a wedding ring.

"No. I just thought that there might be a chance. I mean, how many violent men can one neighborhood really have?" I offer lamely.

We are alone on the main floor—Elena had discreetly ushered the children upstairs as we settled into the living room. In the silence, I can hear his pen scratching at the paper. He asks me a few more questions, about the gardening saw, about what I have and haven't seen. I consider telling him about Emily's suspicions but hold my tongue. Somewhere, far in the back of my mind, I think it could be a reason to see him again.

"Well, thank you for calling. We'll definitely look into it. But a separate question is whether you want to move forward with filing a police report for the assault. According to what we've discussed, it seems that you were on your own property when your neighbor—"

"Oh goodness, no, I didn't call to report this as a crime. No, I just wanted to give you the information because of Teddy's murder," I interrupt. I could just imagine the types of lawyers Jeff would hire, and how much money he would pay them to discredit and embarrass me. And we would have to move.

His nearly archless eyebrows rise to ask for an explanation.

"I just, I shouldn't have been out there, and I don't want to make a scene out of this. If he's really a bad guy, then I'm sure you'll figure it out."

He pauses before answering, "I understand Mrs. Crawford. But I'd like you to consider taking pictures of yourself, of the injuries you've sustained, just in case you change your mind."

"I won't . . . I mean, we just bought this house last year, and I can't. It was probably all a misunderstanding anyway."

What I'm saying is ridiculous, we both know it, but he is kind.

"Well, like I said, if you change your mind, or think of anything else, please don't hesitate to give Detective Bryan or me a call."

He smiles at me as he stands up, the corners of his eyes crinkling to tell me he's probably in his mid-forties at least. I wonder if he really isn't married.

"Could I have your card? In case I need to call you?"

He fishes one out of another pocket and hands it to me with one last smile, warm and—I'm imagining this, I'm sure—faintly interested.

"All right then, I'll be going."

I hurry to follow him and remain shamelessly in the doorway, watching his black sedan pull out of our driveway. I must be losing my mind. Attraction is something I haven't felt toward any man but Sam since before I can remember, and I couldn't have picked a more ridiculous moment. Beat up, with two tiny children, and a husband—who would be interested in that?

More importantly, even if Sam is awful sometimes, even if we sank ourselves into this endlessly demanding house, we are still in it together. That's the whole point of marriage. My mother's life was a cautionary tale of miserably going it alone, and I have no intention of repeating her mistakes. The pathetic opening lines of the oldest letter, postmarked December 1978, come to me as I look out now at our quiet street, Detective Kim's sedan long gone. *It is one year since I left. I have heard nothing from you, and I miss you. We have a beautiful baby girl. She looks like you, and you would love her. If your divorce is finished, I think you should be ready now to meet her. . . .* I'd ripped it into thumbnail-size pieces, along with the others—twenty-five in all, dutifully spaced six months apart over seventeen years, minus a handful of gaps— and thrown them by the fistful into the half-filled trash can in my suddenly dead mother's little kitchen. After that, I remember taking all the food out of her fridge and dumping it on top of the paper scraps, to make sure no one would read her mortifying pleas. Unnecessary, I knew it even then, because no one cared.

No, I've got to talk myself out of Detective Kim—as if I could ever talk him into me. All I can hope for is that he is as competent as he is handsome, or at least smart enough to unearth whatever still buried chain connects the links together. Yesterday, as I was reapplying ointment to my forehead and popping painkillers every few hours, I'd cursed Emily for being so wrong. But before falling asleep, I'd realized that Dylan could be sleeping with Blair and Jennifer at the same time. It seems far-fetched, but not impossible, especially given Emily's comments about his threesome ideas. Teddy could have confronted him violently, as Jeff seems to be planning, and lost. Or maybe Blair and Jeff have a relationship, and Jeff is the murderer. But this seems much less plausible—Jeff was so upset about Jennifer, and more importantly I can't picture Blair having any interest in someone so unappealing.

No matter which sordid story is true, I've become an unwitting bystander, luckily caught in the woods instead of on the trail. Before closing the door, I step out with one foot and stretch my head to look down the block. At the very least, I hope Jeff was home to notice my visitor.

Blair

I saw Detective Kim leaving their house earlier this morning. I'm glad she finally decided to call. My money's on Emily being the garden saw thief, and if she's unhinged to the point of stealing potential weapons, she really needs help. Maybe she thinks poor Alexis is the one fucking her husband now. What a stupid woman. She has no clue, what it's like having a kid. Watching your body sigh and sag in defeat, your hair fall out in clumps, your whole world reorder itself in service of its new master. No sane woman with a newborn is out fucking someone else's husband. Certainly not Alexis.

A text pops up on my phone as I finish rearranging the bar cart in the sitting room. "Met with Detective Kim this morning. Told him everything. He said they'll investigate."

I wonder what she means by everything. A meal will give us enough time to get the whole story out, so I quickly write back. "Wow. Come over for lunch and tell me all about it?"

No answer for at least three minutes. I wonder why she's

thinking about it for so long. Finally, her reply, "I can't today. I'm sorry. How about tomorrow?"

I smile down at the screen and confirm for 12:30.

TUESDAY / JULY 22 / 12:30 PM

Alexis hesitates at the threshold, calling my name. I left the door wide open so she could let herself in, and I'm slightly annoyed to have to put down an armful of takeout boxes and hurry to greet her. The food arrived late, so I haven't had time to transfer it to real dishes.

She's come with a double dozen bouquet of white roses and holds it out to me with both hands when I reach the foyer. "I wanted to bring something, you're always so kind to invite me over. My house is a mess, but I'll definitely return the favor soon," she says sheepishly.

White roses are the last thing I want to see again, but I give her a grin and a hug, then pull back to look at her face. She's got makeup on, but concealer can't hide the nasty patch above her right eye.

"Alexis, what in the hell happened to you?" I ask with one hand still on her shoulder and the other holding the heavy bouquet.

"This past Saturday night I ran into Jeff, and he was drunk." The faint tremor in her voice tells me she's still upset about it.

"Let's get drinks before you finish this story. Sauv Blanc to take the edge off?" and I lead her to the kitchen by the hand.

"Okay keep going, what did Jeff do to you, that bastard?" I ask after we've had a few sips at the island.

Alexis sighs deeply before answering. "He was so drunk, he

slammed me into a tree. He was angry. Did you know that Jennifer and Dylan—"

"Are fucking each other? Yes," I interrupt.

"Well Jeff knows too, he watches them from the trees between our houses. I've seen him out there before, but in the shadows, not clearly. I thought it was Shawn again and just wanted to know why he was out there."

"So you took it upon yourself to confront whichever guy was creepily lurking outside your house?"

"I know, I didn't mean to confront him. He saw me first." She covers her face with her hands, carefully avoiding her wound. "I'm a total wreck now. What if he thinks I know too much and he tries to come back and hurt me? Or the kids?"

"He won't. Jeff is just a jackass, taking his frustrations out on you. But he's not a criminal. You don't have anything to do with his problems, and he knows that. I'm sure nothing else will happen, seriously."

"God, this is such a mess. How did you know about Jennifer and Dylan? To be honest, I thought he had a thing for you, that night Emily had us over for drinks."

A sip of wine gets caught in my throat, and I have to cough before answering. "Why does everyone think that? Listen, he's a shameless flirt, but I shut him down pretty quickly. Absolutely not my type."

"Really? He's so attractive, and, I don't know, seductive? But clearly he knows he is."

I can't help myself. "Well Laura would agree with that. This is all her fucking fault."

"Laura? What does she have to do with it?" Alexis lowers her hands and looks up at me. The whites of her big brown eyes and the tip of her nose are the same miserable shade of pink. I decide there's no reason not to tell her the story.

"As hard as it is to imagine, Laura has had a thing for Dylan since he moved here. She used to fawn over him in the most obvious way, and he'd flirt right back. It was laughable, but innocent enough, until she caught him having sex with Jennifer *in her very own master bedroom* during the neighborhood's Adult Halloween party last year." This last part is fun to say.

Alexis's mouth is hanging slightly open. "Are you serious? How do you know all this?"

"Because I was the first person Laura ran into, in the hallway after she walked in on them. I told her to calm down and keep it to herself. To just throw out the sheets and move on. It's not like he's *her* husband. She pulled it together that night, but then exposing them became her obsession. She and Shawn have upgraded their security camera system three times since that party. What do you think that's for?" I raise my eyebrows at her across the island.

"To record Dylan going to Jennifer's house?" Alexis asks, clearly incredulous. I guess wherever she used to live wasn't this exciting.

"Of course. Laura must be the one who tipped off Jeff and sent him into this ridiculous frenzy. She could have just told Emily a long time ago, but she's a vindictive bitch. I'm sure she was hoping Jeff would do something crazy and hurt them both, but instead you got caught in the middle."

"Wait but why was Shawn helping her? How does that make any sense?"

My smile must look so condescending, but I can't help it.

"Shawn has no idea. You know how hard it is to see what's right under your nose?"

My phone starts buzzing before Alexis can answer. It's the kids' camp, so I excuse myself to answer. All three of them were so angry when I dropped them off a couple of weeks ago, I've been afraid they would do something awful on purpose to get sent home. Especially Whit, he's a counselor this year and the hormones are just oozing off of him. I'd stuffed a box of condoms into his duffle bag and warned him on the drive up that if he had sex, it had better be with a girl at least as old as him.

As I walk to my office to answer, I look over my shoulder and ask, "Lex, can you do me a favor? Those beautiful roses you brought need to get into water. Can you grab one of the big vases from the china closet? It's the third door on the left past the back staircase."

Alexis smiles and gets up from her seat at the island, eager to help, but even at a distance I can see that it costs her. She must still be aching from her run-in with Jeff, and I should tell her to forget it. But she's already walking toward the closet, and I don't want to miss the call.

It's not what I thought, thankfully. It's Whit calling to tell me that he won all the races yesterday during counselor sports day, and that the kids really miss me, and their dad. I close my eyes and try to keep my voice even for him. "Don't worry honey, I'll be up there to pick you up in a couple of weeks, and we'll have a great time at the beach. Are there any cute girls working up there with you?" We stay on the phone for a few minutes. I know it's rude to keep Alexis waiting, but I don't want to let go of Whit's warm voice. It sounds so much like Teddy's did at the beginning. Too soon, he says he has to go.

After he's hung up, I keep the phone up to my ear for a

minute, reluctant to admit he's gone. When I finally come out of my office and walk back down the hall, I see that the kitchen is empty. I turn and see her in the family room, absorbed in our photo wall. "Lex?"

"Oh I'm just right here!" she says, almost startled, and quickly comes back into the kitchen. "I put the vase next to your prep sink."

"Everything okay?" I ask, suddenly suspicious that there may be something she hasn't told me.

"Sorry, I'm still on edge from Saturday night, everything makes me jump," she apologizes as she reaches her fingers up to her wound and blinks too fast, making her thick lashes flutter. Despite the bad clothes, and today's bruises, she really is a good-looking woman. I want to invite her to my Pilates class, or out for a shopping trip. Something to help her find her self-confidence. But now is obviously not the moment for that, so I just smile and lead her out to the patio.

Later, a few minutes after she's gone home, a picture pops up on my phone. It's six bouquets of yellow roses on Alexis's front steps. She texts after it, "Can you believe this? There's no note, but . . ."

I write back right away. "You see? I told you. At least he's a jackass with some manners."

Alexis

What exactly did I learn at Blair's house? I've been turning this over in my mind for nearly twenty-four hours. When she invited me over, I'd decided to push even if it risked being obvious, to get a clear sense of her relationships with Dylan and Jeff. But then we got interrupted by a call from her son, and she'd asked me to fetch her a vase. I didn't consciously decide to open all the doors. I'd just miscounted and found myself staring into a linen closet. At first, I thought it was strange, a linen closet on the main floor, but then I realized it was a closet of table linens, not sheets and towels. Four wide shelves of neatly folded cloth napkins and table runners—by the hints of color peeking out at me I could tell that they were organized by season, with pastels above eye level, followed by bright whites and neutrals for summer, then earth tones with metallic embellishments, and Christmas red and green around my knees.

There were also accessories—a set of cut crystal bunny place card holders on the spring shelf, gold leaf napkin rings, each with a finely detailed spray of acorns and leaves on the autumn shelf. The now familiar wave of envy came, and I let my eyes wander over the colors and textures and details. I could imagine Blair and Teddy sitting close together at the kitchen island over plans for a gorgeous meal, whittling down the list of eager attendees to a few select guests. I wondered what she'd do with all of this now. Put it back to good use, eventually, and maybe remarry.

Before closing the door, my eyes swept up and down the shelves, taking one last appreciative look at Blair's seasonal adornments, and that's when I saw them. On the very top shelf, above the crystal bunnies, and invisible outside the closet frame, the plastic-shine edge of a box I recognized was sticking out just past a neat stack of tablecloths. The baby blue and pink motif brought me back to three years ago, and I reached up to touch the box without thinking. From my tiptoes, I managed to pull it out, and see an identical one behind it, deep into the shelf and also still in its shrink-wrap.

Two at-home genetic tests, the spit-into-the-tube and learn-fun-things-about-yourself kind, never used and stored in a closet of table linens. Unwillingly, my mind went to the wall of pictures in Blair's family room, and I rushed to finish my task, trying every other door along the hallway until I found the closet reserved for multiple china sets and a shelf full of vases at the bottom.

I'd had about two minutes to look at the photos again before she came back, long enough to be sure that my impression from a few weeks ago hadn't been wrong. Birthday parties, formal portraits, children being born—through it all, there were Blair and Teddy looking like cousins, maybe even siblings. The same blue-gray eyes, the same smile—the right side of their mouths going up slightly higher than the left. If I hadn't met Blair's brother on the 4th, I might have assumed this was him.

We'd had a lovely lunch. Blair ordered a whole spread from the gourmet grocer a couple of miles away, too much food for two people, and laid an all-white table on the patio, under a vine-covered pergola with two ceiling fans that I hadn't noticed last time I was there. When we sat down, I accepted a second golden glass of wine and pretended to sip, barely letting the liquid touch my lips. For the first time since Blair and I had become friends, I found myself not worrying about how she saw me, and instead scrutinizing her. We talked about her children, about the landscaping, and about my meeting with Detective Kim. I carefully described what I'd told him and what he'd responded, pushing to really make sure she wasn't concerned about Jeff, or Dylan. She clearly wasn't. After she offered to top up my glass a third time, I said I needed to get back. We sat looking at each other for a moment, and it felt like she was waiting for me to say something. I ignored it, thanked her for lunch, and crossed the street back to my house.

Why did a handful of photos on a wall and two unopened genetic tests, squirreled away in a closet, spark such a strong suspicion? I might just be assuming the worst because of my own shameful family history. A year after Sam and I got married, I'd bought us two of those same tests for Christmas. We'd talked about having children, and I was feeling the weight of the blank space where half my family should have been.

The emailed results had told each of us what we'd already known. Sam was a classic American mutt, with a color-coded map of Western and Eastern European genes that provided scientific support for the family history he already knew well. I, on the other hand, was the full global rainbow, bits and pieces of every continent in my blood. Some of it, like my Chinese maternal great-great-grandmother who'd immigrated first to Mexico and somehow ended up in Honduras, I'd heard of. Some of it, the 50 percent European part, stared back at me like a taunt. I'd known, of course, that my father was white. And even if I hadn't already figured out who he was, an Anglicized version of my mother—the same round face, just with lighter skin and a narrower nose—stared back at me in the mirror every day. The tests were new then, with their most disturbing features still nascent, so there was little else they could tell us. Neither Sam nor I had any of the few genetic abnormalities they could catch, and the section under "identified genetic relatives" was blank for both of us.

But having the basics in email attachment detail—written out and charted and definitive—had sent me to a dark place that I couldn't manage to snap out of. After a few days, Sam had gotten tired of me moping around and insisted that I try to call my father. He pushed me really, knowing I'd found and kept his phone number for years without ever dialing it. I said it was certain the man wouldn't react well, that there was no point. Sam wouldn't listen, and even offered to sit with me and listen on speakerphone, as moral support. I should have refused, but we were newlyweds and I hadn't yet learned to really say no. I'd also never told him about the letters, and still didn't want to.

We called on a Saturday morning from our living room, which in our tiny apartment was also the dining room and kitchen. My hands were shaking as I set the phone down in front of us on the cheap pleather ottoman-cum-coffee table. An old woman's voice answered on the fourth ring, just as I'd started hoping no one was home.

"Hello, hi, may I please speak to Anthony Simpson?" I'd stammered.

A long pause before the old woman answered with a sigh. "Anthony died three months ago. Who is this?"

Panicked, I looked at Sam for what to do next, but he just gave me a useless smile.

"I'm so sorry. My name is Alexis. I . . . my mother used to work for him."

"I see." The woman sounded warmer now. "Anthony had so many loyal employees, there were nearly a hundred people at his funeral. Was your mother able to go?"

"No, she passed away a few years ago. I—"

"Oh I'm sorry to hear that. What was your mother's name, dear?"

"Raisa Rodriguez. She did clerical work in the 1970s—"

"Oh, Lord God Almighty," the old woman interrupted me with a groan. "I thought it was done after all this time. Why did you lie about your name?" But she didn't stop long enough for me to answer. "Please, don't call again. There's nothing here for you. He's gone. Don't call ever again," she repeated herself, and then hung up.

I'd kept my eyes down on the phone, my whole body burning with embarrassment, so I wouldn't have to see the look of pity, soured with a flicker of suspicion, on Sam's face. I know he was imagining how my mother and I had ruined this bitter old woman's marriage, haunting her life with our desperation long after the affair ended.

"Now can you see why I didn't want to call?" I'd said after a few minutes. He'd tried to put his arm around my shoulders, telling me it was okay and asking what she meant, but I'd shaken him off and walked away. The shame was mine alone to bear.

Years before, a few days before my freshman year of college officially began, my mother dropped me off at the Greyhound station. It was the last time I'd see her. We talked every few weeks, but she never came to visit—she said that she was too busy with work, that she was saving up money to come for my graduation. And I never went home over the breaks. We had barely been speaking since I'd turned thirteen, when puberty had let the rage bubble up through the fear and I'd grabbed the belt from her and threatened to run away. That was enough to make her stop spanking me for minor transgressions—refusing to do the laundry because I had too much homework, cursing at her for not giving me $20 for a school party because she didn't have it but wouldn't let me get a job for fear it would lower my grades. It was an empty threat of course, because I was a smart child. I'd seen *America's Most Wanted* and harbored no delusions that anything better was waiting for me—my mother sent me to school and made sure I was always fed, clothed, and sheltered. That she did it without affection, joy, honesty, or whatever else should have been there between a mother and a daughter is what made it so unbearable.

Arriving on campus alone, I'd realized pretty quickly that two dead parents were a far easier conversation than an estranged mother and an unconfirmed father. It was also convenient to say that my mother had died during senior year of high school, after a courageous but short bout with cancer. Long weekends, Christmas, spring break—it all went so smoothly, once I learned to ignore my dorm mates' pitying glances over their shoulders as they hurried to catch their flights and got used to the singularly creepy quiet of a college campus disgorged of its young residents. But whenever I want to kill my appetite, I can still just pull up the memory of sitting alone in the only open dining hall, eating the semester's leftovers with a bewildered-looking crew of international students and miserable doctoral candidates. I knew my mother would never show up at parents' weekend, but I was a little surprised at how easy it was to shed her. Dead and gone, existing only in short, furtive phone calls and in my administrative records as a couple of checked boxes and a name, a mother who was too poor to contribute anything anyway.

It wasn't until Sam's graduation day, at the end of my junior year, that my story changed. After Sam's parents had taken us out to dinner and gone back to their hotel, we finished packing up his dorm room and headed down to his new apartment in Manhattan. Near the end of the drive, as we sped down I-95 somewhere around New Rochelle, I'd gotten a call that my mother was in the hospital. After getting the details, I kept the phone to my ear pretending the other line hadn't hung up, considering what to tell Sam. My mind wouldn't come up with a lie that I wouldn't likely get caught in, so I slowly flipped the phone closed and explained that I was not, in fact, an orphan. At least not yet. I'm still not sure why I brought her back to life—in hindsight, I could have easily invented a dying old friend or distant relative. Maybe because I was disoriented from the exhilaration of the day—the relief of feeling like his parents truly accepted me, the comfort of being a normal student celebrating graduation with a normal family over steak—running headlong into the brick wall of my past. He was more upset than I'd anticipated.

"What the hell Alexis? How am I supposed to react to that? Are you a compulsive liar or what?" He was looking at me instead of the highway and started veering onto the shoulder.

I grabbed the steering wheel and told him that he needed to focus on the road, that I hadn't lied about anything else, and that if he ever met her, he'd understand why I preferred her to be dead.

"What are my mom and dad going to think?" This seemed to really upset him. The previous Thanksgiving, Sam invited me home with him and briefed his parents well—they never asked about my family beyond the town I grew up in, and I loved them for it.

"Please don't tell your parents," I'd said. He didn't respond for three exits, but finally muttered, "I won't, they'd never get over it. Just make sure you don't lie to me ever again."

We drove straight to the Port Authority that night, and Sam drove away without waving—I got on a red-eye bus to Baltimore and to my mother's hospital bed around 5:00 a.m. She'd collapsed from a massive heart attack at work. I waited outside her room while they pulled her off all the machines and she died. She wasn't even fifty years old.

Later the same morning, alone in her apartment, I found that stack of unopened letters, marked "return to sender" and held together with two rubber bands, under her bed. The sender was my mother and the uninterested receiver was Anthony Simpson. I recognized his name immediately and ripped open the letter at the top of the pile, postmarked just a few years earlier in December 1996, in almost eager desperation. My mother and I had never spoken about him, not a word, and I was so hungry for information. It was a single page, handwritten in her elaborate, old-fashioned cursive. *This is the last letter I will write to you. Flor is now eighteen years old. She is enjoying her first semester in college and says she might major in economics. I know she will excel at whatever she chooses, she is very strong-minded as I said before . . .*

The first few sentences were enough to make my stomach turn, but I forced myself to read it all, every letter, from the end to the beginning. From June 1996, *Flor has received a full scholarship to Yale University. I am so proud of her, it is a big accomplishment . . .* Even though it was technically a scholarship plus financial aid, and I'd never heard such positive words actually come out of her mouth. From December 1994, *Flor won second place in the state mathematics tournament, you should have been there . . .* Even though she herself hadn't been there, because she wouldn't take the time off work to come to Annapolis . . . From December 1989, *Her teachers all say that she is extremely bright and should go to a private high school to realize her potential. We cannot afford it, but some of them have scholarships . . .* From June 1984, *Our daughter is very beautiful and asks about her father all the time. I wish I could tell her that he is a good man who loves her, but you have been ignoring me, and her, for so long . . .*

Many of the envelopes looked like they'd been carefully opened and resealed with tape. An occasional line hinted at hope that some letters had actually been kept, and not lost by the postal system in this prolonged back-and-forth. I didn't know how to decipher any of it—maybe he'd read each one but kept only a few, maybe his wife had, or maybe they'd ignored them all. Maybe my mother had started calling once I left for college, or maybe she'd finally gotten the hint and stopped trying.

Regardless, it was infuriating. She'd said more in these pleas to a man who clearly didn't care than she had ever told me in all the years we lived within a few hundred square feet of each other. I couldn't understand why she held on to him for so long, wasting her time year after year carefully documenting our lives in her stiff, error-free English. Every letter was the same—a single page, the first two thirds devoted to me and the last third about her, mostly how hard she was working and how hard things were in general. None of them asked for money, or anything else, really, besides contact. What could she have hoped to accomplish this way? I'd felt so disgusted as I'd ripped them up, more ashamed of who my parents were than I'd ever been before. And that had been the end of it, until Sam and I took the genetic tests. Bright little boxes to shine lights in dark corners I'd tried to forget existed.

All of this—memories I haven't thought about in years—came flooding into my mind yesterday. I'd tried to distract myself by thinking through all that's happened since Teddy's murder, but somehow his story—his and Blair's—feels wrapped up with mine. Maybe too many intrusive questions from the grocery store clerks when my mother took me shopping have made me paranoid, but I can't let go of the fact that Blair's brother looked nothing at all like her, while her husband did.

After getting Carter down last night, I'd used up my last bits of energy to crawl into bed next to Sam but couldn't fall asleep. I just lay there, one arm up against the warmth of Sam's back, my eyes closed with scenes of the summer replaying in my mind. When I finally drifted off, I'd had a horrible dream that we were back on Brad's yacht, at another glittering party, but the decks were swarming with flies and all the guests were panicking and jumping overboard into the dark river. I decided to jump too, and the feeling of the bottom falling out of the pit of my stomach jolted me out of sleep at 6:00. Sam was gone, out for a morning run before work. I could feel the humid air already seeping through the picture window, dampening the curtains, along with the glow of the sunrise, and made a mental note to remind him about the railing he's supposed to build.

Now, Sam has gone to work and Elena's taken the children to the park, so I go into the office and fish my laptop out of the corner. I move Sam's careful piles aside and sit down at the desk, but then think better of it. If I'm going to cyberstalk my neighbors, I probably shouldn't do it on my work computer. Once I find my tablet and settle into a corner of the couch in the den, I open a new anonymous browser window and start searching.

At first, the only thing that occurs to me is to type in their names. But Blair and Teddy Bard just turn up what I already know. Links to Teddy's obituary, social news mentioning the Bards at fundraisers, some political articles about the state legislature. I hesitate, then slowly click through to each link that seems relevant, wandering around the bowels of the internet. Here they are in black tie, mid-cheers in a small group of middle-age couples, at a charity gala in D.C. Here is a headshot of Teddy on his firm's website, smiling with handsome authority. With no need to hurry, I examine the pictures, zooming the screen in as far as it will go. The resemblance is unmistakable. The way the left eye squints more than the right when they smile, the sandy tint to their blond hair—there are even more similarities now that I am looking for them than I'd noticed in the pictures on Blair's family room wall.

Then it comes back to me. I had sent my mother one piece of mail during college in a pathetic attempt at communicating my anger. After reading John Locke for a political philosophy course my junior spring, I'd gone to the bookstore, bought a ninety-nine-cent postcard of campus, and written only one sentence before addressing it to her. *Parents wonder why the streams are bitter, when they themselves have poisoned the fountain.* It sat in my nightstand for the rest of the semester, waiting for a stamp and the courage that wouldn't come, so I never got the chance to mail it.

I won't get anywhere searching for information on Blair and Teddy. If my suspicions are right, it's their parents I should be searching for. My fingers tap the edges of the screen impatiently, willing my foggy brain to remember something about them. What was Blair's mother's first name? She hadn't deigned to introduce herself on the 4th, but Blair had. "This is my mother, Beryl," she'd smiled at Sam and me in the driveway before we'd piled into her Range Rover and driven to the marina in awkward silence. I have no idea what Blair's maiden name is, but they must have had a wedding announcement. Sam had wanted to submit our wedding to *The New York Times*, but I'd refused, claiming it was too obviously striving to be who we weren't. The truth is I would have done it, but for the fact that they required listing parents' names and occupations.

Just a few clicks through the Style section, to the Weddings and Engagements, and a quick search brings up Teddy and Blair's announcement, from June 1996 when I was nineteen and graduating from high school:

> Blair Spencer Edwards, the daughter of Mr. and Mrs. Robert F. Edwards IV of Lower Merion, Penn., was married yesterday to Theodore Davis Bard, a son of the late Dr. and Mrs. James L. Bard of Ithaca. The Rev. Jefferson Ames performed the ceremony at St. Bartholomew's Episcopal Church in New York.
>
> Mrs. Bard, 27, is a design assistant at Muse & Co., an interior design firm in New York. She graduated from Bryn Mawr College. Her father is the chairman of the board and former CEO of Edwards Engineering, a global power equipment manufacturer with headquarters in New York and Hong Kong. The company was founded in 1902 by the bride's great-grandfather Mr. Robert F. Edwards after serving as Secretary of the Navy in Grover Cleveland's second administration.

Mr. Bard, 29, is a legislative aide to Congressman Bruce Sherwood, a Republican representing the 23rd congressional district of New York. He graduated from Cornell University. His father served as chairman of the department of chemistry at the university from 1970 to 1989, and as a president of the American Chemical Society in 1985. Mr. Bard's grandfather, Whitney Theodore White, served as Lieutenant Governor of New York from 1920 to 1922.

A simple and matter-of-fact announcement, no endearing tidbits about the happenstance of their meeting, but enough detail to convey what mattered. Two prosperous, old-money families coming together to continue the tradition. My eyes scan over the lines of the announcement again, searching for something else that is missing besides endearing details—their mothers. They could have at least included their first names. I wonder what Beryl Edwards thought of this. A bright, would-have-been scientist barely even acknowledged in the wedding announcement of the daughter she'd given everything up for. Blair had said her mother was a chemistry major at Cornell when she'd gotten pregnant. My mother had been a secretary in the office of an auto parts company before she'd had me. I only know this because I once found a stiff, faded brochure for the company in the back of a kitchen drawer and asked her about it. She was doing dishes at the sink and answered me without thinking, but after a moment she snatched away the brochure with her hands still soapy and threw it in the garbage can.

I was maybe ten or eleven years old, and burning with curiosity about all the things that went unsaid. So that night, after I was sure she was asleep, I'd tiptoed back into the kitchen and fished the brochure out from under a greasy chicken skin. I'd carefully wiped it off with a wet paper towel and then hid it in the corner of my closet, behind old stuffed animals, with my diary. Having a distant mother made it easy to keep my own secrets, and the brochure stayed safely hidden away until I decided to do something with it. Right before my twelfth birthday, I took the brochure to the public library and asked the least intimidating librarian there to help me find out about the company. I told her the truth, that my mother used to work there and that I wanted to know more about it, and I remember the vertical wrinkles in the middle of her small forehead as she thought about what to do.

An hour of bound business directory volumes, tiny card catalogue drawers, and microfilm later, I knew as much as I ever would. The company, Anthony's Auto Parts, had been a leading area business since the 1960s, and its founder and owner, Anthony Simpson, was still a director of the chamber of commerce. His picture had been in the local newspaper a half dozen times over the years, but all it took was the first grainy photo jerking into the magnified frame of the microfilm reader. He was standing in front of his first store location, in a baseball cap, with a big grin on his face. There was something so familiar about the set of his jaw and the way he cocked his head, but my prepubescent mind didn't want to make the connection. Over time though, without trying, the realization took shape, and I knew, as if I had always known, that Anthony Simpson must be my father.

All those years later, when Sam and I took the genetic tests, the words of my mother's letters silently filled my mouth, pushing down into my throat, gagging me. Whatever had gone on between them, I knew at a minimum that it had not ended well. It had ended with me. Blair's mother, on the other hand, had married her boyfriend and gone on to live an enviable life by all reasonable standards. It seems unfair for her to begrudge Blair her lost career. My modern American history is spotty, but I'm pretty sure most young women in the 1960s still became house-wives, especially if they could afford to. Maybe her prospects would have been different with a degree in chemistry from Cor-nell, but still.

This last thought makes me sit up from my slump on the couch. Beryl had gone to Cornell. Blair told me this at her house that night on the patio. Teddy had gone to Cornell too, but more importantly, his father had been the chair of the chemis-try department. The department that Beryl must have been in before she dropped out. The thought passes like a dark shadow and my stomach drops as if I were back in my dream, falling overboard. Maybe Blair had misspoken. With Teddy's family so closely identified with the university, maybe she'd meant to say another name but reached for the wrong one without even re-alizing it.

My fingers are already tapping out searches for alumni direc-tories, university clubs, any association between Beryl Edwards and Cornell. But I quickly realize that this is as futile as search-ing for "Mrs. Robert Edwards." Beryl Edwards didn't exist at Cornell. The wedding announcement gives me a clue, and the first entry on the third page of search results provides the confir-mation. It's a scan of a slightly smudged, typewritten page from a 1968 edition of the *Sigma Xi Quarterly*'s chapter reports. Near the top of the page, Beryl Spencer, a chemistry major, is listed as the Cornell chapter's vice president. Toward the bottom, Profes-sor James Bard is listed as the faculty advisor.

My heart is racing like it's just been shot full of adrenaline. I know, without understanding, just like when I saw that photo of Anthony Simpson's grinning face on microfiche. A few more clicks, and I have a reprint of the 1967–68 *Cornellian* in my shopping cart on a website I've never heard of. The chemistry club should have a picture in the yearbook. Maybe Beryl and James are there, standing next to each other. For $130, plus shipping, I can get a chance at photographic proof of the connection. My finger hovers over the "buy now" button, and then closes the window. This strange purchase would stick out on my credit card statement, and I have a vague sense of not wanting to leave a trail that anyone could follow.

Blair

WEDNESDAY / JULY 23 / 9:00 PM

Jennifer is smiling, but her eyes and nose are a familiar shade of pink, miserable like Alexis's were when she was sitting in the same spot at my island yesterday.

"I'm so sorry for showing up like this," she laughs as she wipes tears from her cheeks with the back of a white hand. "Jeff invented a business trip so he could run away as soon as the cops left. I can't sleep at the boutique, and I'm going crazy in the house alone at night. You know he nearly got himself arrested, hurting Alexis like that. I feel so awful."

I push a tall glass filled with vodka and ice toward her. "It's Jeff's fault for being an idiot."

Jennifer nods and goes on about Alexis, "She doesn't even look like she ever had a baby, that thin little thing, he could have snapped her in half. She must have been petrified."

"Is he the one who stole her gardening saw too?"

She drinks almost half her glass in one go, like water, before answering. "Yes, God, how embarrassing. He admitted to the cop—you know, the handsome Asian one—that he just saw it sitting outside one night when he was drunk, and took it, but that he'd never planned to do anything except maybe threaten us, or some bullshit like that. He said that it's all because my adultery has been driving him to drink too much. That he'd never actually hurt anyone, not on purpose."

"Is that true? Has he ever hurt you?"

"No, I would've told you if he had. I mean, he yells awful things, but he's never hit me or anything like that. Poor Alexis. Do you think I should call to apologize? I'm just so embarrassed."

"Don't worry about Alexis, Jeff already sent her flowers. Worry about yourself, Jen. What are you going to do now?" It's none of my business, but I know they signed a prenup and most of what they own is in Jeff's name. If they get divorced, she'll be worse off than she was with her middle-aged Jack.

"What is there to do? Jeff called up Dylan right in front of the cop, demanding he come over, so then he showed up apologizing. Emily was right behind him, with that angry teacher face of hers. God, it was so awkward, I wanted to shrivel up and die. Is it too much to ask for a refill?"

We both laugh at that, and I ask her what happened next, while playing bartender.

"Dylan took it too far, I mean he swore to Jeff that he'd never even speak to me again. Such a fucking wimp. I don't know why, but then the cop wanted to talk to each of us separately, and he asked me some weird questions, basically if I had any reason to think our whole mess might somehow include you."

"It's not that kinky of a neighborhood," I joke as I hand her a fresh drink. "I mean, we all know Dylan can't keep it in his pants, but that's Emily's crown of thorns. You should forget about him now. What are you going to do about you and Jeff?"

Jennifer shifts on the barstool. I guess she doesn't like me disparaging her lover, but there was even an exposé about him in some online newspaper a couple of years ago. She must know she's not the first.

"After they all left, I got down on my knees and begged Jeff to forgive me. I'm ashamed of myself. He's not a bad guy, I should be happy, it's just . . ." She doesn't go on, but I know what she means.

"So you think it'll be okay?"

Jennifer just shrugs and picks up her glass again. If she keeps going like this, she won't be able to walk home.

"You know what, I think I'm going to go ahead and throw the summer party after all. Teddy loved it, and we all could do with a little decompression."

She finishes off this second drink before answering. "That would be great, seriously. I haven't been to a nice party in forever."

"But it's going to be a nightmare to pull together so fast. You're still in town next weekend?"

"We're not leaving for Bermuda till the 3rd, so if it's Saturday, we can make it. I mean, unless Jeff changes his mind and cancels the whole thing."

I can tell by the way Jennifer's talking now that she's not in real trouble. Jeff will accept her apology. She's getting away with something pretty awful, and I'm happy for her.

FRIDAY / JULY 25 / 9:00 AM

Detective Kim is at the door again, but without his sidekick. "Good morning Mrs. Bard, do you have a few minutes?"

"Always." This may be my tenth time leading him back into

the kitchen like this, we've seen so much of each other these last two months. "Where's Detective Bryan?"

"Working another case. This won't take long, I just wanted to stop by and give you an update since it's been a while."

It's only been eight days since he and the choirboy were last here. "Is my coffee really that good?" I'm too busy getting mugs and working the machine to check his reaction.

"You know this is an important case for us, Mrs. Bard. Everyone wants to see your husband's murderer brought to justice."

"Have you had any new breaks?" I ask as I come around the island to hand him his coffee.

"Well, I was here earlier in the week, looking into what turned out to be a domestic issue. Do you know what I'm talking about?"

"I sure do. Jeff's bad behavior. I know he's a jealous husband, but what he did to Alexis really was unacceptable." I've resumed my usual position, standing on the far side of the island, as we talk.

"How well do you know the neighbors involved?" he asks casually.

"Jennifer is a good friend, and so is Alexis actually. The rest of them I don't particularly care for."

"And was your husband friendly with any of them?"

I let out a small laugh. "Teddy was friendly with everyone, but he didn't know our neighbors very well. He spent too much time at work and at the club."

Detective Kim looks like he already knew what I just told him and takes his time sipping his coffee before speaking again.

"Your street's seen a lot of activity this summer, but it seems that none of it is related to your husband's murder. Unless there's anything else you've thought of?"

I close my eyes for a breath and then answer. "No, there really isn't. I'm embarrassed to be their neighbor, but Mack and Jeff and the rest of them have nothing to do with Teddy, as far as I know."

He's finished his coffee and folded his hands on the counter. "Well, Mrs. Bard, at this point we've exhausted all our leads. It seems more and more likely that your husband's murder was a random act of violence, perpetrated by a stranger. But we will absolutely keep working the case, so please don't lose hope, okay?"

"It's hard not to, but I understand. I hope this doesn't mean I'll see less of you and Detective Bryan? I've gotten so used to these coffee dates."

Even this doesn't get a smile out of him, just a small nod. "We'll stay in touch, but we won't bother you unless there's something new to discuss. I've been at this a long time, and breaks can come months and even years after a murder, when you least expect it." This sounds like a threat in the guise of reassurance.

"I'll be waiting for that to happen," I say as I collect our mugs for the sink.

"I'll get going then, thanks again for the coffee."

I lead him to the front door and offer my hand for a shake before he steps out. "I appreciate everything you've done for Teddy, Detective Kim. Please thank your partner for me too."

His hand wraps around mine, warm and firm. "I'm sure we'll see you again."

He didn't park in the driveway today, but on the street. I watch him walk past his sedan and over to Alexis's house, before closing the door.

Alexis

Blair beat me to it. I'd tried to invite her over, to even the hospitality scales and to broach the subject of her parents on more familiar territory. Despite my embarrassment over how our house would measure up to hers, I still believed it would be easier for me to bring up something this uncomfortable in my living room instead of hers.

But the same day I'd figured it out, she'd texted me. Her message said to come over on August 2 at 7:00, for a long-running neighborhood tradition—a sunset cocktail party before "everyone" leaves town, an exodus directed mainly toward the string of upscale beach towns scattered along the eastern seaboard between New Jersey and South Carolina. When I'd texted back offering to help her prepare for the party, she'd replied that she was going to be out of town for more than a week, dealing with some of Teddy's business affairs.

So I've had to wait, ten long days, turning over these ideas in my mind. I can't imagine that Blair knew before marrying Teddy, or before having children. But I also can't believe that her mother said nothing, knowing full well the potential con-sequences. How Blair can still be on speaking terms with her is something I'd really like to ask about, but I have to try and not seem judgmental. That I know will get me nowhere with a person like Blair.

I'm already in my closet, thumbing through hangers with dissatisfaction. Carter was born over two months ago, and I still look slightly pregnant. My eyes scan back and forth over the short section of rack that holds my summer dresses. The only real option is another loose-fitting dress, and thankfully I'd bought half a dozen at a Black Friday sale last year. One of them is a shade of dark eggplant, sleeveless and made of a thick synthetic material that looks more expensive than the thin, wrinkle-prone cotton one I wore on the 4th. I have a chunky coral necklace that will go perfectly and distract from my belly. I want to look as good as possible to face Blair, and Jeff too, if he's there. After hearing the backstory from Blair and getting those yellow roses, my fear about him coming after me morphed into something between embarrassment and anger. I shouldn't have stumbled into a desperate man's path, but he should have at least been decent enough to send an apology with all those flowers. I hope he's there, actually, because I want to make clear that I'm just fine, and unimpressed.

I take my time getting ready. We asked Elena to babysit a week in advance so I don't feel guilty, and I can hear squeals of delight coming from Caleb's room where she is reading books to them in careful, heavily accented English. Sam is on his side of the bathroom, shaving after his shower. He spent the week in L.A., starting his client development work, and was just jet-lagged enough to take a nap this afternoon. He'd joked that he wanted to be in great shape in case tonight turned out to be a rager, and since waking up he's been in a wonderful mood. I can hear him humming to himself now in front of the mirror.

At 7:10 we kiss the children good night and head out into the humid evening. I don't even try to hold his hand, but it still feels good to be out here together like this. The setting sun burns against our necks and casts an orange glow over the old trees, the stately houses, the luxury cars parked in the long driveways. Luxury isn't even the right word—four exotic sports cars are parked in front of Blair's, neighbors who preferred to drive their Maseratis a few blocks to the party.

Strains of upbeat music start reaching us as soon as we're in the street. I know how much Sam is looking forward to this, and I won't ruin it by embarrassing myself like I did on the 4th. Anyway, the main reason I'm going is not to have fun—it's to talk to Blair. Tomorrow she's leaving for her beach house and won't be back until after Labor Day, because her children's private schools don't start until the second week of September. I won't see her in person again for weeks.

Sam and I have no vacation plans. His parents have a cabin at a lake near their house, but a trip there seems doomed to end in drowning, and I've refused to go ever since Caleb was born. Besides, Sam has to go back to L.A. at least twice in August, and planning something seems so exhausting. I just can't do it. So I will spend the rest of the summer here, keeping my fingers crossed that none of our three air-conditioning systems break down.

The front door of Blair's house is wide open, and as we come up the walk we can see a sparkling setting of champagne glasses on the foyer table. A middle-aged man in a white shirt and black bow tie hands us each a glass with a smile and gestures toward the back of the house. Sam's eyebrows rise in impressed pleasure. We catch the last few lines of "One Particular Harbour" as we step outside onto the patio.

There are dozens of people here already, scattered in small groups across the patio and on the lawn around the pool. The entire yard is lined with lit tiki torches. Two full bars are set up, one on each end of the patio, and a half dozen servers, dressed just like the champagne man, are slowly weaving their way between the groups of guests with platters of hors d'oeuvres. I'd assumed the music was coming from the same stereo system as the night I'd spent out here with Blair, but then Sam points to the band set up on a small stage at the far end of the pool. The band members are all wearing Hawaiian shirts, and have now moved on to "The Harder They Come."

"Who sings this?" Sam asks me, looking around and smiling at what he sees.

"Jimmy Cliff," I answer impatiently. After my mother died, I'd gone through a long phase of reggae, soca, punta, and every other type of Afro-Caribbean music I thought I should know. She never listened to music with me, but at night after I'd gone to bed she sometimes turned the tape deck on low in the living room, and I'd fall asleep to who I'd later figure out was Toots & the Maytals. Her music drowned out the sounds in the neighboring apartments, and it felt like my mother was sharing something with me, even if it wasn't on purpose. I always slept best on those nights. Sam was there, when I was learning this music, and I thought he'd at least remember the greats.

I open my mouth to tell him so, but he leans in to ask me if I think the band's theme is beach or middle age. I am laughing and telling him he's an idiot when Blair calls out from behind us. "Alexis! Sam! There you are!"

We turn to see her coming outside through one set of French

doors, looking flawless in a flowing white sleeveless jumpsuit. Her lean arms make me wish I'd brought a shawl, despite the heat.

"Good, you both have drinks. You'll need them." She steps in between us and places a light hand on each of our backs. "I need to introduce you to the neighbors worth knowing."

The next two hours go by quickly, and my face starts to ache from smiling too much. A judge who lives a few blocks away interrogates Sam on some point of law that I don't follow. A couple with two children under four who live on Bright Drive seem intimidatingly impressive, until they inadvertently reveal that the investment firm the husband runs was capitalized by his parents and the wife inherited her father's thriving dermatology practice. An executive from Teddy's company and her wife debate the merits of their alma mater, Princeton, relative to ours, for the full length of time it takes the band to perform five songs. Sam occasionally interjects jokes, which make us all laugh but fail to close the debate.

During the fourth song, I spot Jeff and Jennifer on the other side of the pool, talking to another couple. Jennifer is laughing out loud at something, her head thrown back and her black hair cascading around her shoulders, just like it did that night. Jeff makes eye contact but looks away quickly. I try to catch his eye again, to signal that I know and am not afraid of him, but he turns his back and melts into the crowd.

After we finally escape from the Princeton couple, Sam goes off to find a bathroom while I head to one of the bars. One couple at the front of the short line considers what to drink for several minutes. Just as I turn away to try the second bar, the woman glances over her shoulder toward me.

"Oh hi Laura!" I force myself to smile.

She gives me a half nod back, and lets her eyes assess my outfit. Shawn hands her the party's signature drink—a margarita, in keeping with the unmoored beach theme—and says hello to me before walking off. Laura joins me at the back of the now fast-moving line, sipping her drink as I ask for two glasses of champagne.

"Can you believe she is throwing this party?" she says into my shoulder as we walk away from the bar and down the patio steps.

"I heard it was an annual tradition?" I ask, looking around for Sam.

"It is, but her husband just died. I think it's customary to mourn for a little longer, no?" she says, eyebrows raised. We are in the middle of the lawn, surrounded by probably close to a hundred guests, but there is still plenty of space. The humidity dropped after sunset, giving way to a warm, blue night. I have a fleeting desire to tell her that she has no idea, that Blair may have very good reason not to mourn, but I just nod and take a half sip from my glass.

"It looks like the two of you have become fast friends. I'm sure that is a comfort for her," she goes on. I can feel her eyes on me, even as I keep mine scanning the crowd.

"I'm home right now with the baby, so I have time for walks and things. It's a comfort to me too, to have a friend so close by." I force another smile then take a few more sips.

"Well, there are worse friends to have, that I can't deny. Have you heard about the latest train wreck?"

Her eyes are gleaming now, as if she's got wonderful news to share. I shake my head no and finish off my glass.

"You haven't? That's surprising. Look around, do you see anyone from our block missing?"

I start scanning again. It must be well past 9:00. The sky is a midnight blue, and the flames of the tiki torches combined with Blair's landscape lighting create a glowing haze around the guests that make it hard for me to make out faces. A server comes by and gently takes my now empty glass from my hand. I'm not sure when I drank it all, but without thinking I take a quick sip from the second one I'm holding for Sam.

"I can't really see straight anymore," I try to joke.

Laura doesn't laugh. "Dylan and Emily. They're getting divorced."

"What? Oh that's too bad. I wonder what happened." I try to sound surprised.

"I think you can guess pretty well what happened," she answers mockingly.

"What do you mean?" I wonder if she'll tell me the whole story, or a version that absolves her.

"Well, the police paid Jeff a visit last week. But you know that already."

I do know, but I keep my face blank. Detective Kim had stopped by last Friday, to tell me he'd met with Jeff and the other three involved. There was no obvious connection to Teddy's murder, and each of the four had strong alibis. That's all he'd said—he hadn't even come into the house, just stood on the front steps and smiled when I thanked him. I'd wanted to keep him there, to offer him a drink and watch his ringless hands take notes as I shared my salacious theory. I'd wanted to hear the gravel in his voice as he promised to look into it. I'd wanted to, but I hadn't. If I'm wrong it would be another waste of his time. More than that, though, unearthing this potential link between Teddy and his wife hasn't scared or scandalized me. I think I recognize something in Blair, something that is in me too—as strange as that sounds—and I need to see if I'm right. So I'd said nothing to Detective Kim, just thanked him too many times and watched him drive away again.

Laura seems frustrated by my silence but goes on. "It seems that little visit was the push that Jeff needed to sober up and do something. He got the four of them together and told Dylan to stop sleeping with his wife."

I have no interest in telling Laura what happened that night, but it seems pointless to continue feigning ignorance. "But why is he here with Jennifer? As if everything is fine?"

"Because of two important facts, Alexis. First, half of what is Dylan's is Emily's, and none of what is Jeff's is Jennifer's. Second, Jennifer is beautiful and young, and that makes it easy for Jeff to forgive her," she says as if these are the most obvious things in the world. I suppose they are.

"It's a shame, really, but at least it stopped them," she adds before licking the rim salt of her glass and taking a final sip of her margarita.

We stare at each other for a few uncomfortable seconds before I nod and finish the rest of Sam's champagne. I've been talking to her for too long. I need to find Blair before this party ends, to talk to her in private, away from so many sharp eyes.

"Laura," I start making an excuse to walk away when Sam puts an arm around my shoulders.

"Hello ladies, what did I miss?" he asks conspiratorially.

The tiki torch flames are growing and blurring, and I feel unsteady on my feet. I drank too much, and if I don't talk to Blair soon, Sam will probably end up carrying me home half asleep.

"So much. It took you a while, did you get lost or was there a line for the bathroom?" I ask.

"Neither. I ran into a former colleague, turns out he lives just—"

"Okay, well, my turn, for the ladies' room," I interrupt, slurring slightly. "Laura will keep you company till I get back." I smile at both of them and walk away before either can answer.

I make my way unsteadily toward the house, moving slowly enough to keep my balance and not attract any attention. A bow-tied server is standing just outside the French doors manning a small table of coffee.

"Oh thank God," I mutter to myself and smile when he hands me a cup.

I start sipping right where I stand, even though the coffee burns my tongue. The rolling feeling in my legs begins to fade and my vision starts to sharpen. I finish the cup and ask for another. The server obliges, and I take my second cup a few steps away, toward the edge of the patio, to try and spot Blair.

It's still a gorgeous night. The sky is blue-black, with a sliver of crescent moon and a few faint stars. The beach band has moved on to a mellow set, and the sounds of the music merge with the chatter and laughter rising up from the guests into a pleasant thrum. The bow-tied servers are still circulating, now with trays of bite-sized desserts, and I notice that there is another coffee station set up on one side of the lawn. Mack is holding court there, in a baby-pink polo shirt and chinos, as if he were nothing but a harmless country club member. He's surrounded by a group of white-haired neighbors all laughing so hard, they're struggling to keep the drinks in their hands from spilling.

I didn't expect it, but I feel comfortable being here. I've been to dozens of upscale parties—Sam's rich friends have had plenty of weddings, baby showers, and birthdays. But this is the first time that I've been a guest on equal footing with the others. Not someone's college roommate—smart, but impoverished, poor thing. Not Sam's girlfriend—nice enough but kind of awkward, doesn't know how to have a good time. Doesn't know how to relax, how to get comfortable with wealth and privilege, even when it's just on view—not hers of course. Should be grateful for the opportunity.

I've never heard those words exactly, but I've seen it all over their faces. This time is different, even though I know some of these guests would mistake me for a server if not for the uniforms. I'm here because I own a house in the neighborhood—on a desirable, dead-end street no less. It may be in shambles, but it still qualifies. I belong. And not just because we can afford to live here. Now I can see who they really are, and they're not any better than me. The elderly couple that brought us the fern peels away from the small crowd around Mack and stops a server to examine her dessert tray. The idea briefly crosses my mind of going over to them and saying something like, "Hey, guess what? Did you know that Mack is a pervert, and probably a criminal?" I wonder if they'd look as surprised as they did when they finally realized that I was their neighbor. I wonder if they already know.

It's been nearly twenty years since I escaped from the low cloud of sadness my mother and I lived under, but I still thought I was an aberration—a deviation from the normal way families are supposed to grow, so shameful that it couldn't even be spoken. Only now, after these months of living here, do I see that the same dirty sins stain everyone. The clean, bright wash of wealth is just a more effective cover. I laugh to myself at the thought that, until a few days ago, I'd been afraid enough to consider moving. With my vision sharp again, I scan all the clusters of guests one more time to confirm, but I already know Blair is not out here. I would have spotted her white jumpsuit and blond hair against all the shadows.

Fingertips graze my elbow just as I turn to go inside. It's Jennifer, her skin luminescent in a low-cut black sundress.

"Hi Alexis, are you okay?" she asks as her eyes scan my face for signs that I'm not.

"Of course I am," I smile. The scrape is nearly healed, and well-hidden under makeup. "How are you?"

"God, I'm so sorry about what happened. I wanted to come talk to you earlier, but I just can't stand Laura right now," she says, ignoring my question. "Jeff feels terrible too, he didn't mean to hurt you, he just drinks too much sometimes. Are you really okay?"

"I'm fine. I know, it was basically an accident. But he really shouldn't let himself get drunk to that point. What if I'd been a different person, someone who fought back and hurt him?" I grip my coffee cup with both hands to avoid touching my forehead. "It's dangerous for everybody, really."

"You're totally right, he's a fucking idiot," Jennifer sighs. "Listen, you'll have to let me buy you a drink sometime. I at least owe you that, okay?"

"Sure, I'm around."

We smile at each other, and she reaches out to touch my arm again before walking back down the patio steps to find Jeff. I watch her go, then turn to walk inside. The lights are dimmed everywhere except the kitchen, where one group of bow-tied servers is busily preparing more desserts and coffee for another group to whisk outside. A handful of guests are talking in a loose circle near the wall of family pictures. Blair is not among them.

I hand my empty coffee cup to a passing server and move toward one of the powder rooms. The door is slightly ajar, and as I reach to open it, Blair comes down the back staircase from the second floor. She still looks perfect, as if the party just began, and smiles widely when she sees me.

"Lex, there you are! How are you enjoying yourself? I hope you got to try all the hors d'oeuvres before the greedy old fogies gobbled them up," she laughs.

"It's an excellent party Blair, thank you for inviting us," I smile back.

"Well of course, you're my new favorite person around these parts. It wouldn't be a party without you."

Being the object of her affection feels like basking in the summer sun. I might bitterly regret what I'm about to do.

"Blair, later on, can we talk? I want to ask you about something before you leave for the beach," I say as lightly as I can.

"Of course. Let me just make the rounds again before the senior citizens start to expire. It's nearing their bedtime." She reaches out and squeezes my arm as she walks past to rejoin the party.

This powder room has a chic wallpaper of moody peonies and a gold-leaf ceiling. I lock the door behind me and turn to stare at myself in the round mirror. The dark circles under my eyes and the stubborn extra fat swinging from my upper arms stare back at me. I want to ask Blair how to be so effortlessly put together, even if I already know the answers. Worry less, sleep more. Learn how to properly put on makeup. Buy nicer clothes. Maybe have sex every once in a while. Me, my house—we're both in shambles. I wish we were close enough for Blair to help me design some rooms properly. We can't afford whatever she actually charges.

I could keep it to myself—say nothing, and maybe we'd get closer, become real friends. I've managed to make so few, and now Sam and I barely talk about anything other than how to take care of our children and our property, negotiating about money and time as if we were business partners. Going through with this means risking the loss of one of the very few people whose company I enjoy and who seems to enjoy mine. If I somehow misunderstood how the pieces fit together, then she'll probably never speak to me again and tell all the neighbors to do the same. But I have to know.

I finish washing my hands, take a last look at my pitiable reflection, and make my way back to Sam and Laura, who are still standing where I'd left them. Shawn has joined them and is explaining in a too-loud voice how he and Laura are planning an extensive renovation of their basement so their almost-teenagers will never have a reason to party anywhere except home, under their watchful gaze. Oblivious to the looks on our faces, he and Laura drone on about the surveillance features they plan to integrate into their renovation, to "make sure things stay wholesome down there" as Shawn puts it. I wonder if he has any idea that his wife would have jumped into bed with Dylan, if she'd been invited. To force myself to remain in place, I start a game of standing on one foot, then the other, back and forth. Just when it starts becoming unbearable and I think I'll have to find another excuse to walk away, Blair grabs my elbow, pulling me toward her with a wink to the others. I follow her wordlessly back to the house, noticing that the crowd has started to thin but the music has picked up tempo. The remaining guests look like they're ready for more fun.

Blair

Once we are inside, I glance at her over my shoulder and smile. She looks as nervous as I've ever seen her, which is saying something. We keep walking, through the family room and down the hallway opposite the one with the china closet, to my closed door.

"Welcome to my office," I say in a silly voice, flipping on a small, glittering gold chandelier. Teddy got the proper office upstairs, with the big windows, and I had to make the best of the weak northern light in here. So I turned it into the inside of a jewelry box. Mahogany-paneled walls with ornate moldings, a marble-topped desk with lean nickel legs, and a custom Persian rug in an unusual palette of pastel colors. A balance of heavy and light, masculine and feminine, all expensive and gorgeous. This is my favorite room in the house, but I rarely bring anyone in here. I drop myself into one of two cognac-leather armchairs, a furred throw draped perfectly on each, and motion for Alexis to take the other one.

"God it feels good to sit down. What's going on Lex?" I say

with a happy sigh and lean back, letting my cheek rub against the softness of the throw. Alexis looks like a skittish horse, sitting bolt upright at the edge of the armchair, making the leather dent unnaturally, and looking everywhere except at me.

"I, well, there's something I need to ask you about, or that I would like to ask you about. It's about your parents." She pauses and finally makes eye contact.

"My parents? Okay go ahead," I answer doubtfully.

"Blair, I don't know how to say this without—well, let me start by saying I'm sorry. I'm sorry for overstepping and for bringing up painful things."

I don't react.

"I know your mother and Teddy's father were at Cornell at the same time, in the chemistry department. When she got pregnant and dropped out and had you."

My eyes are closed now. I don't want to look at her either.

"I know about the genetic tests too, Blair. I accidentally opened the door to your linen closet. Table linens. I'm sorry."

Her voice is quavering, but the words are out. There is no taking them back. I sigh heavily, open my eyes, and lean forward.

"Lex, what exactly are you saying?"

There is no challenge in my question, just impatience for her to get the whole thing out of her mouth.

"I'm sorry Blair," she says again. "I'm really sorry. I think that your mother and Teddy's father must have had a relationship, and . . . and Teddy's father was also your father. You and Teddy were half-siblings."

This last part comes out in a whisper, as if she's blaspheming in church. As if she's said something that polite people should never say. She's looking down at the rug, too ashamed to look me in the face. I lean even further forward and cross one creamy white jumpsuit leg over the other.

"That's what you know? You know absolutely nothing Alexis."

"If I'm wrong, I really, really apologize. I just—"

"You're not wrong," I cut her off. "You just know nothing. My mother and James Bard did not have a relationship, as you put it. Do you think if I were their accidental love child, things would have turned out this way?"

She doesn't answer.

"No, of course not. My mother is not the best of women, she may not even be a good woman, but she isn't horrible. She wouldn't do that."

"What? Do what?" Alexis is scared, but tenacious. She wants to know.

"Purposefully lead me into living this lie. This disgusting lie. She wouldn't have done that if she weren't already trapped in it. James Bard raped her, Alexis. A full-on, violent assault in the chemistry lab. She had to get a friend to pick the shards of glass out of her back. And she wasn't the only one. Of course not. But she survived, and she moved on. Now you know why she doesn't like me so much."

I smile briefly, up at the chandelier, and keep going.

"Then twenty-five years later, I show up at home, madly in love with his son. Can you imagine? I think she assumed we'd break up. I was living a glamorous life in New York, and he was working like a dog on Capitol Hill. Our lives couldn't have been more different. But we didn't break up."

"Why didn't she tell you before you got married?"

This is a stupid question, but one I've asked Beryl, and myself, many times.

"How could she? My father, who raised me, had no idea.

She'd never told him. Never told anyone. And James had died, but Teddy's mother, Susan, was still alive. It would have ruined both of our families."

"But why did she not just tell you? You could have kept it a secret, between you and her, couldn't you?" Alexis sounds frustrated, regretful even. As if we'd just missed the chance to pry the truth from my mother's lips earlier this evening. I let her question hang between us for a moment before answering.

"I told my mother who Teddy's parents were one day when we were shopping in Manhattan, just the two of us. It was a gorgeous Saturday in the spring, and we were walking by Bryant Park. I remember telling her about Teddy's father, thinking it would endear him to her—*hey Mom, look his dad was one of your professors*—and you know what? She didn't miss a beat. We were surrounded by strangers, and Teddy and I had just started dating, but she still pretended to be happy to hear the name. We were together all day, we had dinner in the city before she took the train home. And of course, there were dozens of times after that. Opportunities that she chose not to take."

I want to look at her, but I'm too disgusted with myself in this moment. "Do you see what I mean? It was a part of herself that she never intended to show anyone, including me."

"But what about your children? She must have—"

I cut her off again, more sharply this time. "Of course, she knew she was letting us take an enormous risk, an unthinkable risk. We were extremely lucky, but still. That's the part I haven't forgiven her for."

Alexis nods slowly and we don't speak for at least a full minute, each of us still avoiding the other's eyes. The muffled murmur of the party is seeping in through the mahogany panels, and I wonder if this is what the funeral reception would have sounded like from inside Teddy's coffin, if he'd been there to hear it.

"So she never said anything to you, not until you were on the cusp of finding out yourselves," Alexis concludes, almost to herself.

I catch her gaze for a moment before responding.

"Exactly. Teddy bought us those kits last year, after his colleague raved about how interesting his results were. He kept joking that we might have Native American ancestry and it would help the kids get into college. He was so excited to take the stupid tests that I mentioned it to my mother on the phone. She drove here the same night and told us both to our faces. . . ."

"And your reactions diverged," Alexis whispers, as if she already knows the rest.

"We were both horrified. Of course we were. And so angry. For a few days, all we wanted to do was comfort each other. But we were also repulsed. Or at least he was. Anyway, it became clear that we were not actually so aligned. Teddy wanted to get divorced immediately, to tell the kids and have them take tests to make sure they were really okay. He wanted to tell his siblings, for fuck's sake. To warn them all that they might be married to other bastard children from his father's rape victims. Can you imagine?"

Alexis winces. I know she feels the way I do—the humiliation of finding out would pale in comparison to others knowing.

"And you disagreed."

"Dammit, of course I disagreed. We were done having kids, we'd been fucking each other for twenty years, why would we need to go and blow the whole thing up now? Embarrass ourselves and our families for what? There's no justice to be had, no way to right the wrongs. I wanted to move on, to shed it like a bad outfit, and go back to living our lives. I managed to convince Teddy to keep quiet for a few months, but he couldn't get over it. The last time we slept together, the only time in those last few months, he freaked out the next morning. Called us deviants and took a thirty-minute shower. It was infuriating."

Without noticing, I've pulled the throw around my shoulders to keep warm. I usually like it chilly in here, but now I'm shivering.

"Is that why you—"

"What else could I do? We were at an impasse. I was not about to let him drag me and our kids down this hole. He was getting ready to file for divorce and call a Bard family meeting to make the grand announcement. He was obsessed. He kept saying the truth had to come out. What truth? I knew he would tell someone soon, and ruin everything."

Alexis looks like she might start crying right here for me, as if she feels the same pain I do.

"Listen Lex, I'm telling you this because you are my good friend. It's pretty reckless on my part, but since we met I've felt that you get me. You're obviously very smart, and I know you're strong. You know that there are difficult choices to make in life. I trust you."

My voice is matter-of-fact and sincere, and I do mean what I've just said. But really what choice do I have? Alexis is clever enough to have figured this out. If I insult her by denying it, I know she'd just keep digging. I have to trust her. Strangely though, I'm not too worried. She understands me better than most of my simpering, small-minded friends. If they'd caught a whiff of this, even just a hint, one of them would have filed a motion to ban us from the club, I'm sure. Teddy hadn't realized how awful the people around him really were.

"If you ever want to talk about this again, I'm here for you. But otherwise, we never had this conversation." Alexis reaches over and rubs my knee. I can feel the heat of her hand through the thin fabric of my jumpsuit.

I start to answer, but a loud knock freezes me mid-word. She pulls her hand back and we both turn to the door. It opens a crack, and one of the bow-tied servers pops his head in.

"Pardon me, Mrs. Bard, I'm very sorry to interrupt but the band would like to know if they should play an extra set. It's already midnight."

"Midnight! We're having too much fun Lex, let's get back out there. I'm going to request that Van Morrison song, it reminds me of you." And to the server, "Definitely one more set."

I grab Alexis's hand and we are off.

Alexis

I'm on my way to the airport. The ride service driver is hunched over the steering wheel, peering out into the gathering darkness as if his headlights aren't strong enough, and we are crawling along ten below the speed limit. I left the house unnecessarily early for this trip, out of the old rhythm when flying felt like taking a drive and I barely gave a second thought to showing up forty-five minutes before takeoff. For this trip, I packed three days in advance, checked my itinerary every few hours, and almost walked out the door without my purse.

My consulting firm asked me to come back two months early to pitch a new, potentially big client in Chicago. Four days away from my children—Carter ever chubbier and more alert, Caleb constantly surprising me with new words—sounded hard, but I didn't want to say no and add another black mark against me on the promotion ledger. So I'd pleaded with Sam to rearrange his travel schedule and stay home this week. Eventually, he agreed, but not before a long and bitter argument that ended with him using the word "divorce" for the first time. He said he was tired of me, of the house, of it all; that this wasn't the life he wanted—no, he wanted to be happy. It felt like an insult, a taunt meant to provoke me into agreeing with him, but I won't throw away everything we've worked for. I'd managed to walk him back from the precipice, and we'd agreed to try couples therapy first. I need to book our first session after I get back.

August was a long month. I spent many evenings drinking alone on our patio after putting the children to bed, thinking about that night. About how easy it had been for me to see that Blair murdered her own husband, her own half-brother, and to understand it. Why was I not repelled? Outraged? Afraid of her? Even worse, I felt like it brought us closer. I wouldn't tell Blair this—I would never tell anyone—but during high school I often fantasized about my mother dying. Not by my own hands, but by a stroke of luck—a car accident, a sudden onset of terminal cancer, a stroke. I didn't care how, really. I just prayed for it to happen, more fervently than for anything else, including getting college scholarships. I don't know why I wanted it so badly, it's not as if she had a life insurance policy or anything to leave me. I suppose I admire Blair, as wrong as that sounds, for making her own problems disappear. But I also pity her.

After my mother actually died, there was no one to tell besides Sam, and he assumed I was fine. I'd killed her off three years earlier, after all. Mostly he was right. I graduated with the highest honors, got a great job, and spent my twenties caught up in the long climb toward success. Late nights in the office, grad school, bars, and apartment parties with Sam—there was never any time to think about her. I didn't want to anyway. But then she started coming to me, unbidden. Bad memories at first, followed by some of the good. How committed she was to combing my curls into pigtails every morning all through elementary school, and to checking that I'd finished my home-work properly every night, even after some of the assignments got too complicated for her to follow. One night when Caleb was still a newborn, I'd cried for a long time in his nursery while he slept on my chest, realizing for the first time how lonely her life must have been.

These past few weeks, sitting by myself out on the patio and watching the summer sky turn from deep pink to purple to blue, I've thought a lot about the questions I would ask her if I could. What cliché promises had my father made to her? Why had she kept writing for all those years, didn't she realize? And most importantly, for me at least, how could she have been so selfish, to keep all of the truth to herself and give me nothing?

Even after figuring out who Anthony Simpson was on my own, I never spoke his name to her. Fear, shame, cowardice—I could scream at her about many things, but, out of an abun-dance of all three, not about him. I was a child though, and she made me that way. There's plenty that I would like to tell her too, about how I feel now. Disappointed that she let herself get fooled. Impressed that she kept living after losing everything. And more than anything else, angry. Angry that she told me so little, that she let her silence sit so heavy that it distorted every-thing around me. But death is as permanent as it is surprising—there is only blank space on the other side of my conversations.

The neighborhood has felt unnervingly abandoned since Blair's party, even though there's nothing to be afraid of any-more. Out on the patio alone at night, I could hear every rustle, and the occasional helicopter over the river sent me jumping out of my seat. It seemed like everyone on the block was on vacation—Laura and Shawn visiting family in South America, Jennifer and Jeff at their house in Bermuda for a month. Even

Emily and Dylan are vacationing during their divorce—they put their house on the market and separately decamped to two of their waterfront properties. Laura is the one who'd told me where they'd gone, while asking—in a voice that sounded like telling—me to pick up any unexpected packages while she was away. Emily hadn't answered either of the texts I'd sent her. I shouldn't have bothered, I know we weren't actually friends.

Blair texts me a few times a week from her own beach house. She invited us to come visit for a weekend, but at the last minute Sam said he had too much work to do and we canceled. She's driving back later this week, and we have dinner plans next Saturday. I've never looked forward to autumn so much—to everyone coming home and the neighborhood coming back to life. I laugh to myself at this idea. I've always thought of autumn as the season when everything starts to die.

"Which airline ma'am?" the driver asks, his eyes on me via the rearview mirror.

We're finally pulling into the airport.

/ 10:00 PM

I'd forgotten how tedious it is to wait. The seating area for my flight is nearly full—all the gates are packed with long-weekend travelers heading home and businesspeople prepositioning for the rest of the week. I've been standing near my gate for almost an hour, reviewing the prep materials for tomorrow's meetings.

My flight is supposed to take off in twenty minutes, but the gate agents have made no motions to start boarding. I know this isn't a good sign and start looking up my flight status on the airline's website. Just before the page loads, my phone dies. I remember with a pang of frustration that I forgot to pack my charger. I wonder what else I forgot. Looking around, it seems like most of the stores are already closed, but I pull up the handle of my carry-on to walk around and check.

"Ladies and gentlemen," the overloud voice of an agent comes through the speakers. "We apologize, but tonight's flight has been canceled due to a mechanical problem on your aircraft. Please head over to one of the service desks located at gates A21 and A40 to reschedule your flight. Again, we apologize for the inconvenience."

This is followed by an immediate wave of grumbling and rustling, as passengers begin to gather up their belongings for the race to customer service. There are no more flights tonight, on any airline. I know this already because I booked the last one out, so I could put the children to bed. As I speedwalk straight to the gate agents, I am silently thankful that I know these routines so well.

"Excuse me gentlemen," I give them my best smile. "Could I ask for your help? Could you please help me check if I've been rebooked? My phone died and I forgot my charger at home, it's baby brain, I have a three-month-old."

The agent who made the announcement purses his lips, uninterested, but holds out his hand for my boarding pass. He aggressively types in my name, and I hear the printer churning something out.

"You're already rebooked on the first flight tomorrow morning. Six a.m.," he says as he hands me a new boarding pass without looking up from his screen.

The benefits of having status. I accept the new pass with another smile at the top of his head, and turn to head home.

/ 10:45 PM

Without a phone, my only option was an old-fashioned taxi. As we pull into my driveway, I worry about waking everyone up, especially the baby, since I have to turn around and leave again in a few hours. The house is dark. Sam didn't even bother to turn on the front porch lights before going to bed. I get ready to punch in the alarm code as soon as I walk in, before it has a chance to go off, but the front door swings open to silence. Maybe he fell asleep on one of the couches. I leave my suitcase and shoes in the foyer and walk through the house looking for him. He's not on the main floor. All I can hear is the creaking of the floorboards under my feet. Before going upstairs, I double back to the kitchen for some water and catch a pile of dirty dishes out of the corner of my eye. I'd forgotten to do them before leaving for the airport. I change course for the sink and turn on the faucet with some resignation. It would have taken Sam less than ten minutes to do these dishes before going to bed. I guess he doesn't care if we get rotting mice and those awful flies again.

Out of habit, I look out the window while waiting for the water to get hot. The only lights on at Mack's are the ones on a timer—his porch and landscape lights. He still hasn't come back from the island he owns off the coast of the Carolinas. Laura told me about it at Blair's party. Another reason he didn't get in trouble, everyone wants an invitation to a private island. My eyes move across Mack's property and down the street, toward Blair's empty house. Her timed lights are on too—but there are also lights on inside the house.

The sink water must be scalding by now, but my eyes are fixed out the window. If this is a break-in, I'm not sure how I'll call for help. We didn't bother to get a landline when we moved in here. Suddenly, Blair's front door opens, and I catch the gleam of her blond head in the porch lights. She's looking up the street, toward my house, and for a brief moment I think she's looking at me.

But then I realize that between us, where her property meets Mack's, the dark is moving. Someone is walking along the curb, avoiding Mack's landscape lighting and keeping beyond the reach of Laura and Shawn's new cameras.

So much time away from us—traveling, late nights at the office, locked upstairs—and so much disdain for me. He became mean, and I accepted it. I'd thought it was work, but he hadn't changed even after making partner.

I wait until he crosses to our side of the street and passes the outer edge of the pool of streetlight, just to be sure.

That feeling when I woke up on the yacht. How giddy he was to go to her cocktail party. He told me to befriend her, she pretended to like me, and I fell for it all.

He'll be at the front door any second. I should have known.

The laundry he did that morning, the only loads he's done since we got married.

Of course I should have known. A woman like Blair wouldn't do her own dirty work. She used Sam instead. I thought I'd understood her fears. I thought I might have done the same thing, in her place. A person can only reasonably bear so much shame, and beyond that, you have to shake it off to survive. Bury it, lie about it, throw it off a cliff into oblivion. Anything to move on. But again, my imagination had been too small—I hadn't realized that anything could include ruining my life too. The day I first went to her house, to bring her cookies from the bakery, I wonder if I'd mistaken laughter for sobbing when she answered the door. If this whole time she's just been laughing at me.

I move quickly, turning off the faucet, running upstairs past the children's bedrooms as lightly as I can, pulling their doors shut as I go past. There's no time to check on them, to make sure they are okay after being left alone by their awful, irresponsible father. He would've never told Elena he was leaving the house, she would have been too suspicious.

I flip on a lamp in our master bedroom to wait. The front door creaks open as I try to catch my breath. I hear Sam stepping in, closing the door, activating the alarm. Then nothing. He must have seen my suitcase. A few seconds later, he comes slowly up the stairs, his heavy steps making each one groan. I'm standing in the middle of the room, in front of our bed. The curtains are open, but it doesn't matter, no one can see in.

He stops in the doorway, just inside the room. He's wearing a fitted dark green T-shirt I bought him last year. The few clothes I buy him are all dark green. It's his favorite color.

"Alexis, what happened? Why are you here?" he asks as if I'm trespassing.

I swallow and try to keep my voice even. "My flight got canceled, so I'm flying out in the morning instead. My phone died so I couldn't let you know."

"Oh," he says, looking down in search of an answer to the question I'll obviously ask. But I don't want to hear it.

"Sam, I saw you." It comes out meekly, the accusation smothered by my own sense of shame. My entire body starts trembling, barely able to hold in all the things I urgently need to say.

"What are you talking about?" he asks evenly, making eye contact now. I guess he's decided to try denial.

"Don't. Blair must have told you already. I figured out that she wanted Teddy dead, but now I see it all. Why did you do it for her? You could have let her get rid of him herself. If she loves you so much, she would have found a way."

We are both keeping our voices low. I think of the day we first saw this house, and our realtor pointing out that a common downside of Cape Cods, this one included, is a cramped second floor. The children's bedrooms are only a few feet away.

"Don't fucking talk to me like that. I see how you run over there every time she calls, like a dog. It's pathetic." He steps forward into the room, and I step back, almost falling into the chair guarding the picture window. The old floorboards under the carpet whine quietly in response.

The humiliation is unbearable, thinking of Blair and Sam together, mocking me. "How long has it been going on? Did you trick me into buying this house? Were you sleeping with her already?"

"You've got to be fucking kidding me. *You're* the one who brought me here. *You're* the one who insisted on this house, on doing all the work. I was here all the fucking time for the kitchen."

His hands are rubbing the back of his head in frustration, and I catch a glimpse of his ab muscles in the gap between his shirt and shorts. It was so obvious. He wasn't just getting into incredible shape for himself, or for me.

"Oh I see, so your pregnant wife was relying on you to get our family's new home ready, and naturally you took that opportunity to start screwing our neighbor."

"Forget Blair, okay? I would have left you no matter what. I'm so sick of it, dragging you along all this time. I can do better than this."

He's trying to shame me into silence, like he always does, but anger makes me spit out the words like venom, even as I keep inching backward, away from him. "Better? By murdering a man you barely knew? Didn't you think you'd get caught? You're a lawyer for God's sake, you know what's going to happen!"

"Now that you think it was me and not her, you want justice to be served. Is that it? You're such a fucking hypocrite." He's straining to hold back his voice, but his hands are already clenched into fists.

He despises me, I see that clearly. But he's never hurt me, or anyone else. At least not before Teddy. Blair must have lied to him. My back is touching the warm glass of the picture window now, and I can feel the sheet shifting in the frame as I brace myself against it. I don't know how long it will hold.

"Sam, listen to me, she used you. She used us both, don't you see that? She—"

He cuts me off before I can get the words out. "I stayed longer than I wanted to, and I asked you for a divorce. It was all going to be fine. But you're fucking up the plan."

"No, I'll divorce you, she—"

"Do you think this has been easy for me? It's been a fucking nightmare. You know I can't go to jail, right?"

He starts coming toward me, and I push my back harder against the glass. "Sam please, the window—" He pauses when I say this, and I realize I've made a mistake. I've given him a good idea. In two long steps, one arm reaches out to grab my shoulder as the other comes across his chest in a quick, fluid motion to elbow me in the temple. The flash of pain is enough to make me collapse, but he's still got hold of my shoulder. Instead of letting me fall where I stand, he shoves me onto the floor behind him, out of his way.

The chair is in the air now, and he's slamming it against the picture window. I want to plead with him, to tell him it's her fault and our children don't deserve this, but I don't want him to know I'm conscious. Besides, he won't listen. He's already gone too far. The window is screeching with every slam, but Sam is impatient. He tosses the chair aside and starts kicking the glass, trying to make it give faster, so he can throw me out of it.

The sound is my signal to force myself up as Sam stops to watch it fall. The scraping and cracking of the massive, single pane of glass breaking free of its rotted frame. It is my only chance. His back is to me, and he is only inches from the wide-open space where the window just was. The sound of glass shattering against brick rises up from outside and fills our room, and this is the moment that I run, straight into him with my arms outstretched, pushing with all the strength I've ever had. Surprise makes my strength suffice—he has no time to grab me or the window frame or anything else. One, two, and the sickening thud of a grown man hitting the ground.

Slowly, I walk to the edge of the window-shaped hole in the wall, the warm night air wrapping itself around me as I carefully lean out to look. The crescent moon emerges from behind a cloud and casts a faint silver light on Sam's body, splayed out on the brick of the patio below me. His head caught the small brick wall separating the patio from the lawn, and his body lies at an unnatural angle to his neck. I count to ten, waiting to see if he moves, but everything is still. There are no crickets, no breezes tonight.

2015

Blair

I underestimated her, truly I did. If we'd been friends before Sam, I would have picked someone else. But we weren't, and all I knew about Alexis was what Sam told me. She was depressed and critical. She was distant, secretive even, and never satisfied. He worked so hard. They'd bought this house and gotten a live-in nanny and a BMW, but she was still unhappy. She sounded awful. I didn't have much patience for his whining, but he was funny and clearly hungry for attention.

It started one weekend in November, before they moved in. I was supposed to be planting purple hyacinth bulbs I'd forgotten about earlier in the fall, but was mostly slamming my trowel against the bricks along the front walk. Teddy and I had just had our hundredth fight about what to do, and I was so angry at him for ruining the holidays. Sam caught me off guard, walking up without me noticing, and asked if I was all right. It was in this moment, looking up at his handsome freckled face and red hair, bright against the gray sky, that the idea came to me.

I smiled and said I was fine, asked when they were moving in. He said it would be a while, renovations were more of a headache than they'd anticipated. He was there that day to talk to his contractor, and since it was a Saturday, he'd decided to run on the trail for the very first time. I invited him to stop by for coffee the next time he was around checking on the progress. It hurts my pride to acknowledge, but it took some convincing. He was careful to be polite, formal almost, and I had to make it pretty damn obvious what I was interested in.

I thought it would benefit us both. Give me an exit strategy if I needed it, and give him a little thrill to distract from his awful life at home. I have to admit it was fun for a while. Before they moved in, we fucked in only one place (the soundproof, windowless movie theater in my basement) at only one time (in the middle of a weekday when I was the only one at home). Thinking about the heat of his body against the cold leather recliners still gives me shivers. I hadn't slept with anyone other than Teddy for twenty years, and it felt like very satisfying revenge for his stubbornness. After the first time, he was scared and called it a mistake. He kept saying that Alexis would find out, that he'd never cheated on her before, not really, but she'd sniffed out some stupid emails he once sent and even something about a girl in college. I guess I should have realized then how smart she was.

But she didn't find out, and he kept coming back. We were pretty careful. After they moved in, I told him to stop coming and instead met him in New York and L.A. a handful of times. There were also the parties, when we were stupid and drunk, but we didn't get caught (my mother seeing us on Brad's yacht doesn't count, she has no right to judge). Not until that night when Alexis was supposed to be gone. But that mistake doesn't really matter to me.

No, what keeps me up drinking in the sitting room even now are the lies I made up about Teddy. How he'd been controlling and abusing me for years, not letting me work and trapping me in our marriage. How the kids grew up petrified of him, and how I had to muster up the courage to leave, now that they're old enough to fight back, before he hurt one of them. The stories felt poisonous on my tongue even as I was saying them. There was no choice though, I had to turn him into a monster to inspire Sam. It worked.

In late April, when I knew Teddy was past the point of convincing, I told Sam that he was getting suspicious I might leave and threatened to kill me. Coming up with the details from there was easy, because I'd thought it all through already. Teddy's running routine hadn't changed in years. We just needed two things: rain and a way to turn off Laura and Shawn's cameras. When Laura told me she was going to upgrade again, I made plans to be out of town for that weekend, and started praying for rain. It came.

Sam followed Teddy out onto the trail, picked up a rock that he'd placed at the second mile marker a few days earlier, and hit him first from behind, in the back of the head. They were almost evenly matched, both over six feet and strong, so we'd talked about how important that first hit would be. To surprise Teddy and knock him unconscious, so they didn't end up in a fight. Then Sam hit him again and again with the rock, aiming for his skull to make sure he was dead before pushing him over the edge. I'd told Sam to be fast and to not hesitate. He'd thought I was worried he might get hurt, might leave some of his skin under Teddy's fingernails, but mostly I didn't want Teddy to suffer.

Things seem to have gone perfectly, but Sam panicked and ran home with the rock still in his hand. He'd had the presence of mind to run into the empty lot next to his house and the good luck to stumble across a dead deer to hide it under. Then he went home, washed the dirt and blood off his hands and sneakers, threw his clothes in the laundry, and went back out for a second run, this time with his phone. We assumed it would take days to find Teddy, maybe even weeks if he got caught in the current and ended up out in the Chesapeake Bay. I was ready to play the part of worried wife of missing husband. It didn't turn out that way, which is good. I didn't want Teddy to be out there alone for long.

Sam is the one who suggested that Alexis and I become friends. He thought it would make our relationship look natural, the unsurprising result of an unhappy couple befriending an attractive widow. He'd always taken the whole thing too seriously. As if I'd want to marry him and become a wicked, old stepmother to those two babies. I could have let him down sooner, but I was in a delicate position. I couldn't let him get desperate.

My plan was to go along with it for a while, and then start hinting at serious money trouble. That would have sent Sam running. Not that he didn't think he was in love. He was, crazily and intensely, in love with me, but also with my money. He kept saying Alexis had turned their house into a financial black hole, sucking him dry between all the overpriced renovations and furniture and whatever else. The last few months, he started talking about moving into my house, saying Alexis would never give theirs up and anyway he'd be happy to leave her with the dumpiest place in the neighborhood. At first, I didn't think he was serious. But the night of my summer cocktail party, as we were re-dressing in my bedroom, he joked that every man there was a member of our country club and then, with a straight face, said he was looking forward to joining in Teddy's place once we got married. If I hadn't pushed him to hurry back to the party, I think he might have gone into Teddy's closet and tried on his watches. So just a few lies—that I couldn't afford the dues anymore, that the house had a huge mortgage, that I was selling the Porsche to pay bills—should have been enough to break the spell. And I was going to start telling those lies soon, before the holidays and more of my mother's glass-house judgments.

Still, I know my plan wasn't a great one. If we'd gone on much longer, he might have blown the whole thing up in panic or pettiness. Some of the nights we met on his business trips, he'd sob and shake with regret, telling me how awful it had been and how scared he was that we'd be caught. I'd have to soothe him like a child, reminding him of how he'd saved me, and it made my stomach turn. Other nights, I'd accidentally offend his increasingly fragile ego. In June, when I'd said I needed another year before we could tell anyone about our relationship, he'd sulked at me to take as long as I wanted because he was building a pool and needed time to enjoy it.

The last night, on Labor Day, I left the kids at the beach and drove home alone in all the traffic just because he'd risked calling me from his colleague's office, saying he missed me. He was waiting for me on my back patio. But instead of sex, he'd wanted to talk, to share the good news that he'd told Alexis he wanted a divorce. I was straddling him on a pool lounger, and without thinking I'd asked why they didn't try counseling first. He pushed me off, saying that's what Alexis wanted too, and then sulked home. I guess she must have seen him coming.

So really, Alexis did me a favor by coming home that night. Herself too, as far as I can see. Sam would have left her without a second thought and come to me, and my money. I miss her though. I don't think I've ever met anyone, besides Teddy, who got me so well. At least she's staying in the neighborhood and not running away. That gives us plenty of time. I think she'll come around eventually. Maybe we can even be friends again.

Alexis

It's not as if I've gone unpunished. My mistakes led to two options—dying, and letting Sam ruin our children's lives without me here to stop him, or making myself a widow and living with the consequences. I chose the latter sentence.

Detectives Kim and Bryan had been suspicious, not surprisingly. Two men falling to their deaths on the same street within months of each other is a pretty big coincidence. But I'd moved quickly, running back down and turning on lights, screaming for Elena from the top of the basement stairs to come with her phone. So it all fit together, just a minor reordering of a ten-minute span of time—I'd come home from the airport, had some water, gone upstairs to check if everyone was asleep, and come across the tragic scene in our room. Sam must have been testing the strength of the window, planning that safety railing he was supposed to build. I'd been badgering him about it for months, I admitted to the detectives. He must have pushed it too hard, and lost his balance, tragically.

Blair will never say anything. I know this. But at the beginning, I worried for weeks that they would find evidence of their affair on his phone, hidden in some app I didn't know about. I had dreams about Detective Bryan knocking steadily on the front door in one of his missionary outfits, with a motive neatly outlined in his little notebook and Detective Kim at his side, shaking his head in disappointment. But that never happened. Months later, right before Christmas when I finally decided to clean out Sam's things, I figured out why. In the top drawer of his nightstand, tucked into the pages of a Woodrow Wilson biography, was a thick, cream-colored note card that I immediately recognized. Deep navy initials engraved at the top, and a single line of text in Blair's flowing script: *Tuesday / July 29 / 4:00 PM / LAX Terminal 7. Can only stay one night!* A sample of their old-fashioned communications. I burned it with a lighter out on the patio, hoping Sam had been smart enough to take care of the others.

Some of the many nights I spend on the Murphy bed in the office or the futon in the sunroom, occasionally the couch in the den—anywhere but our bedroom—I wonder how it happened. If they'd started like we had. Sam is the one who first approached me, after a study session for a math class he shouldn't have been taking, where the teaching assistant asked me to explain how I'd solved a particularly tricky problem. I'd noticed him, of course—a handsome six-foot-and-three-inch redhead is hard to overlook—but being a nerd had always been my entry ticket to life beyond our apartment complex, and I would have cut my own tongue out of my mouth before talking to a cute boy. He'd grabbed my wrist as I walked by his desk and asked if I could help him with the homework over a cafeteria dinner. That night, as I kept my eyes fixed on the frozen yogurt machine slowly chugging vanilla-chocolate swirl into my Styrofoam cup, Sam told me I was the sexiest girl he'd seen in college.

He's the only person I've slept with, but I'd only ever shared the barest details about myself. I can see that now. I never told him how much anger I felt toward my mother, and myself for feeling it. I never told him how I'd changed my name, or how Caleb and Carter both have her eyes. I never told him how afraid I was of being lied to, of being made to feel worthless, not even when I left him for six months. But it's too late to talk about that now.

Blair came to the funeral and gave me a light, silent hug. She must have told Sam something awful was going on between her and Teddy, but I doubt it was the truth. I erased her number from my phone during the service. Dylan and Emily's house was already under contract by then, but many of my other neighbors came. Jennifer wept gracefully, Jeff shook my hand and didn't make eye contact, and when Mack put his hand on my back I pulled away and excused myself for the ladies' room. Only Laura was tactless enough to ask me what I was going to do about the house. I told her the truth, which was that, despite the painful memories, Sam and I bought it to raise our family in, to improve little by little into something we were truly proud of. I have no intention of going anywhere else.

Sam's firm was surprisingly generous. In addition to his life insurance policy, they gave me two years of his salary. There's nothing more tragic than a young widow and her children, a senior partner had said at the celebration of life his firm held for him over the winter. I'd nodded in silent agreement. The money has helped, a great deal. I've only had to go back to work part-time, without caring about the financial implications. Sam's parents offered to move in with us, ostensibly to help me, but I think more to find solace in the presence of their grandchildren. We compromised with long visits, and they've been here for the past three weeks already. That's part of my punishment too.

Elena, of course, is also here. She'd told the police that she'd been fast asleep until my desperate screaming woke her, but I'm not sure if that's true. She doesn't seek me out to share her family's sad stories anymore, and when we're in the kitchen together, I've felt her shrinking back when I move toward her. It could be the workings of paranoia or guilt, but in case it's not, I increased her salary by $300 a week and never ask her to work on the weekends anymore.

This summer I'm going to redo the patio and relandscape the backyard. Elena, the cleaning lady, and I weren't able to completely scrub the stains from Sam's body off of the brick, and it really upsets his mother every time we are out there. We'll continue to be the only house in River Forest without a pool though. This is my solace—one major project every six months, starting with replacing all the windows this past December. I've been careful to plan it out, and it feels good to see the house coming back to life.

If I'd never fallen in love with this house, if I'd been a different kind of wife, maybe Sam and I would have been able to save our marriage. Or maybe this was inevitable, me ending up like this, fooled and alone, like my mother. I've come to realize, though, how much better off I am than she was—I have my career, money, Elena, and Sam's parents. She had nothing, because it was all taken away from her.

It doesn't make me understand, but it does make me sure that I won't repeat any more of her mistakes. At the very least, my children will grow up feeling how deeply and achingly I love them every day of their lives, and not the pain of what I've been through. They will also have a father—not an unspeakable blank, and not a murderer. Just a wonderful, successful man who died in an unfortunate accident. And there's no shame in that.

Acknowledgments

It seems to me that writing acknowledgments is like pre-broadcasting the acceptance speeches of all awards show nominees—a bit awkward for the eventual losers. But whether this book sinks to the bottom, rockets to the top, or floats along somewhere in between, its mere existence feels like a miracle to me as a first-time novelist, and I am deeply grateful to so many people for their help along the way.

Thank you to my brilliant agent, Helen Heller, for asking all the right questions the first time we ever spoke. I'll never forget that feeling, and this book wouldn't exist without you. Thank you to Charles Spicer for taking a chance on me and, along with Sarah Grill and the whole wonderful team at St. Martin's Press, for expertly and patiently guiding me through every single step of the publishing process. Thank you to my real neighbors, for being far kinder and saner than anyone in River Forest.

Thank you to my dear friends, especially my conscripted early draft readers, for your encouragement and time and considerable intelligence—Monica, Supreet, Katie, Liz, Miriam, Laura, and Bram. Thank you, Frank, for the book you sent me—it meant a lot. Thank you to every member of my precious